THE LAWMAN: WHITE LIGHTNING

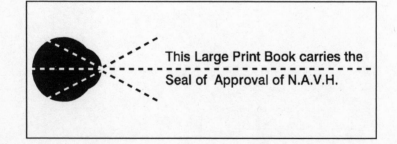

This Large Print Book carries the
Seal of Approval of N.A.V.H.

THE LAWMAN: WHITE LIGHTNING

LYLE BRANDT

THORNDIKE PRESS
A part of Gale, Cengage Learning

Detroit • New York • San Francisco • New Haven, Conn • Waterville, Maine • London

GALE
CENGAGE Learning®

LIBRARY OF CONGRESS CATALOGING-IN-PUBLICATION DATA

Brandt, Lyle, 1951–
   The Lawman : White Lightning / By Lyle Brandt. — Large Print edition.
      pages cm. — (The Lawman) (Thorndike Press Large Print Western)
   ISBN 978-1-4104-6487-3 (hardcover) — ISBN 1-4104-6487-3 (hardcover)
   1. Slade, Jack (Fictitious character)—Fiction. 2. United States marshals—Fiction. 3. Distilling, Illicit—Fiction. 4. Murder—Investigation—Fiction. 5. Oklahoma—Fiction. 6. Large type books. I. Title.
PS3602.R364L398 2013
813'.6—dc23   2013033181

285
W

Published in 2013 by arrangement with The Berkley Publishing Group, a member of Penguin (USA) LLC, a Penguin Random House Company

Printed in the United States of America
1 2 3 4 5 6 7 17 16 15 14 13

For Ben Johnson

1

Bill Tanner lay in knee-high grass, atop a long ridge lined with sawtooth oaks, and scanned the lower ground before him through binoculars. He had a clear view of the ranch below, its large two-story house, the barn, and other outbuildings. He was particularly interested in the barn just now, and the four wagons lined up side by side in front of it.

The glasses Tanner used were new — at least, to him — from the Bausch & Lomb Optical Company. Tanner had never owned a pair of binoculars before, and the model he pressed to his eyes now had been introduced this very year, from the factory in Rochester, New York. He liked them better than the one-eye spyglass he'd been using since he joined the U.S. Marshals Service five years earlier, for comfort and their magnifying power.

At the moment, for example, Tanner saw

nine men moving around the wagons, half a mile out from his shaded vantage point. Eight of the hands were working, while the ninth one supervised, giving directions now and then. It didn't take much sense to load crates on a wagon, but the foreman wanted everything just so. Four crates across each wagon bed, seven in line between the driver's seat and tailgate, making twenty-eight for one level. Stacked up three deep, that came to eighty-four per wagon, and Tanner reckoned there'd be eight or nine bottles per crate, packed in excelsior.

Tanner did the simple arithmetic in his head, coming up with a minimum 672 bottles per wagon, and maybe as many as 756. Two dollars per bottle, wholesale, meant the four wagons in front of him would earn the shipper more than twenty thousand dollars.

Good money, Tanner thought. Thirty-odd times his yearly salary, bare minimum.

"I'm in the wrong damn business," Tanner muttered to himself, half smiling. But at least he wasn't on his way to prison, like the men working down range.

He had been watching them load wagons for an hour, lying in the grass, shifting a little now and then to keep his legs from going numb, feeling the buckle of his gunbelt gouging him. His chestnut roan was tied well down the slope behind him, out of sight and earshot from the men he'd trailed from town, out to the ranch. Tanner was confident they hadn't seen him, had no inkling they were under observation at that very moment by an officer intent on putting them away.

Not all at once, of course. The wagons would be heading off in different directions when they left the spread, their cargo under canvas, each one with a driver and a shotgun rider. Tanner would lose three of them in transit, but it didn't matter. He had names for everyone involved, picked up eavesdropping and in idle conversation over six nights of idling in saloons. He could match the names to faces, and he had no doubt that one or two of them, squeezed hard enough, would tattle on the men in charge.

Case closed.

And none too soon, all things considered. Tanner had no scruples about drinking — liked to pull a cork himself, in fact — and it was hard for him to work up much enthusiasm over violations of the law imposing tax on liquor, though it was his bounden duty to enforce it. But the rotgut being loaded on the wagons down below had caused no end of trouble in the territory, lately. Costing lives, in fact, and that would have to stop.

He had the plan worked out. Wait for the wagons to be battened down and start on their way, and follow one that led him in the most convenient direction. Overtake it on the trail and get the drop on its two passengers — the tricky part — and take them into custody. The wagon and its cargo would suffice as evidence to justify search warrants, and he'd come back with reinforcements for the rest.

Easy. Unless something went wrong.

But Tanner wasn't worried. He could handle two men, plug the guard if necessary — hell, plug both of them if they left him no other choice. Try not to kill them, since Judge Dennison was touchy on that score, sometimes, but the first rule of marshaling was always come back home alive, yourself. If some of these boys felt like dying for a load of moonshine, Tanner thought he could accommodate them.

How much longer for the loading, now? The two-man team on Tanner's left had roughly half their cargo stowed and squared away. The others weren't as fast, despite the foreman riding them to finish. It was almost noon, and all of them were slowing down. Not dogging it exactly, but he thought they'd likely break for lunch before they finished.

Lunch. It made his stomach growl, and Tanner lowered the binoculars, opened the buckskin bag that lay beside him in the grass, and palmed a corn dodger. Stuffing the whole thing in his mouth, he chewed it slowly, raised the glasses to his eyes again, and focused on the job at hand.

"You see it? On the ridge?" Jed Walker asked.

"I see it," Grady Sullivan replied. Sun glinting in the distance, maybe off a spyglass lens. "Keep working. Just act natural."

"What are you gonna do about it?"

"Something," Sullivan replied and eased off toward the barn, careful to keep from glancing backward as he went. Inside the barn, Lon Burke and Mickey Shaughnessy were lounging by the wall of crates still waiting to be loaded, smoking hand-rolled cigarettes and snickering at something till they noticed Sullivan approaching.

"I need you two saddled up," he told them.

"What's the matter?" Shaughnessy inquired.

"We might have someone spying on us from the ridge, off west," said Sullivan.

11

"Might have?" Burke frowned. "You isn't sure?"

"I'm pretty sure. Go check it out, the two of you. But careful-like. Ride south until you're out of sight, then double back around and come in from behind," said Sullivan.

"What if it's nothin'?" That from Shaughnessy.

"Then you'll have got some exercise for once. It wouldn't kill you," Sullivan replied. "Get to it."

Lon said, "Sure, Boss. Only, if there *is* somebody . . ."

"Bring him back to me. Alive. I'll wanna talk to him."

"He may not care to come with us," said Shaughnessy.

"Persuade him, then. But when I say *alive,* that's what I mean. No accidents."

Sullivan left them to the chore of saddling up their mounts and moved back into the April sunshine where his teams were busy working, four men toting crates from barn to wagons, while the others got them lined up square and proper in the wagon beds. Five minutes later, Shaughnessy and Burke rode out behind him, turned their horses south and spurred them to a lively trot.

Sullivan guessed that it would take twenty minutes, maybe half an hour, to complete

12

the circuit at their present pace. They'd have to slow down, coming up behind the watcher — if there *was* a watcher — to avoid alerting him. Or them, whichever it turned out to be. Sullivan wondered for a moment if he should have sent more men, then put it out of mind.

He made a show of taking off his hat, sleeving the perspiration from his forehead, which permitted him to glance off westward without seeming to. Another flash of sunlight, bright on glass or metal, and he tried to think of any explanation other than a spy watching his people load their crates. Came up with nothing innocent and hoped the men he'd sent remembered what he'd told them about bringing the intruder back alive.

They had him cold on trespassing, for starters, grounds enough to question him and see what he was up to. Where it went from there depended on the watcher's story and identity. Whatever he was up to, though, Sullivan couldn't think of any answer that would save his life.

You simply couldn't know some things and live.

He started thinking past the kill now, keeping an eye on Jed Walker to see that he didn't go stirring things up. If the workers started acting nervous, sneaking looks up toward the ridge, they might scare off the spy before Sullivan's men could drop in and surprise him.

And that wouldn't do at all.

Disposing of a body wasn't difficult. The spread he supervised sprawled over some twelve hundred acres, ample room for one more shallow grave. Sullivan wasn't sure they'd want to plant the prowler, though, if leaving him displayed somewhere would send a message to potential future trespassers. Much would depend on who he was and why he'd come to spy on them.

An idea came to Sullivan. He'd have to run it past the boss and get approval, but the more he thought about it, it seemed workable. Some of the burden fell on Burke and Shaughnessy, trusting the pair of them to follow orders, bring the prowler back alive and fit to answer questions. If they messed it up and shot him, Sullivan decided, they would have to dig the bullets out themselves, to make his scheme pay off.

Pulling out his pocket watch, he checked the time and guessed the cook would surface soon, clanging his triangle to signal lunch was served. Sullivan had been smelling stew the past two hours, his mouth watering, but now he was distracted, thinking that he'd likely miss his midday meal. Or if his men came back while everyone was eating, they could leave their captive hogtied in the barn and let him sweat a little, wondering what lay in store for him.

One hard last ride, screaming his life away.

Because they couldn't simply ask what he was doing on the spread and take the first answer he gave as gospel. Everybody lied, particularly when they found themselves in trouble. It would take some time and effort to extract the truth, squeezing until Sullivan satisfied himself that there was nothing left to learn. Nothing to stop the wagons rolling on their way, although he guessed departure ought to be delayed a bit, until they made sure that the spy was working by his lonesome.

Otherwise . . .

Sullivan didn't want to think about that, at the moment.

Look on the sunny side, he thought. And nip their problem in the bud.

Tanner saw the work crew's foreman leave his men and head into the barn, returning moments later with a sour expression on his face. Through the binoculars, it seemed that he was almost close enough to touch, and Tanner wished there was some way to pair the glasses with a camera to take long-distance photographs for evidence. Maybe one of the new kinetoscopes, invented by that fellow Edison he'd heard about, away up north.

Tanner wondered how a jury would react to seeing criminals caught in the act, on film. There'd be no arguing by some defense attorney over whether they'd been present at the crime scene, what they'd done, no claims lawmen on the witness stand were spinning fancy tales to lock away the innocent. Like now, for instance. He could film the wagons being loaded with their contraband and have a photographic record of the men responsible, with no room for a claim he'd been mistaken.

Maybe someday.

At the moment, though, he lay and watched the work continue. Soon after the foreman left the barn, two riders followed him, turned left out of the wide front door, and moved off to the south. He tracked them with the glasses for a while, until they passed from sight beyond one of the spread's cornfields.

Some errand for the boss.

Corn was the only crop the ranch produced, and precious little of it ever reached a dinner plate. The bulk of it went into mash, which went into a vat with rye meal, barley salt, water, and yeast, then was heated and distilled, producing whiskey that could knock your socks off — or, in cases where the purity was not controlled, leave drinkers blind or dead.

Bill Tanner had consumed his share of whiskey, and some more besides, but he was not concerned about the purity of what was being loaded on the wagons in his view, per se. His job today involved collecting evidence that liquor had been made, bottled, and sold without the proper taxes being paid to Uncle Sam. To prove that charge, he'd need some of the booze.

A wagonload ought to suffice, together with the men assigned to drive and guard it. After that, a raid to take the still and bag the men in charge, then he could move on to another case. Maybe pick up a commendation for his trouble if he made the job sound dangerous in his report. A little fudging did not harm, and truth be told, there *was* an element of danger when it came to hunting moonshiners. Tanner had heard of marshals getting killed on liquor raids — three in the past twelve months alone, but farther east, in Tennessee. It was the same as any other crime, he thought. Where there was easy money to be made, some folks would kill to keep it rolling in.

And he'd be keeping that in mind when it was time to brace the teamsters with their load of who-hit-John. Be ready with his Schofield — better yet, his Winchester — when he confronted them, and take no chances that they'd come up shooting to avoid arrest. Killing was a part of law enforcement Tanner didn't relish, but he meant to be the one who walked away from any showdown with a felon, if he had a say in how it all turned out.

A raucous clanging noise reached Tanner's ears and made him turn his glasses toward the farmhouse, where he found a slender figure in an apron banging on a metal triangle suspended from a wooden beam. A Chinaman, no less. The cook's lips moved, presumably some variation on the theme of "Come and get it," but his voice didn't carry as far as the ridge.

Turning back toward the barn, Tanner watched as the foreman and crew made their way toward the house, stopping off at a pump in the dooryard to rinse off their hands. When they'd all passed inside, he set down the binoculars, wriggled back six feet or so, and rose for a stretch with the nearest oak blocking his view of the house.

If he couldn't see them, Tanner figured they couldn't see him.

He'd left his canteen propped against the tree and raised it now, to wet his whistle. As it turned out, lying in the shade and watching other people sweat was thirsty work.

Too bad I haven't got a little taste of 'shine, he thought, but it would likely make him sleepy and the last thing that he needed was to doze off at his post and let the whiskey wagons roll away without him. Old Judge Dennison would have a fit, and then some, if he botched the job after a week of following the moonshine trail.

The whicker of a horse reached Tanner's ears, coming from somewhere down the slope in front of him. He couldn't see his roan from where he stood, was stepping out to find a point where he could spot it when a *second* animal let go a whinny with an altogether different tone.

Tanner was reaching for his Schofield when he heard the *click-clack* of a lever-action rifle to his right, and someone said, "That wouldn't be the smartest move you ever made."

The marshal was a tough one. Grady Sullivan admired that in a man, though at the moment, it was also irritating. They'd been working on him for the best part of an hour — knuckles mostly, working up from there

19

— and hadn't even got his name yet, for their effort. Not that naming him was worth much, in the long run. More important was the reason he'd been spying on them in the first place, and it wasn't any secret.

Whiskey.

Knowing that, they could have killed him outright, but it wouldn't do. Sullivan had to know whether the lawman had discovered them by accident, or if someone had put him on their trail. It was ridiculous to think he'd just been riding past — on private property, no less — and thought he'd stick around to watch some fellows loading wagons up with crates labeled CORN SYRUP, so he must have had a tip from someone, somewhere.

That was what they needed. Trace it back to the informer, then find out if he — or she — had spread the word around to anybody else. Their operation wasn't secret, in the strictest sense, and couldn't be when there were paying customers involved, but squealing to the law must be discouraged. An example was required to put busybodies on notice.

Sullivan heard screaming from the barn and went back in to see how they were making out. Lon Burke stepped back from where they had the marshal tied up to a wagon wheel, against an upright beam. The knife Burke held was dripping blood from where it had incised the captive's naked chest.

"Still nothing?" Sullivan inquired.

"We'll break him," Burke said. "Don't you worry."

"I'm not worried." Moving closer to the prisoner, Sullivan knelt and asked him, "Are you worried, Marshal?"

"Should I be?" the lawman asked him, through clenched teeth.

"I'd say so," Sullivan replied. "You've horned in on a deal too big for you to handle. Now you're done. The only question left is whether you go quick and clean, or slow and messy."

"My choice, is it?"

"Absolutely," Sullivan assured him. "Someone pointed you at us. Give me the name, and this all stops. I guarantee you won't feel anything."

"That simple?"

"Just like falling off a log."

"Thing is," the marshal said, forcing a smile of sorts, "there isn't any name to give. I worked it out myself."

"That's crap. You didn't find this place by chance," said Sullivan.

"You're right. Lucky for me, the idjits

you've got working for you left a trail a one-eyed man could follow through a dust storm. Anybody ever tell 'em that they shouldn't brag about their crimes in public?"

"Bullshit!" Mickey Shaughnessy stepped forward, looking twitchy nervous. "Grady, we don't talk the business up to anybody!"

That was bullshit, obviously, since they had to advertise the product where it mattered, to saloon keepers and such. Who else was in position to alert the lawman? Any customer who stocked their whiskey, any lush who drank it and inquired about its source, maybe some preacher with an ax to grind against John Barleycorn. The whole damned territory and a couple of adjacent states, the way their business was expanding.

Still, he couldn't let it go. The boss would want to know that Sullivan had left no stone unturned — no bone unbroken — in his bid to make the lawman sing. Sullivan rose, knees creaking. Told the captive, "Have it your way." To the others, "Get back to it."

"I was thinking we could try a branding iron," said Burke.

"And have it traced back to the Rocking R?" asked Sullivan. "Jesus, the closest you come to a brainstorm is a drizzle."

The others cackled over that, until the foreman raised his voice. "Shut up! When you get done with him, I want him looking like a bunch of Injuns had their way with him. Keep that in mind."

"I know just how to do it," Burke replied, anxious to please.

"The rest of you," said Sullivan, "get back to work. I've never seen a goddamned wagon load itself."

He left them all to their appointed tasks and walked back to the house. The boss was waiting for him on the front porch, coffee mug in hand. "Well, Grady?"

"Nothing yet. They're keeping at it."

From the barn, another scream rang out to punctuate his words.

"I don't like seeing badges on my property," the boss informed him.

"No, sir."

"I pay you to keep this kind of thing from happening."

Sullivan nodded. Knew there was no point stating the obvious, that he could not predict when someone would alert a lawman to their operation. What the big man needed was a chance to vent his spleen, and Sullivan was handy. When he calmed down, saw the threat had been contained, he would rest easier. They all would.

23

"It's a good idea you had, about the Indians."

Sullivan nodded, kept his mouth shut, knew it wouldn't do for him to crow about it.

"But we have to know who sent him," said the boss.

"I'm working on it, but he may not break."

"Hell, everybody breaks. You know that well as I do."

Sullivan kept quiet, heard the noises coming from the barn, and wondered whether that was true.

2

Since he'd given up the full-time gambling life, some years ago, Jack Slade had been surprised to find himself an early riser. It was nothing he'd expected, much less planned, but there it was. Instead of sleeping in after a long night at the poker table, he was up and at it with the chickens, more or less, and hungry as a bear just coming out of hibernation.

Part of that was knowing he'd have work to do before the day got too much older. There was always something since he'd been persuaded to accept a U.S. marshal's badge. He'd thought it would be temporary when he took the job at first, but Slade had finally accepted that it wasn't working out that way. The question in his mind at six o'clock this Wednesday morning was how long he could continue on his present path.

Manhunting. Risking life and limb for fifty bucks a month. So far it had cost him . . .

what? Assorted wounds that ranged from superficial to a shooting that had nearly killed him. And his wife.

Thinking of Faith pushed Slade into a sour mood but didn't stop his stomach's grumbling. When he'd dressed and finished shaving, buckled on his gunbelt, and squared away his hat, he locked the small room's door behind him and walked downstairs and out of the hotel that passed for home. The morning clerk wasn't behind his counter — no one there to wish Slade a good morning, which he thought was just as well.

Outside, the air was warm already, Main Street merchants busy setting out their wares. A couple of them greeted Slade in passing and he answered back, giving the friendly ones a kind of smile with no feeling behind it. Enid was a decent town and growing with the rest of Oklahoma Territory, but of late Slade had begun to question how and why he'd thought that he could plant roots here.

Or anywhere.

It was his fault that it had started to unravel; he accepted that and knew he'd have to live with it. A lawman's life was no good for a woman left at home while he was gone for days or weeks with no certainty that he would ever make it back at all. Worse yet, when bloody work spilled over onto the domestic side of things and put the lady's life in danger.

Last time, supposed to be his wedding day, the shooters hadn't actually come for Slade. In fact, he doubted whether they'd known who he was or gave a damn. If that had been the *only* time, it might have made a difference, but Slade and his intended had been down that road before, and more than once.

Too often.

There was nothing Slade could do about it now, no turning back the calendar, erasing scars and ugly memories. He had to live with who and what he had become.

Or did he?

Other men had taken off a badge before it got them killed or maimed. Slade knew that for a fact. He'd met some of them in his travels, guarded men who watched the world through wary eyes and generally kept a weapon handy, just in case. That part would be no different than when he made his living with a deck of cards, something that still amused him when he had the time to spare. Who said he couldn't change his life again?

But that meant leaving Oklahoma Territory. Leaving Faith.

She'd closed the door on their relationship, was selling off her ranch and moving east, which should have made it easier for Slade to go. As long as she was still in Enid, though, he found it difficult to sever that last tie. To grind hope underneath his boot heel, even when he knew that it was dead.

Slade crossed the street to Galleon's restaurant, maybe one-third of the tables occupied as he walked in. The waitress, Clara, met him with a smile and showed him to a table by the window, knowing from experience that Slade enjoyed a free show with his breakfast. People normally intrigued him, even as they went about their routine daily tasks. He often practiced judging moods by the expressions on their faces, picking up on attitudes and gestures, but the street scene didn't hold his interest today.

Slade ordered two fried eggs with bacon, flapjacks on the side, and coffee, black. The food was on his table, piping hot, when he saw Luke Naylor across the street, walking from the direction of the courthouse. Naylor saw Slade through the window, raised a hand, and waited for a wagonload of lumber to pass by before he crossed.

Naylor was five foot ten, rangy, with curly

dark hair showing underneath his flat-brimmed hat. He wore matched Colts and kept his round badge polished to a satin shine. Ten months and counting as a deputy and Naylor still seemed to enjoy the work.

He entered and sat across from Slade without waiting to be invited. "Thought I'd find you here," he said. "Judge wants to see us when you're finished."

It was early for a summons, early for the judge to be found in his office. Slade swallowed the mouthful he was chewing and asked Naylor, "What's the trouble?"

"Not sure, but he's worked up over something."

Slade surveyed the food remaining on his plate and said, "Ten minutes ought to do me, if you want to go and tell him."

"Might as well have coffee while I'm here," Naylor replied and raised a hand to Clara as he eased back in his chair.

Go on and make yourself at home, Slade thought and dug into his meal.

Judge Isaac Dennison was in his early sixties, strong and stocky, though he limped a little from a gunshot wound he'd suffered when assassins tried to kill him at the courthouse some time back. He kept a walking stick around, whether he needed it on

29

any given day or not, and since the shooting he had carried a .32-caliber Smith & Wesson Lemon Squeezer, the "safety hammerless" model, in a shoulder holster under his left arm. There'd been no call to use it, but he wasn't taking any chances.

Dennison was standing at his window, in the wall behind his desk, when Slade and Naylor reached his chambers. From that window, Slade knew that he had a clear view of the six-man gallows standing in a walled-off courtyard, where the prisoners condemned by Dennison were hanged the second Saturday of every month. Slade also knew that while the judge derived no pleasure from a hanging, he was always at his post to watch the show.

Seeing it through for justice to the bitter end.

Slade rapped his knuckles on the open door and waited for the judge to turn, acknowledge them, and ask them in. It took a moment, and the old man's face was solemn when he swiveled, raised a hand to indicate the chairs standing before his desk. Slade doffed his hat and crossed the room, taking the chair to Naylor's left.

"Bill Tanner's dead," the judge informed them, as he eased himself into his high-backed chair.

The news pained Slade. He'd liked the older marshal, though they hadn't socialized to speak of. Tanner was — had been — a married man with two kids and a small house on the eastern edge of town. Slade thought about the people left behind and asked, "What happened?"

"That's a question that I need you two to answer," Dennison replied. "A farmer on his way to market found him, what was left of him, out by the reservation. Didn't recognize him, since whoever killed him left him naked, but the farmer brought him in to Mattson."

Enid's undertaker.

Craning forward in his chair, Naylor asked, "He was nekkid?"

"No sign of his clothes or other gear," said Dennison. "It would appear that he was stabbed to death and . . . mutilated."

"Redskins?" Naylor asked.

"That still remains to be determined," Dennison replied. "Did either of you speak with Tanner recently? The past week, say?"

Slade shook his head. Naylor said, "No, sir."

"They've had some trouble on the rez," said Dennison. "There's whiskey getting in from somewhere. Untaxed whiskey, so whoever's peddling it has broken two laws,

31

just for starters."

"Moonshining and selling it to Indians," said Naylor, showing off his knowledge of the statute book.

"And now, just maybe, murdering a U.S. marshal," Dennison continued. "Or, if Tanner *was* killed by a Cherokee, maybe inciting them to bloodshed with the liquor."

"You say there's been other trouble on the rez?" asked Slade.

"Some drunken fighting," Dennison replied. "I'm told they've had one killing and some minor injuries. You know the agent out there, don't you, Jack?"

"Yes, sir. Frank Berringer."

They'd met when Slade went looking for the men who'd turned his wedding day into a massacre. The same gang had been stealing horses from the reservation, killed a tribesman in the process, and Slade's vengeance trail had started there.

"What do you think of him?" asked Dennison.

"Can't say I liked him much," Slade said. "He's competent enough, I guess, but lets you know he looks down on the Cherokee like problem children. Treats them that way, too, from what I saw. It wouldn't take much alcohol to stir them up against him."

"He's been talking to the army," Dennison

informed them. "I sent Tanner to investigate because it feels like an explosive situation in the making. Now he's dead, and I intend to see the man or men responsible out there." He cocked a thumb over his shoulder, toward the window and the courtyard gallows.

"Is there anything to go on?" Slade inquired. "Was Bill filing reports?"

"I got one cable from him," Dennison replied. "From Stateline, on the Kansas border. He was cagey, said he thought that he was getting close but didn't mention any names. I got a sense that he was worried about sharing too much in a wire that anyone might see."

Slade hadn't been to Stateline, but he knew it was an agricultural community straddling the Kansas-Oklahoma border, hence its name. The split, he guessed, might cause some law enforcement problems, but he wouldn't have to fret about it with a U.S. marshal's badge.

"We ought to pay a call on Berringer," Slade said, "before we head for Stateline. See what's on his mind and what he plans to do about it."

"Try to reassure him that he has our full support," said Dennison. "If that won't calm him down, to hell with him. We'll find whoever killed Bill Tanner by ourselves."

Back on Main Street, Slade asked Naylor, "Have you ever been to Stateline?"

"Once. Wasn't much to it, but it's likely grown since then."

"How far away is it?"

Naylor considered it, then said, "We leave right now and sleep out overnight, we could be there tomorrow afternoon."

"About the same, then, from the rez," Slade calculated.

"Give or take a few miles. Will they put us up there?"

"Probably. They found a room for me the last time."

Naylor seemed to be on the verge of saying something, but he caught himself, maybe remembering the reason for Slade's last trip to the reservation and the bloody trek that followed it. Long seconds passed before he cleared his throat and managed, "Meet you at the livery in, say, an hour?"

"Suits me," Slade replied. "You have a coffeepot?"

"Sure thing."

There wasn't much for Slade to pack: some vittles for the trail, a canteen full of water, ammunition for the guns he would be carrying, a change of clothes. No one for

34

him to say good-bye to, either, as he rode with Naylor out of town. That part reminded him of all the years when he'd been drifting, gambling, dodging one scrape or another, rarely making plans beyond tomorrow. He'd have likely kept on living that way, rootless, if he hadn't got the telegram about his twin brother's death. Murdered for his land in Oklahoma Territory, as he'd learned, by men who thought they were above the law.

The rest, as someone said, was history. He'd come to Enid, met Judge Dennison, and grudgingly accepted the jurist's ultimatum: either wear a U.S. marshal's badge while tracking down his brother's murderers — and do it in accordance with the law — or risk a visit to the gallows if he bagged them any other way. Slade had agreed, reluctantly, and met his brother's fiancée while searching for the killers.

Faith Connover had surprised him. Not so much for her beauty and resilient spirit in the face of tragedy, but for the feelings she had stirred in Slade. Guilt followed close behind desire, the image of his brother and betrayal constantly before Slade's eyes, a struggle that took time to reconcile.

But first, Faith had been kidnapped by the same men Slade was hunting, and his quest for justice had become a race to save her life. Maybe she would have been endangered if he'd never got the telegram or come to Enid, but he couldn't say that. Not for certain.

Slade had rescued Faith that time, and she had warmed to him over the months that followed. He'd surprised himself by sticking with the marshal's job, wondering why each morning when he pinned the badge on, slowly realizing that he stayed for Faith. If it turned out she wouldn't have him, that the idea made her skin crawl, it all would have been wasted time. Slade was having trouble with it, too, but edging closer to the notion that there might be something more between them than a void left by his twin.

And it had worked . . . up to a point. But Slade's work had endangered Faith again, when some fanatics with religious murder on their minds had trailed him back to Faith's ranch, outside Enid. Slade was shepherding a family marked for slaughter, and the showdown had imperiled Faith again — forced her to fight beside him for her life, in fact. To kill in the defense of strangers and her property.

More strain and ugly memories.

The last time hadn't actually been Slade's

fault, as it turned out. Faith had dismissed one of her ranch hands when the others caught him stealing and peering at Faith through her windows at night. The slug had nursed a grudge, teamed up with brutal border trash somewhere along the way, and sold the gang on the idea of looting Faith's ranch. Faith and Slade were at the altar, on their wedding day, when the banditos struck. And when the smoke cleared, both of them had been unconscious, gravely wounded.

Rotten luck or Fate?

Slade had bounced back from the shooting faster than his lady love. She'd still been comatose when Slade began the vengeance ride that carried him from Enid, south through Texas, into Mexico, and more than halfway to the gates of Hell. On his return, leading the scum who'd set it all in motion to a trial before Judge Dennison and hanging in the courtyard, he'd found Faith awake — and finally determined that she'd seen enough of him and the violence that had marred their life together.

She was selling up and heading out. They hadn't spoken since the day she'd told Slade her decision, though he ached to plead with her, beg for another chance. The thing that held him back was knowing that the ugly memories would always stand between them, coupled with the fear of some fresh trouble waiting down the road.

Now, as he prepared for another manhunt, Slade found himself wondering if Faith would still be there when he returned. *If* he returned. Would she take off without a parting word? And would it matter either way?

Slade had half an hour left to kill when he was finished packing, so he walked the long block west to Mattson's funeral parlor. It felt morbid, but he wanted to examine Tanner's body, see what had been done to him and what they might be up against. Whether a viewing could determine *who* had murdered Bill, red men or white, Slade wasn't sure. If nothing else, he thought that it would put him in the proper mood for hunting.

Holland Mattson was a tall, thin man with a shock of gray hair that pomade could barely tame. His long face and chin curtain beard brought Abe Lincoln to mind, the impression enhanced when Mattson opened his mouth to speak in a sonorous baritone voice.

He met Slade in the front room of the *home,* a euphemism Slade had never understood, since no one living occupied the place. Mattson, his pallid wife, and robust adolescent son lived two blocks over, near the heart of town, away from Holland's work and its attendant smells. Still, *home* it was, according to the sign out front, and Slade was disinclined to raise the issue with the man in charge.

"Marshal, you've come to see your colleague, I presume?" the undertaker said.

"That is correct." Something about the man caused Slade to speak more formally than usual.

"You are aware that he was . . . badly used?"

"I heard."

"I haven't had a chance to work with him, you understand, since he arrived last night. It's bound to be closed casket, I'm afraid."

"Thanks for the warning."

Mattson led him through one door, into a room with caskets on display, then through another to the undertaker's workshop. There were two reclining customers on tables separated by a yard or so, both draped in sheets. The one on Slade's right as he entered seemed to be a woman, from the shape.

"Mrs. Wolinsky. Did you know her, Marshal?"

"No."

"The grocer's wife. Just thirty-one. Ironically, she choked on a Brussels sprout. And here . . . your fellow deputy."

Slade stood between the tables, facing Mattson on the other side of Tanner's shrouded form. "All right," he said.

Mattson peeled back the sheet, from Tanner's head down to his feet. As advertised, the corpse was nude and mutilated. Tanner had been scalped, his nose and lips removed. The carving on his chest and stomach might have had some pattern to it, once upon a time, but scavengers had done their part to make a mess of any symbols etched there. Moving on, the deputy had been emasculated and his feet were gone.

"How much of this was done by men?" asked Slade.

"Men or *a* man," Mattson replied. "The scalping, obviously. There's clean knife work all the way around the cranium, you see. The feet, of course. If they'd been chewed off — by coyotes, say — you wouldn't see that neat transection of the ankle joint."

"Neat?"

"As opposed to being gnawed and broken off. As to the rest, the wounds you see were first incised by hand, then drew the normal prairie scavengers."

"You wouldn't know if he was dead before

40

they started carving him, by any chance?"

Frowning, the undertaker said, "You won't appreciate it if I try to spare your feelings, I assume."

"Just give it to me straight."

"Retraction of the muscles on a deep cut indicate the victim was alive, as here," said Mattson, pointing toward one side of Tanner's ravaged chest. "In death, we see no elasticity."

"So this was torture, not just murder," Slade replied.

"I fear that your assessment is correct, Marshal."

"And nothing here to tell me whether it was done by Indians or white men?"

"Um. Perhaps the feet," said Mattson. "I confess my knowledge of the savages is incomplete, but I recall hearing from someone that they take the feet of victims slain in war, sometimes, to hobble their opponents in the afterlife. A crude preventative against postmortem haunting, as it were."

"Do you remember where you heard that?"

"Not offhand. I'm sorry."

"Never mind," Slade said. "It's something, anyway."

"If you desire a bit more time with the

departed . . ."

"No. That's plenty. Thank you."

Mattson drew the sheet back over Tanner, gently, almost reverently. It may have been an act for his sole benefit, but Slade appreciated it, regardless. He'd seen stiffs dumped into holes without a fare-thee-well, or left topside to feed the buzzards, and had ridden off from some himself.

"Has someone told his family?"

"No one has been in touch, as yet."

"He's covered, though? I mean, the funeral?"

"All settled, by the court," Mattson replied.

Suppose that it would be the same for me, Slade thought, then put it out of mind. He didn't like to dwell on death before a hunt, unless it was the other guy's.

"Okay, thanks for your time," he said and put the place behind him. Halfway back to his hotel, to fetch his gear, Slade still imagined that the smell of lifeless flesh and Mattson's damned embalming chemicals trailed him.

Someone would have to pay for what he'd seen. Pay with their lives, whether they went to trial or chose to fight it out. Now that he'd seen what they had done, Slade felt that he was equal to the job.

3

The livery and blacksmith's shop stood six blocks north of Slade's hotel. He got there with his gear as Luke Naylor was saddling his snowflake Appaloosa gelding. The younger marshal grinned at him and said, "I thought you might've gone back for a second breakfast."

Slade replied, "I went to Mattson's. Killed my appetite."

That wiped the smile off Naylor's face. "You went to see him?"

"Thought it best. I find it helps me focus, knowing just how far the other side will go."

Naylor glanced toward the hostler, working some distance away, and lowered his voice as he asked, "So, what did you think? Was it renegades?"

Slade knew he meant renegade tribesmen, but still hadn't made up his mind. "Some kind of vicious bastards," he replied. "I couldn't tell you whether they were Indians."

Naylor frowned. "What did they . . . do to him?"

Slade saw no reason not to share. If anything, it might keep Naylor sharp while they were on the hunt. He said, "Whoever jumped Bill took his hair, which *could* be Indians, or not. Cut up his face and body. Kept his feet."

"His *feet*? What kinda deal is that, for Christ's sake?"

"Couldn't tell you," Slade replied. He didn't feel like passing on the undertaker's speculation about native laming rituals, when he had nothing to support it. Naylor seemed to be half set on blaming Indians for Tanner's murder, as it was, and there was nothing to be gained by aggravating his suspicion.

Slade moved to the stall that held his roan mare, took her bit-less bridle from the wall, fitting the padded noseband and the crownpiece quickly into place. Ten minutes later she was saddled, and he'd stowed his long guns in their scabbards — a Winchester Model '73 on his right, chambered for the same .44-40 cartridge as his Colt Peacemaker, and a matching Model 1887 lever-action shotgun to his left, loaded with twelve-gauge buckshot rounds.

"You always take two shoulder guns?" asked Naylor, watching him.

"You wear two pistols," Slade observed.

"Figure I might get into something where there's no time to reload. I never want it said I died because I ran a bullet short."

Slade smiled at that. "With me," he said, "it's different tools for different jobs. Up close, far off. You never know."

"That's true enough. You ready?"

Slade swung up into his saddle. "As I'll ever be," he said.

They left the stable, turning north on Main Street, Slade on the outside and Naylor closer to the sidewalk. Passers-by ignored them for the most part, as most people seemed to do with lawmen if they weren't in need of help. Slade's acquaintances would speak to him, of course, if he was walking down the street, but when they saw him riding out of town it changed somehow. As if they guessed where he was going, what he'd have to do on their behalf, and didn't want to soil themselves with that side of society.

Slade took the opportunity to study people as he rode, knowing most wouldn't meet his eyes. Passing Doc Abernathy's office on his left, he saw the front door open, a woman emerging, the doctor behind her. They paused there a moment, the woman saying something, Abernathy nodding, answering.

Slade felt his heart skip as he recognized Faith Connover. She turned in time to see him passing by, looked startled in her own right, quickly averting her eyes. Slade brought the fingers of his left hand to his hat brim nonetheless, then drew his gaze away from Faith, continuing along his way. He felt Naylor looking at him, but the younger man was wise enough to hold his tongue.

They rode in silence until they were clear of town, broken when Naylor asked, "This BIA man that we're off to see now, what's your take on him?" referring to Frank Berringer, the local reservation agent for the Bureau of Indian Affairs.

"I wouldn't want to prejudice you," Slade replied.

"Afraid I might not take a liking to him?"

"Doesn't matter to our business, either way," Slade said. "I've only met him once, but he impressed me as the sort who likes to lord it over those less fortunate. A man who likes his privilege and power. If the choice was mine, I likely wouldn't trust him with authority. Of course, the bureau didn't ask for my opinion."

"No, they wouldn't. So, you think he's down on redskins?"

"I think he divides the world, inside his head. There's people who control him and can make him miserable if they choose to. Others, he can push around without much consequence."

"In other words, a bully."

"But refined about it, if you follow me," Slade said. "You wouldn't find him in a lynch mob. Doesn't like to soil his hands. He gives the orders, leaves the dirty work to his tribal police."

"Or the army," said Naylor.

"Or them. I still can't figure why he's calling them to hunt for Tanner's killer when they didn't even find Bill's body on the rez."

"Maybe he's scared the problem will get out of hand."

"Assuming that he even *has* a problem," Slade replied.

"You heard the judge. Somebody's getting whiskey to the Cherokees," said Naylor. "It must look bad for Berringer, you think about it."

Slade *was* thinking. He replied, "So, what he needs to do is put a lid on drinking where he has authority to stop it. Hunting 'shiners off the rez is our job, not the cavalry's."

"Judge sounded riled about it, too," Naylor remarked.

"He should be," Slade replied. "Unless the president proclaims a state of martial law, Judge Dennison's in charge of law enforcement for the territory. It gets hazy on the reservation, when the army sticks its nose in, but he does his best to hold the line. You know the Posse Comitatus Act?"

"It rings a bell," said Naylor. "Couldn't quote it for you."

"I never heard of it until I started marshaling," Slade told him. "Congress passed it fifteen years ago. It limits local government from calling on the army to enforce their laws without an order from the president or act of Congress."

"But the bluecoats still chase Indians," Naylor reminded him.

"Because the Indians aren't U.S. citizens," Slade said, "and Washington considers any crimes committed off the rez an act of war against the government. Moonshiners, now, they aren't rebelling against anything except the tax on booze."

"So, if a pack of Cherokees killed Tanner . . ."

"It could be an army problem," Slade allowed. "Unless we find them first."

"But if it's white men —"

"Then the army has no interest in the case," Slade finished for him. "They're all ours."

"I hope we find 'em, either way," said Naylor. "Bill seemed like a decent guy, the few times I had dealings with him."

"Decent sums it up," Slade said. "And nobody deserves to go the way he did."

"Nobody?"

"Well . . ."

"I thought so." Naylor chuckled. "I can likely think of one or two, I put my mind to it."

"Don't think too hard," Slade said. "I wouldn't want to wind up hunting you."

They rode another mile or so before Naylor spoke up again. "You ever work a moonshine case before?" he asked.

"Nope. It's a first for me," Slade said.

"I had one, back around the Christmas season," Naylor said. "A family was cookin' up by Alva, on the Salt Fork of the Arkansas. Came from Kentucky, as it happened, where the business went back through their generations. Mostly sold their product up in Kansas, though. They lived around too many Injuns — Osage, I believe they were

49

— to want 'em liquored up."

"How many of the family were in on it?" Slade asked.

"Old grandpa called the shots," Naylor replied. "There was his son, and he had three boys old enough to work the stills."

"You took them by yourself?"

"They didn't want to go, I grant you," Naylor said. "I had to wing a couple of 'em, then they saw that I meant business and they came along."

"Lucky for you," Slade said.

"I guess. The lads were all for roastin' me until they saw their daddy and the old man bleeding. Then, of course, I let their females off the hook. I figure they were just as guilty as the menfolk, but it just seemed petty, charging them."

"You have to watch your back with women, sometimes," Slade suggested, thinking of Kate Bender and the hatchet she'd have split his skull with, given half a chance. After he'd spoken, though, Slade wondered whether Naylor thought it was a reference to Faith, then decided he should let it drop without explaining.

"Do you know much about whiskey?" Naylor asked him.

"Just the kinds I like."

"I mean the making of it."

"Never gave that part much thought," Slade said.

"I hadn't either, till the job at Alva," Naylor said. "It's kind of interesting, though. Let's say they start with corn. You need at least four bushels, dried and ground to meal. Soak that in eight to ten gallons of water, then toss in a couple pounds of malt, two sticks of yeast, two gallons of hops, and a half bushel of barley. Mix it up and you've got mash, which needs to sit fermenting for five or six days."

"And then what?" Slade inquired, relieved to have the subject changed.

"You put it in a big old copper kettle," Naylor said, "and heat it up. The steam comes off through a condensing coil and drips into tub. The first batch comes out clear, around 110 proof, and they call that the *high shots.* Later on, it turns gray and they switch out the tubs for what they call the *low wines,* maybe half as strong."

"I've never seen gray whiskey," Slade remarked.

"See, that's the thing. Before you sell the booze, you have to proof it down. They pour some of the high shots in a bottle, then start adding low wine until beads form in the middle of the mix. If they sink to the bottom, your liquor's too weak. If they rise to the top, it's too strong. Then you test it."

"By drinking, I guess?"

"Not so fast," Naylor said. "First you pour a smidgen in a bowl and light it with a match. If you get blue flame, then it's safe to drink. Turn up a yellow flame, forget it. That's wood alcohol and it'll blind you, maybe kill you."

"That's a lot to know," Slade said.

"And it goes on from there. They keep the mash, then sweeten it with fifty pounds of sugar for the second batch. Third round, a hundred pounds, fourth time, hundred and fifty. After that, you start again with new mash. Age the liquor in a keg, if you've a mind to, or just sell it raw, soon as you get it in a jug."

"What proof is that?" asked Slade.

"Eighty's about the average," Naylor replied.

Meaning forty percent alcohol by volume. Enough to get a Cherokee — or anybody else — stoked up for fighting, if they didn't pass out first. Slade knew that federal laws banning sale of liquor dated from the turn of the century, buttressed by a statute passed in 1832, forbidding sale of alcohol on reservations. He understood the primal fear of raiding parties fueled by "firewater," but wasn't sure if red men acted any worse than whites when they were drinking heavily. As for blaming murder on a whiskey jug, he'd seen both men and women flare into a rage when they were drunk, but Slade had always thought the liquor simply brought out traits they covered up, to some extent, in daily life.

Forget it, he decided. Their assignment was to find the man or men responsible for cooking untaxed whiskey and then peddling it illegally to Indians. Lump the crimes together, and a violator might be fined or sentenced to a year in prison for each individual offense. A hundred violations, then, could mean a hundred years in theory, but the courts tended to minimize the penalty or make the sentences concurrent. Add the murder of a marshal, though, and you were looking at a short drop from the gallows.

If the evidence could make it stick.

And they had none, thus far, besides the injuries Bill Tanner suffered as he screamed his life away in agony. Slade needed more than Holland Mattson's theory about amputation of the feet to pin the crime on Cherokees, but if the killers had been white men, he had even less to go on. Tanner's wire from Stateline to Judge Dennison remained the only clue, and it contained no names, descriptions, or directions to a suspect.

So they were starting more or less from scratch, and at a disadvantage, too. If Tanner *had* been killed by moonshiners, it meant the men that Slade and Naylor had to find were on alert. They'd know that Tanner's death would spark a more intense investigation, and they might well know he'd sent a telegram from Stateline to Judge Dennison. Slade wondered if that wire had triggered nervous men to strike, uncertain whether they had been exposed or not.

He couldn't say, but the idea gave him a place to start when they arrived in Stateline. After talking to the local law, they'd need to have a chat with the town's telegrapher. From his reaction, Slade thought they could tell if someone else had had access to the cryptic message Tanner sent. If so, and if the operator didn't want to share a name — well, there were ways to loosen up his tongue.

Before they finished up in Stateline, Slade decided, they would have at least a fair idea of what had happened. If that knowledge led them to the killers, white or red, he would be satisfied. Justice would take its course.

And Slade would have more time to think

about what he should do with the remainder of his life.

The reservation set aside for Cherokees was one of twelve in Oklahoma Territory, the remainder being set aside for Pawnee, Osage, Ponca, Kickapoo, Creek, Nez Perce, Comanche and Apache, Cheyenne and Arapaho, Chickasaw, and Choctaw. Oklahoma Territory had been formally known as Indian Territory until May of 1890, when Congress changed its name and started letting more white settlers populate the districts' unassigned lands. Conflict between the races had been unavoidable, but nothing on the scale that some alarmists had predicted from the outset. Still, there was a fine line between nervous tolerance and open war, and it was patrolled by Slade and other deputies, the army standing by to ride if it appeared civilian officers had lost their capability to keep the peace.

Cherokee land lay northeast of Enid, in the same direction Slade and Naylor had to ride toward Stateline. There was no sign to alert them when they reached the reservation, but his previous excursions had shown Slade the basic landmarks. Shortly after crossing over, Slade told Naylor, "We could meet tribal police at any point from here on in."

"We're there already?" Naylor looked around, not agitated, but on guard.

"Ten, fifteen minutes in," Slade said. "That live oak with the lightning scar's a marker you can guide by."

"Oughta be a sign or something," Naylor said, "so folks can tell."

White folks, he meant. Slade said, "The reservation's neighbors have a pretty fair idea of where it is."

"But someone passing through could have a problem. We should ask the judge about —"

His words dried up, and Slade glanced over to find Naylor staring off to the southeast. Scanning in that direction, out two hundred yards or more, Slade saw three mounted riders watching them, immobile on a ridge top.

"Here we go," he said.

"Uh-huh."

Naylor was reaching for his Winchester when Slade said, "Stop it! I already told you they're police."

"How can you tell from this far out? Could be a hunting party or . . . you know."

Hostiles. The younger deputy *was* nervous now, not sweating yet, but with a tenor to his voice that gave away his strain.

"First thing, there's three of them," Slade said. "If they were hunting, there'd be one — or two, at most, and then spread out — to keep from scaring off the game. If they were hostiles, they'd be off the rez somewhere, not sitting there and hoping for a white man to ride by."

"You seem to know 'em pretty well. Let's hope you're right, eh?"

"Just sit easy. Let me do the talking when they get here."

"What? They're coming over?"

And as if his words evoked the action, Slade saw the three Cherokees start down the near side of the slope, nudging their horses to an easy trot. All three were armed with rifles, though he couldn't tell what kind from that far out. Most members of the tribal police, some twenty in all, carried pistols as well, while on duty. They would be the Indians whom Berringer trusted the most, which wasn't saying much. Most of their time was spent arresting drunks and wife beaters, but renegades who fled the reservation were beyond their jurisdiction. If they'd nabbed a white trespasser on the rez, Slade guessed that Berringer would tell them to apologize.

Which could instill a certain attitude, he

thought. Best if they walked on eggshells now and made it clear they'd come to see the man in charge.

Up close, Slade saw the Cherokees *were* wearing six-guns and the stamped tin badges he remembered from his last trip to the rez. He saw the riders checking out his badge and Naylor's, understanding that they'd been outranked, and not much liking it.

The middle one, a little older than his flankers, wearing braids over a denim shirt and balancing a .50-70 Sharps carbine on his right hip asked, "What brings you marshals here today?"

Slade caught a blink from Naylor, showing his surprise. He'd probably expected Cherokees to grunt and mutter in a language barely comprehensible.

"We've come to speak with Agent Berringer," Slade said, "about the whiskey being smuggled to your people."

"You wish to arrest the men responsible?" their spokesman asked.

"That's right. And there's the matter of a murdered deputy to talk about, on top of that."

"The yellow-haired marshal," their greeter replied. "We heard that he was killed."

"And found not far from here," Slade

answered, pushing just a little.

"You think Cherokees did this?" the trio's leader asked, frowning.

"Or someone wants us to believe that," Slade replied. "I try to keep an open mind."

"You are Marshal Slade, the friend of Little Wolf?"

"I'm hoping he has more than one," Slade said. "But, yes. We've done some hunting."

"Hunting men who kill our people."

"Ours, too. What they pay us for."

"I will take you to Agent Berringer." The spokesmen gave some orders to his two companions, speaking Cherokee. They peered at Slade and Naylor for another moment, then rode off to westward. "We are seeking stolen horses," the remaining Cherokee explained.

"No luck, so far?" Slade inquired.

"I think they are no longer on the reservation." With a sidelong glance at Naylor, he continued. "Sometimes whites come here and steal our animals."

Slade half expected Naylor to make some remark and was relieved when he did not. "I've known some white men who'd steal anything that wasn't nailed down tight," Slade said. "You get a line on any rustlers who've been hitting you, get word to me in Enid and I'll run them down."

Addressing Naylor for the first time, their appointed guide said, "Two guns. Are you fast with both?"

Naylor gave Slade a little frown, then shrugged and said, "I do all right."

"I think two guns would pull my pants down. Let us go now."

Slade had managed not to laugh and guessed that Naylor would be wondering if he'd been made a fool of by the Indian. If so, he didn't make an issue of it, saying to the Cherokee, "I didn't catch your name."

"Joe Mockingbird. And yours?"

"Luke Naylor. *Marshal* Naylor."

"Agent Berringer has hoped someone would come to see him about whiskey. Captain Gallagher is coming, too."

"Today?" asked Slade.

"We don't know when," Joe Mockingbird replied.

"I'd like to ask you something," Slade pressed on, "without giving offense."

"People say that when they intend to be offensive," said their guide.

"I've known a few like that," Slade granted. "What I need to know deals with the other marshal's death. The way he died."

"I'll answer if I can," said Mockingbird.

"Okay. When he was found, he had no feet. They'd been cut off, it seems, not eaten by coyotes. That sound familiar to you?"

Mockingbird considered it, then said, "I think Apaches do that. Maybe the Comanches, too. Not Cherokee." He glanced at Naylor with a little grin and said, "Unless somebody wants foot stew."

"Foot — !" Naylor caught himself, cheeks coloring, and said, "I get it. That's a real rib tickler, that is."

4

The reservation's seat of operations was a small town built around the agent's residence. Its public buildings were a one-room school that doubled as a meeting hall, a church, a stable with a blacksmith's shop attached, a dry goods store, a barn for grain and cattle, and a stout log jail. Beyond those clustered buildings, clapboard houses had been built with no great thought to streets, as far as Slade could tell. Privies were ranged along the outer limits of the settlement, like pointy-headed sentries, forcing those whose homes stood at the center of the town to run in the event of an emergency.

Joe Mockingbird led Slade and Naylor to the structure that contained the bureau agent's home and office, all in one. Somehow, it seemed that word of their arrival had preceded them. Roughly a hundred Cherokees stood watching in the small town square, or from their nearby doorways, as the three horsemen rode in.

And waiting on the front porch of his quasi-mansion was Frank Berringer.

He looked like power: stocky, six feet tall, a nearly-square head crowned with ginger curls planted atop broad shoulders with sparse evidence of any neck. His deep-set eyes surveyed the new arrivals from beneath thick eyebrows that were mirrored by his lush mustache. He wore a three-piece suit of charcoal gray, with gleaming spit-shined boots. The gold chain of a pocket watch secured his straining vest.

"Ah, Marshal Slade," he said, when they were close enough for conversation. "Still in harness, eh?"

"Looks like it, Mr. Berringer."

"And your companion is . . . ?"

"Luke Naylor," Slade replied, then rounded off the introduction. "Luke, Frank Berringer."

Luke nodded, kept his mouth shut, sizing up the man.

Berringer peered at Mockingbird as if the Cherokee had just appeared from nowhere, then said, "We won't keep you, Joe. There's work to do, I think."

Mockingbird wheeled his animal around and left without a word or backward glance at Slade and Naylor. Other members of their silent audience began dispersing, too, appearing sullen and uncomfortable under scrutiny from Berringer.

The agent smiled without conviction as he said, "Well, gentlemen, won't you come in? We should be dining soon. I hope you brought your appetites."

"We'll need to get our horses settled first," Slade said.

"Of course. My oversight." Berringer turned back toward the open doorway of his residence and called out, "Ashwin! Rajani!"

Two young Cherokees appeared in answer to the summons. Both wore cautious poker faces, standing at a semblance of attention in the presence of three white men, two of them with guns and badges. They could have passed for brothers, separated by a year or two in age.

Berringer examined them, as if he hoped to find fault with their spotless servant's garb, then said, "Convey these horses to the stable. Tell Hemadri to take special care of them."

The two youths bobbed their heads in unison, came forward, and received the reins from Slade and Naylor. Slade took time to thank the one called Ashwin, who cracked his façade enough to show a measure of surprise at common courtesy.

"Now, if you'll follow me," said Berringer. He turned, preceding them into his home. The place was just as Slade remembered it, spotless, a man's retreat with no sign of a woman's touch. "I'm pleased to see you gentlemen, but sorry for the circumstances, naturally."

"Bill Tanner spoke to you, I understand," said Slade.

"About our difficulties, yes. Kindly accept my most sincere condolences for his untimely end." Berringer led them to his study, indicating deep chairs with a gesture of his hand. "Something to drink?"

"What have you got?" asked Naylor, speaking to the agent for the first time.

"Bourbon, Irish whiskey, cognac, sherry," Berringer replied.

"No lack of alcohol," said Slade.

Berringer cocked a woolly eyebrow and replied, "Of course, this is my personal supply. And drinking is forbidden to the *Indians,* not to their . . . supervisors."

Wondering what he had meant to say before he checked himself, Slade said, "It sets an odd example, though."

"You think so, Marshal?" Berringer pretended to consider Slade's idea, then frowned, dismissing it. "I think it best for subjugated people to accept the day-to-day realities of life."

"I'll try that Irish," Naylor interjected, with a smile.

"Of course. And Marshal Slade?"

"Nothing for me right now, thanks."

"As you wish."

Berringer poured two double shots of Irish whiskey, handed one to Naylor, then sat facing them in yet another padded armchair. Slade watched him sip his drink, then said, "About this liquor problem you've been having . . ."

"Straight to business. Good. We have, in fact, been plagued of late by smugglers of illicit alcohol. The impact on my charges, as you may imagine, has been detrimental."

His *charges*, speaking of the Cherokees as a personal burden of duty.

"We're behind the times on what's been happening," Slade said. "I understand you've had one killing tied to liquor somehow."

"That's correct. A drunken brawl two weeks ago that led to stabbing. A buck called Avinash was killed. I understand his name meant 'Indestructible.' Ironic, don't you think?" Berringer smirked and took another sip of whiskey. "Several others suffered minor injuries during the fracas. We have two in custody for manslaughter."

"How long has this been going on?" Naylor inquired.

"The whiskey smuggling? To my knowledge," Berringer replied, "about two months. At first, I thought the cases of intoxication we encountered were produced by native beer the tribesmen make from sarsaparilla roots and berries. As it turns out, though, I was mistaken."

"And you've caught no one bringing in the liquor?" Slade inquired.

"Not yet," said Berringer. "After the fatal melee, I interrogated the survivors. Two of them reluctantly admitted that delivery was made by white men, but they either didn't know or would not share with me the names."

"Bill Tanner thought he had a lead in Stateline," Naylor said.

"Oh, yes? He must have learned that after he was here," said Berringer. "At least, he failed to mention it."

"We're interested in the smuggling and mean to stop it if we can," Slade said. "First thing, of course, we need to find whoever murdered Marshal Tanner and collect them for Judge Dennison."

"Priorities, of course," said Berringer. "Do

you suspect my Cherokees?"

"The only lead we have right now," Slade answered, "is the damage that he suffered."

"There was mutilation, as I understand it," said the agent. "Scalping, was it?"

"And some other things," Slade said. "I need to ask about the feet."

"I beg your pardon?"

"Someone chopped 'em off," said Naylor.

"Oh?"

"Our undertaker, back in Enid, had the notion that was something Indians might do," Slade said. "To keep a vengeful spirit from pursuing them?"

Berringer frowned. "Well, now. It's nothing that I've heard associated with the Cherokee," he said. "But then, I haven't made a detailed study of their odd native customs. Here, you realize, we stress the Christian values that have made our country great."

As if on cue, an older tribesman dressed in butler's garb appeared and said, "Dinner is served."

Berringer's house had indoor plumbing — no sprints to a privy in the middle of the night for him — so Slade and Naylor washed up in a small room off the kitchen, then proceeded to the dining room. The

68

table there had seating for a dozen people but was set for three. Frank Berringer presided at its head, while Slade sat to his left and Naylor on his right.

The agent poured wine all around, not asking Slade this time, and sipped his while another Cherokee, this one apparently the waiter, served them large bowls of potato soup. Slade spotted onions in the mix and gave the cook due credit for his effort.

While they ate the soup, Berringer talked about his trials and tribulations at the agency. "The Cherokee are childlike, for the most part," he explained, "but even children may turn savage if they're not restrained, eh, gentlemen?"

Slade chewed a mouthful of potato, letting Naylor take the bait. "I knew a kid like that, one time," Luke said. "He damn near bit my little finger off. Still got the scar."

Berringer eyed Naylor's upraised finger with a fine disdain, saying, "Of course, the danger from a tribe of full-grown savages, no matter how childlike in mind, is that they won't be satisfied with simply gnawing on your finger. If their heathen impulses are not constrained . . . well, who knows what may happen in the way of tragedy?"

"Your school helps out with that, I guess," said Slade.

"To some extent," the agent granted. "Though I must admit, we aren't producing any scholars here. The brighter ones can learn to read and write, if they apply themselves sufficiently, but this peculiar talk of higher education for the red man I've been hearing? I mean, really. What's the point?"

"Never got past the seventh grade, myself," said Naylor. "Guess I've done all right."

"And that's the key," said Berringer. "An individual must recognize his limitations. Why encourage hopeless fantasies when they are just a waste of time and energy for all concerned?"

The soup was gone, and Berringer summoned their waiter with a little silver bell. The Cherokee cleared off their bowls and soupspoons, coming back after a moment with their main meal for the evening. It looked like venison, with sweet potatoes and some green beans on the side.

"We're living off the land here, as you see," said Berringer. "The Cherokee have learned to farm, after a fashion, and they're still proficient hunters. Don't believe the gossip that you hear about privation, gentlemen."

Slade would have bet a month's pay that no Cherokee was dining from a menu such as Berringer's tonight, but he kept the opinion to himself. Instead, he said, "I wonder if you could arrange, before we leave, for me to see my friend."

Berringer looked up from his meal and frowned. "Your friend, Marshal?"

Slade held the agent's gaze and answered, "Little Wolf."

"Ah, yes. Well, I'm afraid that won't be possible."

"Why's that?" Slade asked.

"Because we haven't seen him for . . . oh, what? Three weeks now, I would say. Perhaps a little more."

"You're saying that he's disappeared?"

"I wouldn't state it so dramatically," said Berringer. "He's what I'd call a restless sort. It's not the first time he's been absent without leave, as you may be aware."

"You wouldn't be referring to the time he helped me track those fugitives to Texas," Slade replied, not making it a question. Neither did he mention that the chase had taken Little Wolf and him across the border into Mexico without official sanction from the governments on either side.

"No, no," said Berringer. "But I'm advised there was at least one prior occasion when he left the reservation for some reason of his own, never explained."

"That rings a bell," Slade said. "In fact, it was the first time that he saved my life. And helped me bag the Bender family."

Berringer blinked at that. "The Benders? Out of Kansas?"

"Out of anywhere they chose to go, until we stopped them. Me and Little Wolf."

Berringer sipped his wine, then said, "I had not heard that part of it."

"Don't worry," Slade replied. "It wouldn't be the first time files were incomplete."

"Indeed, sir. At the risk of bearing tales, my predecessor's record-keeping skills left much to be desired."

Slade brought the conversation back on track. "I'd be disturbed to learn that Little Wolf had come to any harm through no fault of his own."

"I have no reason to believe that is the case," said Berringer. "Of course, once he's beyond the reservation's boundaries, there's nothing I can do to find or help him."

"There were no incidents before you lost track of him?" Slade inquired. "I'm thinking of that trouble that he had before our trip to Texas, with the other fellow's family."

"You'd be referring to the death of Mayank, also known as Moon," Berringer said.

"I don't recall getting the name," Slade said.

"I likely didn't mention it," the agent granted. "Little Wolf was serving sixty days before he joined you in your manhunt. Is that proper terminology?"

"It's close enough," said Slade.

"Is he a tracker?" Naylor asked. "This Little Wolf?"

"The best I've seen," Slade said.

"Too bad he isn't here, eh? We might need the help before we're done."

"Too bad," Slade echoed. "But there's nothing to be done about it, I suppose."

Their waiter came to clear away the plates and wine-glasses, returning shortly with another liquor bottle and some smaller glasses on a silver tray.

"Brandy," said Berringer. "The perfect end to almost any meal."

"Another first for me," said Naylor. "Fill 'er up."

The waiter poured while Berringer pressed on. "I trust you'll stay the night with us," he said. "To start for Stateline now . . . well, you'd be forced to camp before you've gone five miles."

"Sounds good to me," Naylor replied. "I'll take a roof over my head when I can get it."

Nodding, Slade said, "Thank you for your

hospitality."

"Nonsense," said Berringer. "You're helping me — and all of us — by following this liquor business to its end. And finding justice for your friend, of course."

"Well, if you've got a cabin not in use . . ."

"No, Marshal Slade. I wouldn't hear of it," said Berringer. "I have spare rooms made up for visitors. The odd inspector from the bureau, military officers, that sort of thing."

"Well, if it's good enough for them," said Naylor, "we'll get by all right."

"I'll have Rupali show you to your rooms." Berringer rang his little bell again, a double chime this time. "Her name translates as 'Beautiful,' I'm told, but you can judge that for yourselves."

The young woman who stepped into the dining room a moment later was, in fact, quite pretty in her starched maid's uniform. Slade wondered if her duties were confined to cleaning and conveying visitors to vacant rooms, but there was no good way to ask — and no point riling Berringer.

Rising as Naylor did, Slade bade their host good night and trailed Rupali to his bedroom for the night.

It was a smaller room than the one Slade

had at the hotel in Enid, but its furnishings had obviously cost a good deal more. Taxpayers' money, Slade supposed, since Berringer was no innkeeper with a capital investment in the place. He'd want to make a good impression on the bigwigs sent from Washington to check his operation — maybe check his bookkeeping — and make his job secure.

That thought turned Slade's mind back to Berringer's young maid. He wondered if the dignitaries passing through would find some comfort there, or with some other comely woman under Berringer's control. There was no reason to assume it, but he hadn't liked the agent's last remark about Rupali. Something in the tone of it had set his teeth on edge.

Forget it, he decided. *Focus on the job.*

So far, they had gained nothing in their search for evidence or information that would lead them to the bootleggers and Tanner's killers. Slade still couldn't say if Tanner had been slain by Indians or white men, though it was a safe bet that the whiskey cookers would be white. No reservation could conceal a moonshine operation — not unless the supervising agent was involved in some kind of conspiracy. And Berringer, for all his faults, did not strike

Slade as someone who would deign to tend a still.

As for Little Wolf's disappearance, there was nothing Slade could do about it at the moment — or at all, unless he had some kind of lead to where the Cherokee had gone, what had become of him. He *was* the kind to roam about at will, Slade knew, if it was feasible. And once he crossed the reservation's boundary, anything might happen. Little Wolf might have encountered roaming gunmen or a farmer who shot first at Indians and thought of asking questions later, if at all. He might be locked up in some rural jail for nothing more than having bronze skin in a white man's town.

Or maybe he had ridden off and just kept going, Slade surmised. Maybe the ride to Mexico and back had given Little Wolf ideas. A taste of freedom that he wanted to recapture and try to make permanent — or anyway, to last as long as possible, on his own.

And why not, if he had the chance? Slade saw no reason to begrudge him that, though many others whom he met along the way might disagree.

As Slade prepared for sleep, he turned his thoughts back to the job at hand. There was a chance, he realized — although a slim one

— that Bill Tanner's murder might be unrelated to the moonshine ring he'd been investigating. It would stretch coincidence beyond the breaking point, but it was *possible* he'd stumbled into renegades while working on the case and had been taken by surprise. If hostile tribesmen were to blame, it scuttled any link to Stateline or the 'shiners. Suspects could be drawn from any of the tribes confined on Oklahoma reservations — or, in theory, a band just passing through from Texas, maybe all the way from Mexico.

That was unlikely, granted. Unless something came along to prove that angle, Slade would work the murder as a part of his ongoing whiskey case. It made more sense, but also complicated matters. When they got to Stateline, he and Naylor, there'd be no one they could absolutely trust. Not local law, the mayor, or anybody else.

What else was new?

How often had he ridden into strange towns, wondering if he would find a friend among the people there when it came time to do his job? Would they support the law or find excuses to be elsewhere, not give a damn?

At least this time he wasn't going in alone. Luke Naylor had a few rough edges, but on balance he seemed competent enough. Slade hadn't worked with him before but had no fear Naylor would let him down. Whether he'd go the distance . . . well, that was another question altogether. One Slade couldn't answer at the outset of a job.

They had arranged to be up early in the morning, off straight after breakfast on their way to Stateline. Even so, they would be camped out overnight before they reached their destination sometime Friday. That was more time for the killers to make tracks, if they were running — or to finalize their preparations for a showdown if they figured other marshals would be following along in Tanner's tracks.

Trouble for Slade, whichever way it went.

But he would find them, even if it meant he had to ride to Hell and back.

Hadn't he done that, more or less, already?

Turning down his bedside lamp, Slade let his thoughts stray from the job. He needed sleep, and in those moments prior to dropping off, his mind still turned toward Faith. He wondered whether she had finished packing up her things, if there'd been any offers on her ranch, if she had finalized the details of her getaway from him and all the ugly memories that haunted her.

Slade wished her luck with that, though

personal experience had taught him running didn't help much. You could leave a place behind, never return, and maybe even block it from your waking mind, but there were always dreams — or nightmares — to recall what set you running in the first place. Slade, while he was drifting, had become an expert at departing, but he'd hear a snatch of music sometimes, catch an old familiar scent, or see a stranger on the street who brought another face to mind, and it would be as if he'd never left.

He wished Faith luck forgetting him, if that was what she needed to be whole and lead a life that brought her joy. Slade didn't want to think that happiness might lie beyond her grasp forever after what she'd been through with his brother, then with him. That pained him more than losing her — which he supposed was proof of love, for what that might be worth.

Nothing. Not now.

Whatever Faith had felt for him was lost to pain and gun smoke, images of dead and dying strangers, enemies, some of her better friends. If he could turn the clock back, do it all again, Slade thought he would've handed in his badge after his brother was avenged and kept on going, back to drifting and the poker tables where he might lose money but no one had ever laid a finger on his heart.

All second-guessing now.

Whatever he decided, there was still one job to finish. Bill Tanner deserved whatever Slade could do for him, for justice of a sort, although it wouldn't bring the fair-haired marshal back.

They could send his killers on to join him, with a rope or with a bullet, if they didn't care to wait around for trial.

It wasn't much, but it was something, and Slade took it with him into sleep.

5

Slade woke before dawn on Thursday, spent a hazy moment trying to recall his fractured dreams, then gave it up and used the water closet down the hallway from his room. Returning, he stopped briefly outside Naylor's door, listened for any sounds of movement, then passed on without knocking

Give him time. A little more, at least.

Cold water had to do for washing up and shaving, but it fit with Slade's normal routine and helped clear out the final cobwebs from his drowsy brain. He thought about the ride to Stateline, calculating how far they could go before they had to camp at dusk, and figured they should reach the border town midmorning Friday, if they met no obstacles along the way.

And once they got to Stateline, they would have to watch each step, each word, while they determined who was trustworthy and who was not. Assuming it was even pos-

81

sible to tell.

Approaching any town for the first time, a lawman never knew what he would find. In some, the people shared a common goal or desire and showed the outside world a firm united front. Others were scarred by deep, bitter divisions, and a wily man could play one side against another if it suited him. Maybe one element tried lording it over the rest, and all the underdogs required was someone to encourage them, give them a little push toward mutiny.

Stateline's division — half in Kansas, half in Oklahoma Territory — hinted at a world of possibilities that wouldn't be revealed until Slade saw the place and judged it for himself. And if somebody tried to take him down while he was doing that, at least he'd know that someone in the town had secrets to conceal.

Secrets worth killing for.

A thump from Naylor's room next door told Slade the other deputy was up and moving. Slipping his boots on, he heard Naylor's door open and close, footsteps receding toward the water closet, coming back again while Slade was strapping on his pistol belt. He'd take the long guns and his saddlebags downstairs to breakfast, maybe leave them in the entry hall for easy access once they'd finished and were on their way.

Five minutes more, and he was out. Naylor emerged, sniffing the air, and asked, "That ham I smell?"

"Let's go find out."

Berringer beat them to the dining table, seated at his normal place with coffee steaming in a mug as Slade and Naylor entered. "Gentlemen," he said, smiling. "I trust you both slept well?"

"Wish I could take that bed along with me," Naylor replied.

"You'd need a wagon, I'm afraid," the agent said.

It had been ham that Naylor smelled, along with fried eggs and potatoes, thick rye toast, and strong black coffee, served by the same waiter from last night. Since there was only one course to the meal, Berringer left his little bell alone, told anecdotes about the Cherokee that passed for jokes, and cleaned his breakfast plate.

Outside, in pale daylight, they found their saddled horses waiting for them, guarded by the same youths who had taken them away the previous evening. It seemed that Berringer had certain members of the tribe picked out to serve him, although whether they were privileged thereby or simply drew the low card, Slade could not have said.

He checked the bridle on his roan, made sure the saddle cinches wouldn't chafe her, then stowed his long guns and turned back to Berringer. The agent wore a little smile, half quizzical, and said, "My boys are fully capable of saddling a horse, Marshal."

"Looks like it," Slade replied. And to the blank-faced Cherokees: "No slight intended. When it's my butt on the line, I don't take anything for granted."

Naylor took a moment, eyed his riding tackle cautiously, then mounted up. When Slade was in his saddle, reins in hand, he turned to Berringer a final time and said, "If you hear anything we ought to know, contact Judge Dennison in Enid. He can get a wire to Stateline with the message."

"Certainly. I wish you luck. Godspeed."

When they were out of earshot, Naylor said, "Godspeed? I would've thought that man's religion was himself."

"You never know," Slade said. "He thinks the Cherokees need saving, but I have to wonder if that just means turning them as white as possible."

"Good luck with that."

"Scrape off the paint, it's all political," said Slade. "Things change in Washington, friend Berringer may find himself out of a job."

"He knows that, too," said Naylor. "Hell, they all do. Did you ever know a bureau agent in your life who wasn't cashing in some way?"

"I've only known this one," Slade answered. "I keep hoping that he's not the rule of thumb."

"Better than some of them, I'd say. We had one down in Texas who was leasing out Apaches to pick cotton, pocketing the cash. Another one I heard about kept the allotment set aside for beef and fed the Injuns horse meat, sometimes dog. Those two got booted out after a while, but nothing ever happened to 'em, otherwise."

"Way of the world," Slade said. "We've got our hands full with another part of it."

They had a hundred miles to cover, from the agency to Stateline. Call it thirteen, maybe fourteen hours at a steady trot, but Slade didn't intend to wear the horses out to reach their destination after nightfall. Even with the urgency he felt toward solving Tanner's homicide, it wasn't worth leaving themselves afoot on unfamiliar ground, where they might need mobility to stay alive.

Besides, the ride gave Slade a chance to think and get better acquainted with his trail companion. As he learned over the next few miles, Naylor was twenty-five years old and Texas born, a farmer's son who didn't take to plowing, milking cows, or slopping hogs. He'd tried his hand at cowboying, then figured out there was no future in it for him. He'd been appointed a U.S. deputy in Austin, then accepted transfer to the territory when it came his way. He was a fair hand with the twin Colts, by his own account, and while he savored tracking bad men, Naylor didn't have the attitude of some lawmen who yearned for opportunities to throw their weight around.

"You figure we're enough?" asked Naylor, when he'd finished laying out his brief biography.

"Enough for what?" asked Slade.

"To handle what we're up against."

"We don't know what that is yet," Slade replied. "Don't undermine yourself by worrying ahead of time."

"I've just been thinking about Tanner."

"Good. That ought to keep you sharp. But don't imagine that you'll end up the same way."

"Could happen, though," said Naylor.

"Anything *could* happen," Slade reminded him. "We could be struck by lightning from a clear sky, or a prairie fire could overtake us on the trail. You could wake up tonight with rattlers in your bedroll."

"Thanks for that," said Naylor. "Nice of you to cheer me up."

"The other side of fretting is that we could have the job wrapped up in no time, run the 'shiners out, bust up their stills, and bring whoever took Bill Tanner down to face Judge Dennison."

"You really see that happening?"

"The day I pinned this badge on," Slade replied, "I gave up telling fortunes."

"Hey, speaking of that, I heard you took the job to nail your brother's killers. That the straight of it, or just a campfire story?"

"Straight, far as it goes," Slade said and laid it out for Naylor, sketchy on the details, steering absolutely clear of Faith and their relationship.

When he was done, the younger deputy said, "And you stuck around when it was done. No itch to get back on the move?"

"I've seen a lot of territory," Slade admitted. "And I won't say one place is the same as any other. That's a crock. Some places, you can take your ease and never give a second thought to trouble. Others . . . well, I reckon you've seen those."

"A few," Naylor acknowledged. "But to stay in Enid when you've been to Dallas, Denver, any of the big towns, something had to hold you."

They were edging into something Slade did not plan to discuss with Naylor, or with anybody else. To cut it off, he said, "You get to be my age, the thought of staying put begins to make more sense. A steady salary, a roof over your head that you can count on."

"Goin' out to sniff around for killers. Gettin' shot at for your trouble. Yeah," said Naylor. "I can see how that appeals to an old-timer like yourself." He laughed and added, "You've got what, ten years on me?"

"At least," Slade said. Some days it felt like forty.

"I don't know," said Naylor. "Enid's good for now, you know. But it's a place I work *from,* if you follow me. I like the traveling. The hunting."

"Just make sure you're not the one who's being hunted," Slade advised him.

"There you go. That sunny disposition."

"It's a funny thing, I grant you," Slade replied. "Older you are, the more it seems you've got to lose. Should be the other way around, if it made any sense."

"Who ever said that life makes sense? My older brother is a preacher, if you can believe it, down El Paso way. He makes a living spittin' fire and brimstone at the faithful, Sunday mornings. Couple hundred of 'em eat it up."

"I take it that you're not a praying man, yourself?"

"Depends," Naylor replied. "One time I prayed I wasn't out of ammunition, and I found some shells. Does that count?"

"Only if they fell out of the sky."

"Guess not, then." Naylor turned more serious and said, "Last time I saw my brother, we had words about him sellin' things nobody gets to see or take advantage of while they're alive. I doubt that he's forgiven me, or maybe ever will." A pause, before he said, "Don't get me wrong. I wouldn't say there's *nothing* on the other side, okay? I just don't know. Nobody does, who's still around and breathing, right? Guess that's the part of it that rubs me the wrong way."

"Well, hopefully," Slade said, "we won't find out on this trip, anyway."

"Amen," said Naylor, with a crooked smile. "Amen to that."

"How long ago did this come in?" asked Grady Sullivan.

"Within the hour," Percy Fawcett said. "I sent for you directly, sir."

Sullivan read the telegram a second time,

brow furrowing at what he saw. Of course, it had to happen. There'd been no way to avoid it once the door was opened and he'd stepped through, following the big man's orders.

"You'll keep this to yourself," said Sullivan, not asking.

Fawcett bobbed his head, which made his wire-rimmed spectacles slip down his stubby nose. "Of course, sir. That's the rule."

"And we all know how much you care for rules, now, don't we, Percy?"

Fawcett's sunken cheeks flushed crimson as he pushed the glasses up his nose, eyes twitching free of Sullivan's relentless stare.

When he was satisfied the small man had been duly cowed, Sullivan left the Western Union office, walking east along the Kansas side of Border Boulevard. The street divided Stateline more or less in half, as did the boundary that separated Oklahoma Territory and the Jayhawk State. That split made for peculiar politics and commerce, even sparked a minor feud from time to time, but none of that concerned him at the moment.

He had business with the big man, and it couldn't wait.

Sullivan's destination, two blocks down from Western Union, was the Sunflower

Saloon. It was a good-sized place, the bar and gambling apparatus all downstairs, with ladies and their cribs above. Most nights there'd be some kind of altercation over cards or a doxy, now and then involving guns, normally stopping short of homicide.

You couldn't say that for the Sunflower's competition, catty-corner on the Oklahoma side. The Swagger Inn was a bucket of blood, complete with loaded dice, marked cards, and hookers who were scary if you met them in the sober light of day. The boss man over there, Sean Swagger, hailed from Indiana, Illinois — one of the *I* states, anyhow — and had a reputation as a cutthroat in his younger days. Some hinted that the killing wasn't all behind him, but it didn't matter so long as he kept it on his own side of the street.

Sullivan pushed in through the Sunflower's bat-wing doors, jangly piano music greeting him despite the morning hour. The saloon was open twenty-four hours a day, dealers and strumpets working shifts around the clock, to take in every dollar that they could. The big man would be in his counting room by now, after his standard breakfast — steak and eggs — checking the past night's take.

Sullivan didn't like to be the bearer of bad

news, but it was better faced immediately, while they could prepare themselves, than being put off in the fragile hope that it would all blow past and leave them undisturbed.

Too late for that.

A storm was coming. Sullivan could feel it drawing nearer, and he wondered who'd be standing after it had passed.

The barkeep saw him coming. "Beer for breakfast, Grady?"

"Not this morning. Is he in his office?"

"Same as always."

Sullivan turned toward the west end of the long oak bar, past poker tables and a roulette wheel, to reach a door marked PRIVATE, by the staircase that the painted ladies used, leading their customers to paradise. He knocked and waited for the summons from within, then entered, closed the door behind him, moving to a spot before the big man's desk.

"You've got a sour look," Flynn Rafferty observed, sitting behind the spacious desk with greenbacks in both hands. "Something you ate? Or something eating you?"

Sullivan offered him the telegram. The big man took it, read it silently, and then once more, aloud. "*Two marshals coming.* That's the message? Christ, that penny-pinching bastard could have given us their names, at least."

"He likely thought we'd recognize them by their badges," Sullivan replied.

"And so we will. Given the choice, though, I'd prefer to do without the pleasure of their company."

"Coming from Enid when the wire was sent, they won't get here before tomorrow morning," Sullivan suggested. "I could meet them on the trail. Discourage them."

"That's good," Rafferty said. "But delegate it, will you? Someone you can trust to do the job unsupervised."

"It wouldn't take me long," said Sullivan. "Ride out this evening, come straight back when it's done."

"A military officer knows when to share the burden of command," said Rafferty.

"Wasn't aware I'd joined the army."

"Weren't you? We're expanding, branching out," the big man said. "You know *that*, certainly."

"Yes, sir."

"Opening new territory means resistance from established opposition, eh?"

A silent nod from Sullivan.

"If I'm the general commanding our advance, that makes you — what? My colonel?"

"Long as I don't have to wear a uniform," said Sullivan.

"Nothing like that," the big man answered, smiling. "But I can't afford to have you riding off to every skirmish."

"U.S. marshals. Two of them."

"If they knew anything about our operation, there'd be twenty coming. Or the cavalry."

"I guess. But when they find these two . . ."

"Why should they *find* them, Grady? Better, don't you think, if these two simply disappear?"

"Like they were never here," said Sullivan.

"A mystery. Something for old Judge Dennison to ponder, sitting in his courthouse."

"While he's picking more to send."

"It buys us time," the big man said. "And when the next ones head our way, we'll think of something else. You with me?"

"Absolutely, Boss."

"All right, then. Pick your men and send them on their way."

At dusk, still thirty miles or so from Stateline, Slade and Naylor found their campsite. It was on a low ridge lined with bur oaks, ample grass for grazing, and a spring that

94

burbled out of rocks a few yards distant from the spot they chose for sleeping. High ground let them scan the countryside while daylight still remained. Nightfall would blind them, while their campfire shone out like a beacon if they didn't find a way to screen it.

"Maybe over here, between these oaks," Naylor suggested. "We'd have cover from the east and south, at least."

"Suits me," Slade said. He'd staked his roan where she could graze and reach the spring at will, with Naylor's mount to keep her company.

They spent a quarter of an hour scavenging for dead wood on the ridge, gathered enough to keep a fire up through the night, and Naylor lit the kindling with a wooden match. He put the coffee on and they got settled on their blankets, eating from their saddlebags. Jerky and corn dodgers for Slade, Naylor devouring some kind of sandwich he had brought from home.

"Smoked ham and cheese," he said around a mouthful. "Got another for the morning, too."

Slade wished he'd thought of something similar and made a mental note to try for some variety on the ride back from Stateline. As to how long they would be in town, or what they'd find upon arrival there, he didn't have a clue.

Naylor appeared to read his thoughts, asking, "You think the 'shine is being made somewhere around Stateline?"

"We know Tanner was there," Slade answered. "Anything beyond that's just a guess."

"But something had to draw him there," said Naylor. "Right? I mean, he didn't close his eyes and point his finger at a map, deciding where to go."

"Not likely," Slade allowed.

"So, something that he picked up from the reservation, maybe?"

"Not from Berringer, or he'd have shared it with us," Slade replied.

"One of the Injuns, then. Would they have talked to him?"

"Could be. Bill had a way of being affable." Slade caught a glimpse of Naylor's frown. "Friendly," he translated.

"Maybe he got *too* affable and some of 'em resented it."

Slade sipped his coffee. Shrugged. "I couldn't rule it out," he answered, "but it doesn't sound like Bill."

"We're back to 'shiners, then. One of the Cherokees knew something, passed it on. Next thing you know, he's sending telegrams from Stateline."

"Just the one, and nothing in it we can hang our hats on. *Getting close,* he said. No names or pointers."

"So we wait and see what happens when we ask around. Talk to the Western Union guy, their lawmen, anybody else in a position that could help us out."

"Best we can do," Slade granted. "I was thinking we should check out the saloons and see if anyone gets twitchy. If the operation's growing, chances are they've stepped on someone else's toes along the way."

"Could work," Naylor agreed. "But if they're playing rough, the townsfolk could be scared."

"In that case," Slade replied, "we offer them a way to end it. Maybe find a weak link in the chain and try to work a deal with someone on the inside."

"Just so long as we can hang on to our hair."

"I'm planning on it," Slade assured him. "Till it falls out on its own, at least?"

"You come from baldies?" Naylor asked him.

"Not that I'm aware of, but I left home young," said Slade.

"Already anxious for the road."

"Seemed like a good idea," Slade said.

"Then, once you're on it, going home seems like more trouble than it's worth. At least, it did to me."

"You ever miss your folks?" asked Naylor.

Slade sipped his coffee, thought about it. "I was mad as hell when I lit out," he said, at last. "It took a while for that to fade, and by that time I didn't think they'd want me back."

"How come?"

"Some of the things I'd done. Was doing. My old man took a hard line, sort of like your brother."

"Not a preacher, though?"

"He could've been, but felt a calling from the soil instead. I didn't see a future in it for myself."

"Funny how people start and where they finish," Naylor said. "Now here we are."

"Not finished," Slade reminded him. "Just getting started."

"Right. I wouldn't want to hex us."

Darkness settled over them as they sat jawing, drinking coffee, killing time. After a while, a quarter moon raised a coyote chorus in the distance, somewhere to the north, the voices tangled up and wailing.

"Ever wonder what they're saying?" Naylor asked.

"Not lately. Something about who they'll

98

have for supper, I suppose."

"As long as it's not us."

"I'll drink to that."

"Speaking of which," Slade said, reaching into his saddlebag, "I brought this, just in case we caught a chill along the way."

Naylor's smile broadened at sight of the bottle. "Whiskey for a 'shine hunt. Get us in the mood, eh? Sounds all right to me."

6

"Two marshals," Lou McCreery said. "So Grady sends the five of us?"

"You figure that's too many, or too few?" Hoke Woodruff asked.

"Won't know until I see 'em, will I?" Lou replied.

"You're soundin' shaky, Lou," Bob Kerrigan suggested.

"Hell I am!"

"He's right," Eddie Gillespie said. "I'm purty sure I heard a shiver in your voice there."

"Hell you did!"

"Knock off that shit," said Woodruff. As the leader of the hunting party, it was his job to keep order in the ranks and see their job completed without any fumbling. "You want to measure pricks, wait till we're done and you're back at the bunkhouse."

They rode on in brooding silence for a quarter mile or so, then Harry Stroud said,

"Five on two feels right to me. Gives us an edge."

"Plenty of edge," McCreery said. "But killin' marshals . . ."

"They's the same as anybody else," said Kerrigan. "I didn't hear you tellin' Grady no."

"You sure as hell did not," McCreery answered. "I'm just sayin' —"

"Sayin' *what*?" Woodruff demanded. "Spit it out, for Christ's sake."

"That the marshals won't stop comin'," Woodruff said. "One dead already, and tonight we make it three. You think Judge Dennison is gonna fold and cut his losses here? Or will he keep on sendin' more and more, maybe call out the cavalry?"

Woodruff wanted to laugh at that but swallowed it. He couldn't tell these yahoos everything he knew for fear they'd blab it far and wide. Instead, he told them, "Let the big man think about what happens after. You just follow orders, right? Do what you're told, collect your pay, and shut your claptraps."

"You got no call to be so tetchy," said McCreery.

"Keep it up, I'll show you tetchy," Woodruff said, "and then some. I get sick and tired of —"

"Campfire," Stroud announced, pointing ahead and slightly to their left, which made it southwest from the trail they had been following.

Woodruff squinted in that direction, didn't see the light at first, then caught a flicker of it. Hard to say, when they were still a mile or more out from the spot, but it appeared to be on higher ground.

"That's what I mean, goddamn it!" Woodruff said. "You get to yappin' and we damn near miss it."

"Jesus, Hoke, we didn't —"

"Keep your voice down!" Fairly hissing at them now, clutching his reins so tightly that the leather straps felt welded to his hands.

"How do we know it's them?" Gillespie asked him, in a whisper.

"We go up and see. How else?" Woodruff replied.

"But if they ain't the marshals —"

"I said go and *see,* not call 'em out, unless we see their badges. Use your head, will you?"

"So we're just gonna sneak up there and have a look-see?" asked Gillespie.

"That's the plan, unless you've got a better one," said Woodruff.

"Nope. I's just thinkin' that they'll hear us comin' from a ways off."

"Might, if we was riding," Woodruff said. "I figure we'll walk in, leave Harry with the horses farther back, to keep 'em quiet."

"I can do that," Stroud replied, sounding relieved to be left out of any shooting. Woodruff made a mental note of that, for next time when he needed someone he could count on, striking Harry from his first-choice list.

"You need to check your weapons, do it now," Woodruff instructed. "I don't want a bunch of noise when we close in there."

Three of them drew their revolvers, spun the cylinders to verify full loads, then put the guns away. Woodruff had no need to examine his own Smith & Wesson Model 3, kept fully loaded as a matter of routine. He knew some shooters liked to keep an empty chamber underneath the hammer, but to Woodruff that was just a testament to carelessness. He'd never dropped a pistol in his life and didn't plan on starting now.

He'd dropped some men, though. Right around a dozen.

And tonight he planned to add a couple more.

They flipped a silver dollar for first watch; Slade lost with tails and edged back from the fire a bit as Naylor bedded down. Edging around one of the bur oaks blocked the low flames from his line of sight, allowing his night vision to adjust. The quarter moon helped out a little, in its field of stars, but spotting any kind of danger from a distance clearly wasn't happening. He'd trust his ears instead, staying alert for any sounds of an approaching predator, and hope he didn't doze before the time came for his switch with Naylor.

As a rule, staying awake on watch wasn't a problem, but his sleep had been disturbed of late by dreams of Faith, both loving her and losing her. A kind of weariness had settled over Slade the past two weeks, not the fatigue that came from strenuous activity but an annoying sense of lassitude he might associate with riding through a desert, no clear end in sight.

Slade's mind kept circling back to Faith, wishing he knew a way to make things right with her, fearing it was beyond him. He'd been ready to consider turning in his badge after they married, finding out if he could be of any use around the ranch, but that idea had vanished in a cloud of gun smoke and he realized there wouldn't be a second chance. When Faith made up her mind on something serious, there was no turning her around.

Which brought him back to thinking of himself again, wondering whether he should stick around or give his notice to Judge Dennison, start counting down the days until he was a free man once again. Funny, it didn't feel like freedom when he thought about it, though.

It felt a bit like being lost.

But first things first. Whatever Slade decided, he still had a job to do, and it was likely going to be dangerous. Whether Bill Tanner had been killed by Indians or moonshiners, Slade planned to run them down and see them pay.

Naylor would do all right, he thought, as long as youthful overconfidence could be restrained. He didn't seem to have a reckless attitude per se, but it was easy to let down your guard when you had worn the badge a while and won a fight or two. Slade wished Naylor had seen Bill Tanner's corpse, to sober him a bit, but maybe his description of the body was enough to do the trick.

Or maybe he was underestimating Naylor, after all. Slade wondered whether he was jealous of the younger deputy — the years still stretching out before him, with a cornucopia of opportunities. Was Slade hearing the echoes of his own mortality from Tanner's death and the proximity of youth?

If so, he had to keep a rein on that.

A fatalistic attitude, he realized, could be lethal to a lawman. When you started taking death for granted, it was easier to hesitate. Not giving up, exactly, but delaying a reaction in a crisis situation, even by a fraction of a second, could be all the break an enemy required to make the kill.

A call of nature interrupted Slade's dark thoughts. He rose and moved away from camp as quietly as possible, out past the horses to a point beyond the burbling stream. No need for cover in the night, even if he was being watched by several thousand stars.

Hoke Woodruff huddled with the three men he had chosen to accompany him on his slow hike up the ridge through darkness. Heads together with their hat brims touching, he warned his companions in a graveyard whisper, "First one of you makes a noise from here on in, I'll gut you like a hog."

To punctuate the threat, he drew a bowie knife and passed its twelve-inch blade before their faces, glinting starlight. No one tested him by answering. Convinced that they had got the message, Woodruff sheathed his blade and started up the slope to higher ground.

Damn, but he still couldn't be sure whose camp they were approaching, whether the expected marshals or some drifters heading anyplace but where they'd been. He had to take it slow and easy now, make sure who he was dealing with before he made a move. Not that he minded shooting strangers, but tonight it wouldn't do. If they surprised and killed the wrong folks in this camp, it meant a load of wasted time, scut work disposing of them, and a likelihood that they would fail to do the job they'd been assigned.

The last part was what worried Woodruff most. He didn't want to think about returning empty-handed, telling Grady Sullivan they couldn't find the marshals after all. Embarrassment was only part of it. When Sullivan got riled . . . well, it was best to be somewhere away from him, preferably out of pistol range.

So Woodruff kept his fingers crossed — or would have, if it didn't slow down his quick draw. He tried to place each step precisely as he climbed the slope, uncertain of the ground before him, painfully aware of its potential pitfalls. Loose rocks could betray him, or a patch of mud, a twig rolling beneath his boot. He wouldn't have to fall exactly, to betray their presence near the camp. Just sliding down the ridge could do it, set the others scrambling after all his warnings to be silent, and the blame would fall on him.

The trick was getting close enough to watch the campers without being seen. To hunker down beyond the reach of firelight and discover who or what they were. Badges would mean he'd found the troublemakers he was looking for. No badges . . . well, it *still* might be the lawmen, if they'd taken off their vests or put on jackets, but he couldn't just rush in, guns blazing, if he wasn't sure.

Besides, he had a second job beyond disposing of the marshals. Grady wanted answers from them. How much did they know, if anything, about the Stateline deal? Was there a snitch inside the operation? Maybe more than one? The last cop hadn't talked, but Woodruff knew some methods shared by an old Injun fighter, who in turn had learned his craft from Chiricahuas. Anyone who didn't crack within the first ten, fifteen minutes must be made of stone.

Another thirty yards, and Woodruff strained his ears to pick out any voices, but the camp was quiet. Catching them asleep might make things safer, but it complicated spotting badges, under blankets. He might

have no choice but to confront them, risking gunplay, if he couldn't learn what he
required by spying from the dark.

Get on with it, he thought, biting his lower
lip. *You're wasting time.*

Luke Naylor normally dropped off to sleep
without a bit of trouble, but tonight was
different somehow. Maybe his talk with
Slade, or just imagining what all Bill Tanner
must have suffered in his final hours of life.
Naylor would've denied it, if someone had
asked him to his face, but he was feeling
jumpy. Nerves on edge.

And now, trying to sleep, there was that
damned noise in the night.

The horses, he first thought, but knew that
wasn't right. There was no whickering, no
sound of hooves on grass, and it was coming from the wrong direction anyway. They'd
picketed the horses west of camp, beyond
the spring, and Naylor would have sworn
the scuffling sounds he heard were coming
from the north, maybe a bit northeast.

He cracked an eye and looked around for
Slade, but saw no sign of him. Maybe the
noises came from him, scouting around the
camp's perimeter to keep himself awake.
That fit the *kind* of noise Naylor had heard,
but didn't make much sense to him. He

couldn't picture Slade off roaming through the darkness for no reason, when he might step on a snake or twist his ankle in a gopher's hole.

"Goddamn it!" Naylor muttered, throwing back his blanket, turning toward the gunbelt he had coiled and set aside when he turned in.

"Just leave 'er where she sits," a strange voice told him, as a man stepped into view, out of the dark.

Correction: *four* men, with the others trailing back a step or two behind the one who'd spoken. All of them had six-guns drawn and cocked them now. The sound of hammers locking back grated on Naylor's nerves, setting his teeth on edge.

"You ain't supposed to be alone," the leader of the party said.

"Oh, no?"

"Two marshals, we was told. And here I see two saddles, two bedrolls. So where's the other?"

Naylor tried to feign confusion. "Did you maybe pass him, coming in?"

"We didn't pass nobody, mister. Are you gonna tell us where he is, or do we have to squeeze it out of you?"

"Hold on there, partner," Naylor answered. "I was fast asleep up here until I heard you all bumblin' around out there. You woke me up. The hell am I supposed to know where anybody went or what they did while I'm in dreamland?"

"Marshal, if you're prone to jokin', I can promise you this ain't the time," the mouthpiece of the quartet said.

"Four guns to none," said Naylor, "doesn't put me in a joking mood."

"Best tell us where your partner is, then, hadn't you?"

Naylor figured his right hand was at least twelve inches from the nearest of his pistols, too far to be useful if the strangers cut loose from their present range. The only thing that he could think of was to stall for time and hope Slade reappeared from wherever in hell he'd gone.

"I'll say it one more time," he offered. "I was sleeping when you made the noise that roused me. If you want to find my partner, best thing for you all to do is call him." And with that, he hollered out, "Hey, Jack! You wanna get your ass back here to camp?"

"No need to shout," a voice said from the darkness.

Then all hell broke loose.

Slade had barely finished buttoning his fly when he heard voices from the camp. Luke

Naylor's first, and then a voice he didn't recognize. The words eluded him at first, but Slade assumed they represented trouble in the making. With Bill Tanner's grim example fresh in mind, he didn't feel like giving strangers in the night the benefit of any doubt.

He doubled back to camp, Peacemaker drawn and cocked, his sense of urgency and caution vying for control as he advanced. Long strides, but careful not to make a misstep and announce himself to whoever had dropped in for a chat. Behind him, Slade's roan and his partner's snowflake Appaloosa both stood silently, watching him and waiting to see what would happen next.

Slade reached the last bur oak before the fire, staying in shadow as he counted four new faces in the camp. Naylor was sitting upright with his blanket thrown aside, his twin Colts visible but too far out of hand to do him any good right now. He'd need a suitable diversion if he planned on reaching them, and even then he would require a healthy dose of luck.

Slade got in on the tail end of the conversation, Naylor telling the four guns, "I'll say it one more time. I was sleeping when you made the noise that roused me. If you want to find my partner, best thing for you all to

112

do is call him." Suiting words to action then, he yelled, "Hey, Jack! You wanna get your ass back here to camp?"

"No need to shout," Slade answered, leveling his Peacemaker.

The shooters spun to face him, couldn't help themselves under the circumstances, and it wasn't a negotiating situation. Slade squeezed off a round that struck the nearest of his targets in the chest and dropped him thrashing on the grass, then ducked back out of sight behind the oak as other guns cut loose.

He didn't bother counting, couldn't tell if Naylor'd reached his Colts or been cut down while he was trying. Slade rolled to his right, around the bur oak's trunk and out the other side from where he'd fired a moment earlier. Two of the four intruders still were on their feet and moving, one looking for him, the other fanning shots in Naylor's general direction while the younger marshal ducked and rolled to save his skin, returning fire without a chance to aim.

Slade nailed the pistolero who was stalking him, a gut shot, but it wasn't good enough. The wounded man dropped to his knees, cursing, but braced his six-gun in a firm two-handed grip and sent a bullet whistling past Slade's head. Thumbs drawing back the hammer, and he might get luckier this time unless —

Slade's next shot drilled the target's forehead, blew out through the back somewhere, and sent his slouch hat sailing. Gunfire hammered from his right, and Slade twisted in that direction, ready with his Colt, but Naylor didn't need him. Rapid-firing from a place low on the ground, he made the final gunman jerk and dance before he fell.

Slade's ears were ringing, but he still made out a voice calling from somewhere in the darkness to the north. "Hoke? Harry? *Anybody?*"

Scrambling to his feet, Slade ran in that direction, but he wasn't fast enough. Before he'd covered half the estimated distance, he heard rapid hoofbeats fading in the night, first there, then gone. He saw more horses milling in confusion, riderless.

Damn it!

"It's me," he called to Naylor, as he hiked back into camp. "Don't shoot."

"You took your time," said Naylor. "Figured I was done there, for a second."

"Sorry. Had my hands full," Slade replied. "One got away."

"I guess that's bad," Naylor surmised.

"It can't be good," Slade said.

■ ■ ■ ■

"Don't know how much you heard," said Naylor, as they searched the bodies, coming up with nothing to identify the dead.

"Only the last bit," Slade replied. "About my ass."

"The one who did their talking for 'em said they were expecting two of us. *Two marshals, we was told,* the way he put it. So my question would be —"

"Told by who?" Slade finished for him.

"That's exactly right."

"Someone in Stateline, I imagine."

"Yeah, but *who* told *them?*"

Slade thought about it. "Any warning had to come from Enid, way I see it. Hard to see a rider reaching Stateline, passing word in time for guns to turn around and meet us here, but they're connected by the telegraph. Someone in town knew what we've been assigned to do and sold us out."

"It wouldn't be the judge," said Naylor.

"No. But someone in the courthouse could've done it. Or somebody that a courthouse worker spoke to, talking out of turn."

"Maybe the undertaker?"

"I don't picture Holland Mattson having any truck with moonshiners," Slade said, "but I can't tell you it's impossible."

"Another marshal?"

That gave Slade a sour feeling in his stomach, worsening because he couldn't absolutely rule it out. Instead of answering, he said, "We need to bring their horses into camp before they wander off."

"What for?" Naylor inquired.

"To load these four at first light, for the trip to Stateline," Slade replied.

"You want to take 'em in?"

"Sure thing. And see who's waiting for them. Maybe who looks disappointed when we turn up with the bad boys draped across their saddles."

"Right. Okay. Sounds like a lot of work, though."

"Could be worse," Slade said. "They might be packing you."

"You always this much fun to travel with?" asked Naylor.

"Hard to say," Slade answered him. "I'm normally alone."

The dead men's horses hadn't strayed when Slade and Naylor reached them, each man leading two back to the camp, where they were hobbled near the roan and Appaloosa. Slade refused to load the animals with their late riders yet and leave them standing under deadweight all night long, which left them only one alternative. They dragged the corpses out of camp and far enough away to spare themselves from any trouble with coyotes in the hours that remained till sunrise.

"We've got some answers due in Stateline," Naylor said when it was done.

"We do," Slade said, "but we should take it easy. Stick to what we planned, after we drop those four with whoever's in charge. Find out what happens when we light a fire under the pot."

"You're pretty sly," said Naylor.

"When I need to be. Like now."

"Hey, thanks for helpin' out before. I likely could've taken 'em, you know, but why hog all the glory?"

"Right," Slade said. "Especially when there's enough to go around."

"My thought exactly," Naylor said.

And Slade suspected there would be more opportunities in Stateline, too. Someone was anxious to prevent them getting there — which made him all the more determined to proceed.

7

Flynn Rafferty was in his office at the Sunflower Saloon, counting the money stacked atop his desk, when knuckles beat a tattoo on the door. He reached into a pocket of his suit coat, closed his hand around the small Apache pistol that he carried there, and called out, "Enter!"

Grady Sullivan came in, trailed by a harried-looking fellow with a day's growth on his cheeks and jaw, traces of trail dust on his clothes. They stood before the big man's desk, the nervous one with hat in hand. Flynn thought his name was Eddie Something. Gilligan? Gilhooley?

"Well, what is it?" Flynn demanded.

"Go ahead," said Sullivan. "Tell him what you told me."

"Um . . . Mr. Flynn . . . thing is, we missed 'em, sir."

"Missed who?" he asked, before it hit him and he felt the first small spark of anger flaring in his chest. "You mean . . . ?"

"The marshals. Yes, sir. I was told to watch the horses, now, you understand. It weren't *my* fault."

"What happened?"

"Well, I couldn't see much from the spot where Hoke told me to wait —"

"Hoke Woodruff," Grady interrupted.

"Yes, I know him," Flynn replied. Thinking, *The goddamned idjit.* And to Eddie Something: "You. Keep talking."

"Yes, sir. Um . . . the other boys left me and walked up to this fire we seen, top of a ridge there, and I couldn't hear 'em talkin' to whoever was in camp, you know. I kinda seen 'em with the firelight there behind 'em, but it wasn't clear. After a couple minutes, someone started shootin', then they all did, but I couldn't leave them horses after Hoke gimme the order, so I . . . um . . ."

"You left them to it," Flynn suggested.

"Yes, sir. That's about it. For a minute there, I thought they might be winnin'. Then this fella what I never seen before comes runnin' down toward where I was, and I . . . well, I . . ."

"Took off," Flynn said. "And what about your friends?"

"They's dead," Eddie replied. "I mean, they'd have to be, sir. All that shootin' of a

119

sudden, then it cut off quick. They couldn't be alive no ways."

"You'd better hope not," Flynn informed him.

"Sir?"

"They won't be very well disposed toward you, now, would they? After you abandoned them? If they're alive and talking to the law?"

The dusty gunman blanched at that, wringing his hat with anxious hands. "They's dead, all right," he muttered, as if trying to convince himself. "I'm sure of that."

"Well, then, your problem's solved. But mine remains. Leave me to speak with Grady, will you?"

"Yes, sir. Absolutely, sir."

"Wait at the bar," Sullivan ordered, as his flunky reached the office door, prepared to exit.

"Right. Okay."

Alone with Sullivan, Flynn said, "Goddamn it, Grady! What the hell?"

"I know, Boss."

"Oh, you *know*. Well, that's all right, then."

"Sir, I didn't say —"

"Shut up! Best case, we've lost four men and put the marshals on their guard. Worst case, some of the clumsy bastards are alive

120

and talking to the law right now."

"They wouldn't give us up," said Sullivan.

"Oh, no? You want to bet your life on that, one of them looking at a noose unless he gives them someone higher up the ladder? *I* don't."

"There's another possibility," said Sullivan. "With all that shooting Eddie heard, maybe they took the marshals with 'em."

"Wouldn't that be great?" Flynn sneered. "And then some moke can find them all together, our boys and the two dead lawmen. That's fabulous!"

"I can ride out and see if —"

"No! *Hell,* no! Forget that. If there's any chance to put this off on someone else, you'd only make it worse by mixing in the middle of it. Shit!"

"One other way it could've gone," said Sullivan.

"Oh, yes? What's that?"

"Well, Eddie didn't see much. Nothing, really. We aren't even sure Hoke and the boys *did* find the lawmen. Suppose they happened on somebody else's camp and got shot up."

"If Woodruff was that stupid, you're a goddamned fool for putting him in charge," Flynn said.

"Yes, sir."

"First thing to do is tie up your loose ends. This Eddie What's-his-name . . ."

"Gillespie."

"If he spills this shit to anybody else, it could be *our* necks in a noose."

Sullivan nodded, stony-faced. "I'll take care of it."

"See that you do. And let me know the minute those two deputies hit town."

Ants had found the corpses overnight, but Slade and Naylor brushed them off as best they could before they hoisted the dead meat onto the abandoned saddle horses. There was no way to decide which man had ridden what horse when they were alive, but none of the four animals protested overmuch as they were loaded up. With camp already broken and the early light of day to guide them, Slade and Naylor led the captured animals — two each, trailing their reins — northeast, toward their intended destination.

"One of two ways this can go, I figure," Naylor said, once they were under way.

"What's that?" asked Slade.

"The local sheriff, constable, whatever, either recognizes them or doesn't. If he *does,* it stands to reason he can tell us who they worked for. If he doesn't —"

"Then he can't. I follow you. Unless he lies."

"He does," Naylor replied, "we've got a whole new world of trouble on our hands."

"Except we may not *know* he's lying, right away," Slade said.

"He'd try to pull the wool over our eyes, you mean."

Slade shrugged. "Can't say until I've met him, but it's possible."

"I have a way of readin' people," Naylor said. "It's like a gift."

"Could come in handy," Slade allowed. He bit his lip to keep a smile from twitching up.

"It's bound to shake somebody up, we come in leadin' this bunch, eh?"

"I wouldn't be surprised," Slade said.

"Show 'em we're not that easy."

"So they'll send more guns next time."

"You think?"

"I don't suppose they'll change their minds and ask us to be friends," said Slade.

"Not likely, is it?" Naylor fiddled with his reins a bit then asked, "Compared to other scrapes you've been in, how was this?"

"We're both alive. I'd say we did all right."

"Better or worse than usual, I mean?"

Slade wished he'd let it go but had to say something. "There isn't any *usual*. It doesn't matter if you have a dozen fights in one town, on the same street. Every man you face is different. They can surprise you. If you let that slip your mind, you're courting trouble."

"Understood. I told you, back a while, how much I like the hunting. Thing is, this was just my fourth — no, *fifth* — real fight. I mean, where there was killin' or close to it. You've been through way more than that."

"I've had my share and then some," Slade agreed.

"It ever get your stomach riled or interfere with sleepin'?"

"With the first one, I was queasy after. That was over cards. Time passes. You get used to it."

"Or quit," said Naylor.

"That's another way to go."

"Can't see me doin' that," the younger deputy replied.

"Long as you're set to see it through, you'll be all right," Slade said. Thinking: *Like me. No one who loves you. Nothing to look forward to except —*

"Don't worry," Naylor told him. "I won't let you down."

"It never crossed my mind."

"Funny if there turns out to be a bounty on these boys, eh?"

"Won't matter," Slade reminded him, "since we can't claim it."

"They could change that rule," Naylor replied. "I wouldn't mind."

"Another way to go, if you get tired of marshaling," Slade said. "Turn bounty hunter for the cash."

"I thought about it, but I like havin' the law behind me when I'm hunting. Keeps it clear that I'm on the right side."

"There's that," Slade granted.

"Do you think more people hate a bounty hunter or a lawman?"

"*Hate* would be a little strong, I think," Slade said. "For most folks, anyway. We make a lot of people nervous when they see us, thinking of the sneaky little things they've done, maybe the laws they've broken, wondering if something might catch up to them."

"Some people hate us, though," Naylor persisted.

"Oh, I'm sure they do."

"Some folks in Stateline, maybe."

"Guess we'll find out soon enough," Slade said.

Their first glimpse of Stateline was a smudge on the horizon, growing as they traveled on, until Slade could make out the

125

shapes of individual buildings. Away to their right, his eyes tracked the telegraph poles with their lines linking Stateline to Enid and points farther out. He wondered if the message marking Naylor and himself for death had traveled on those wires, deciding that it was the only explanation that made sense.

Technology.

Slade sometimes felt as if the world had passed him by and was receding in the distance at a lightning pace. They had a telephone exchange in Enid, though subscribers couldn't talk to any other cities yet. Slade was aware of other new inventions catching on, within the past five years or so: the gramophone, an electric tabulating machine, and Kodak cameras with rolls of film, their pictures printed out on photographic paper. The innovation that concerned him most was cordite, a propellant advertised as "smokeless" that was now replacing black powder in some cartridges.

A world of wonders, but when felons ran amok it still required a lawman to corral them, bring them in, or put them down. The four dead men riding his dust to Stateline had already learned that lesson, but it wouldn't do them any good. Not in the present life, at least.

They entered Stateline from the western

end of Border Boulevard, five minutes shy of ten o'clock. A sign announced the street's name, causing Slade to wonder who had picked it out and how much he'd been drinking at the time. The town was bustling, people passing in and out of shops whose window signs hawked better, cheaper merchandise than that stocked by competitors across the street. It seemed, indeed, to be a town divided but with no signs of defeat on either side.

Slade spied a marshal's office on his left, tucked in between a lawyer's office and a barber's shop, near the center of town. There seemed to be none on the Oklahoma side, but a flick of the reins brought him over to Kansas in no time. They stopped outside the office; those who could dismounted, stretched, and left the other silent riders draped facedown across their saddles.

In a minute, maybe less, a man of forty-some-odd years emerged, hatless, star on his chest, gun on his right hip, right hand on the gun. He sized them up, noted their badges, and approached them slowly, flicking glances at the dead men draped on horses. "Have some trouble on the prairie?" he inquired.

"A bit," Slade said. "We're better off than they are."

"So I see." He thrust a hand at Slade, saying, "I'm Arlo Hickey, marshal for the Kansas side of Stateline."

Slade introduced himself and shook the older lawman's hand, then Hickey passed it on to Naylor for another pumping and exchange of names. The ritual complete, Slade said, "We're hoping you might recognize these fellows, Marshal."

"Go with first names, can we? Otherwise, we'll all be *marshal*ing each other till the cows come home."

"Suits me," Slade said.

"Same here," from Naylor.

That decided, Hickey walked around the horses, lifting heads and peering into faces as he went, a frown tugging the corners of his mouth down. Slade watched him for signs of recognition but saw nothing he could rightly call a giveaway.

"Don't know 'em," Hickey said, at last. "Did they try'n jump you on the trail?"

"In camp last night," said Naylor. "One of 'em let on he knew that we were coming."

"Well, that's more'n I could say," Hickey replied. "We had another marshal come through here, I'd make it eight, ten days ago. Showed up one day, then left without so much as adios."

"Blond hair on that one?" Slade inquired.

"Was, for a fact. Can't say that I recall his name, though."

"It was Tanner."

"Was?"

"He's dead. Murdered," Slade said.

"Who done it?" Hickey asked.

"That's what we're looking into," Slade replied. "Last place that anybody heard from him was here."

"Well, I swan. That's a puzzlement. You say *heard* from him here?"

"By telegraph," Slade said. "We'll need to see your Western Union man. But first, if you could take these fellows into hand . . ."

"Sure can. We'll get 'em bedded down in potter's field, no markers 'less we hear from next of kin sometime. That don't seem likely, does it, now?"

Hickey gave them directions to the livery, a good-sized stable on the Oklahoma side, one of the few things Stateline didn't duplicate. The hostler was a wiry, sad-eyed man who charged a reasonable rate and promised that their animals would be well tended through their stay.

Next stop, the Stateline Arms, a three-story hotel standing a block west of the livery, in Kansas. Slade and Naylor signed for top-floor rooms, deposited their trail

129

gear, then went down and got directions from the desk clerk to the local Western Union office.

It was warm this Friday morning, getting on toward midday. Slade considered rolling up his sleeves, then let it go. People who passed them on the street may have been curious but hid it well, averting eyes from Slade and Naylor in most cases, otherwise presenting nods and smiles that stopped a few yards short of welcome. Slade noted that, as in Enid, few of the men carried firearms — at least, in the open — and those who did were a different sort, cowboy types as distinguished from townsmen. The pistol packers eyed Naylor and Slade more warily, as seemed to be the rule in most towns.

Stateline's little Western Union office was another operation that had not been duplicated. It stood on the Oklahoma side of Border Boulevard, next to a hardware store with spades and pitchforks in its window. Slade went in, followed by Naylor, their arrival heralded by tinkling bells over the door. The operator came out of a back room, putting on a cap that bore the company's winged logogram. Beneath a florid face and double chins, he wore a bow tie, dark blue vest, and a white shirt that strained across his paunch. Slade wondered if the color in his cheeks was due to hyper-tension, alcohol, or the appearance of two lawmen at his counter.

"Gentlemen . . . er, officers . . . how may I help you?" he inquired.

"Sharing your name would be a start," Slade said.

"It's Fawcett. Percy Fawcett."

Slade completed the preliminary introductions, clammy handshakes all around, then said, "There was another marshal in last week. He sent a wire off to Judge Dennison, in Enid."

"Yes, sir. I remember him, but can't recall the name offhand."

"Bill Tanner."

Fawcett nodded. "If you say so, I'll assume that is correct."

"A short time after sending off that cable," Slade said, "he was murdered."

"M-m-murdered? What's that got to do with me?"

"I'm not a great believer in coincidence," Slade said. "We need to know if anyone besides yourself saw Marshal Tanner's telegram, or if you mentioned it to anyone."

The fat man's ruddy face went pale. "I never!" he protested. "Why would I?"

"Maybe someone pressured you," Naylor suggested. "Maybe paid you."

"N-n-no, sir! There is such a thing as ethics in this business."

"Ought to be in every business," Slade replied. "First thing you learn, wearing a badge, is that some folks regard the rules as flexible."

"If everyone was honest," Naylor added, "we'd be out of work."

"I deny your accusation categorically!" said Fawcett, with a not-so-subtle tremor in his voice.

"It's not an accusation," Slade informed him. "Yet."

"In that case —"

"But if it turns out you're lying —" Naylor said.

"That makes you an accessory to murder," Slade finished the warning.

"I resent this," Fawcett blustered. "There's n-n-no call for insinuations that besmirch my honor. I perform my duties to the highest standard p-p-possible. Ask anyone!"

"We plan to," Slade replied.

"If you remember something, sudden-like," said Naylor, "you can reach us at the Stateline Arms."

"There's nothing to remember," Fawcett said, as they retreated toward the exit. "And you needn't come back here unless you have a telegram to send!"

"Seems like the nervous sort to me," said Naylor, once they were outside. "Or guilty."

"Safe to say he's hiding something," Slade agreed.

"And I'd say we spooked him. Maybe he'll go running to the ones he tipped to Tanner's wire."

"Be ready if he does," Slade said. "After last night, they may try anything."

"I'm more alert," said Naylor, "when my belly isn't growling. Lunch?"

"Sounds good," Slade said. "I'll buy."

"They're here," said Grady Sullivan.

"Together with the men you sent, I understand," Flynn Rafferty replied. "Facedown across their saddles."

"So, you heard already."

"Bad news travels fast."

"What are we gonna do about it?" Sullivan inquired.

"Nothing, for now," said Rafferty. "They talked to Hickey and he's playing dumb."

"You sure he's playing?"

"I believe he's smart enough to know which side his bread is buttered on," said Rafferty.

"He ain't the only one around who knew them boys."

"Drunkards and sluts."

"They still might talk."

"It's your job to make sure they don't," said Rafferty.

"Yes, sir. But if we start to throw our weight around right now —"

"Use common sense. Don't give the marshals anything to work with."

"Are we getting rid of them or not?" asked Sullivan.

"In due time, Grady. Did your mother never tell you patience is a virtue?"

"Too much patience gives 'em time to work against us. 'Fore you know it, you're in handcuffs, climbin' up the scaffold."

"Funny thing," said Rafferty. "I never took you for a worrier."

"I've got more reason, lately. Did your townies tell you that the marshals talked to Percy Fawcett?"

"They did not. But I can't say it comes as a surprise."

"They're one short step away from us," said Sullivan. "If they crack Fawcett . . ."

"Once again, it's your job to ensure they don't. Stop by and visit Percy. We already know that he's suggestible."

"And yellow. Wouldn't take much to persuade him he should give us up."

"Then you must strengthen his resolve," said Rafferty. "I leave the method to your own discretion, within limits."

"Meanin'?"

"Meaning that I don't want anything spectacular, bizarre, or even noteworthy. Try talking to him first."

"And if that doesn't work?" asked Sullivan.

"Be more creative. If it's necessary to remove him, try to make it look as if he left town of his own volition."

"Huh?"

"His own free will. Who knows, maybe the marshals frightened him enough that he took flight."

"You think they'd buy it?"

"They'll consider it, at least. Investigate the possibility. Whatever time they waste, we use in preparation."

"So," asked Sullivan, "you're saying he should snuff it?"

"As a last resort," said Rafferty. "If you decide he can't be trusted to cooperate."

"And make it seem like he lit out."

"Which would require discretion on your part. No witnesses, of course."

"Unless I need help packin' up and movin' him."

"Use your most trusted men, in that case."

"Can't," said Sullivan. "They're over at the undertaker's now."

"You have my every confidence," Rafferty lied. In fact, he was beginning to suspect that Grady might be showing fatal signs of strain, himself. Something to think about, once they'd resolved their more immediate concerns.

"All right, I'll see to it." Grady went out and closed the door behind him, leaving Rafferty alone to think about the trouble he was facing.

Clearly, Sullivan's attempt to blame rogue Indians for the first marshal's death had failed. It hadn't been a *bad* idea, per se — in fact, Rafferty had approved it — but it hadn't kept the new lawmen away from Stateline. Now, after the failed attempt to stop them on the trail, they'd be even more suspicious of the town and its inhabitants.

Goddamn that Percy Fawcett!

He'd been smart enough — greedy enough — to share the contents of the first deputy marshal's telegram, but hadn't thought to fake transmission in the first place, which might well have nipped their problem in the bud. For that alone, Rafferty wished him dead, but he could let it pass if Fawcett did as he was told from this point on.

If he did not . . . well, then, the fat man would have made his choice.

Rafferty had a thriving business to protect. An empire in the making, if he played his cards right. He was not prepared to pull up stakes and start from nothing in some other town, building his trade from the ground up. At forty-five, he didn't have the patience to start over. Not when everything he'd ever dreamed of was within his grasp.

He would fight for what was coming to him — which meant fighting to the death.

8

Slade and Naylor tried the Grub Stake restaurant, a block from their hotel and on the Oklahoma side of Border Boulevard. They took a table at the window and both ordered steaks — Slade's rare, Naylor's well-done — with fried potatoes and a side of beans. The food was good and plentiful, the waitress who delivered it was cute, and the coffee that she brought along with it was strong and black.

"Must be a funny place to live," said Naylor, talking with his mouth full. "Everything divided up the way it is."

"Could get confusing," Slade agreed. "The other side of that is if you break the law, you only have to walk across the street to make your getaway."

"No lawman working this side," Naylor noted.

"Makes you wonder."

As he spoke, Slade glanced out through

the window, toward the Kansas side, and saw a man of middle years, dressed in a three-piece suit and bowler hat, observing them. The watcher saw Slade looking back at him and raised a hand, fanning the air as if in greeting or farewell.

Naylor followed his gaze after a moment, frowned, and asked, "What's that about?"

"Beats me."

Slade watched the stranger for a moment longer, then beckoned him across the boulevard. The man stopped waving, frowned as if in consternation, then checked left and right for traffic before scurrying across the street. He slowed on reaching the restaurant's sidewalk, delayed another moment on the threshold, then came in.

The waitress came to meet him, smiling. "Table, Mayor?" she asked him.

"Not today, Arlene," the new arrival said, doffing his hat. He tipped a nod toward Slade and Naylor, saying, "I just need to have a word with these two gentlemen."

"Alrighty, then." She whirled away to deal with paying customers.

He approached the table, hat in hand. "Marshals, I apologize for interrupting you. I meant to wait until you'd finished and were on your way, but . . . well . . ."

"The lady called you 'Mayor,' " Slade said.

139

"Um, yes . . . well, on the Kansas side, that is. Name's Warren Jain." He eyed the third chair at their table. "If you wouldn't mind . . . ?"

"Feel free," Slade said. He introduced himself and Naylor, neither of them dropping forks or knives to shake the mayor's hand.

"What brings you into Oklahoma, then?" Luke asked, wearing a half smile as he chewed a slice of steak.

"I heard that you'd arrived in town with some . . . ah . . . shall we say, unfortunates?"

"Unfortunate for them that they weren't better shots," said Naylor.

"Yes. Regrettably, we're plagued by wicked elements. Thank heavens you were able to prevail."

"Unlike a friend of ours who passed through Stateline recently," said Slade.

Jain's face took on a mournful cast. "I was informed of that, as well. Condolences. I understand he ran afoul of savages?"

"Some kind or other," Slade replied.

"I'm not sure I follow," said the mayor.

"We're looking into it," Slade said. "Also a moonshine racket."

"Oh? In Stateline?"

"Wherever the evidence takes us."

"Evidence? Um . . . what I mean to say

is . . . may I —"

"We can't talk about it," Naylor interrupted.

"Ah. Of course."

"About your two saloons," Slade said.

"Not *my* saloons, Marshal."

"The town's saloons, then. Can you tell us who's in charge of them?"

"Why . . . um . . . yes. Yes, I can. Sean Swagger runs the Swagger Inn. His name, you see? And at the Sunflower, the man in charge is Mr. Rafferty. Flynn Rafferty."

"Big men in town, are they?" asked Naylor.

"They both make a decent living, I suppose," Jain granted.

"Decent, as in *profitable,"* Slade suggested.

"Well . . . yes. I suppose some folk could argue that their business isn't decent, in the strictest sense."

"Church types," said Naylor.

"Absolutely."

"But you don't appear to have a church in Stateline," Slade observed. "At least, we didn't see one, riding in."

"Um . . . no. There is a gap in our community, where biblical instruction is concerned," Jain said.

"Seems curious," Slade said. "In my experience, most towns attract at least one

141

preacher by the time they double up on bars, hotels, and such."

"I hadn't really thought about it," Jain replied.

"Just a point to ponder," Slade suggested.

"Yes. Well . . . um . . . if I can be of any help to you while you're in town — across the street, of course, not over here — don't hesitate to ask."

"Appreciate it, Mayor," Slade said, as Jain rose from the table and made off, planting his derby squarely on his head.

"That's one odd bird," said Naylor. "Got the feeling he was pumpin&' us for information, 'stead of offering to help."

"I wouldn't contradict you," Slade replied, watching Mayor Jain hurry across the street without a backward glance.

Stateline's Western Union office was locked up tight when Grady Sullivan arrived. A hand-lettered sign dangled on string inside the glass front door, advising that the operator would be BACK AFTER LUNCH. With no idea of when the telegrapher had left his post, and nothing more important than ensuring Percy Fawcett's silence at the moment, Sullivan set off to check the town's three restaurants.

He tried the Grub Stake first and got a

rude surprise. No sign of Fawcett, but Mayor Jain was seated at a window table, jawing with the marshals who had hauled Sullivan's dead men back to town. That made him nervous, and he nearly doubled back to warn Flynn Rafferty, but then decided it could wait. For all Sullivan knew, Rafferty might have *sent* the mayor to see them, to feel out what they knew so far.

Sullivan crossed the street, hoping Jain hadn't seen him peering through the Grub Stake's window. Next, he checked the Borderline Café, ducked in to scan the faces of its diners that he couldn't make out from the street, and came out empty-handed. One to go, the Lone Star Barbecue, and if he missed out there, Sullivan guessed that Fawcett must have gone back home for lunch. Which helped him not at all, without the fat man's address.

He was simmering as he approached the Lone Star — and saw Percy Fawcett eating alone at a table for two. The telegrapher was gnawing on a pork rib as Sullivan entered and moved toward his table, waving off the waitress who had tried to intercept him. Seeing Grady loom above him, Fawcett made a little choking sound that didn't sound like "Howdy," dropped the rib, and scrubbed his plump lips with a napkin.

"Mr. Sullivan," he managed, when his mug was nearly clean. "W-w-would you care to join me?"

"Don't mind if I do," said Sullivan. He dropped into the empty chair and leaned toward Fawcett, kept his voice low-pitched for confidentiality. "You had a couple visitors today, I hear."

"Y-yes, that's true. A pair of U.S. m-m-marshals."

"Let me guess. They asked about a certain telegram you sent a while back, for a friend of theirs."

"That's r-r-right." The fat man's eyes were darting here and there, as if in search of eavesdroppers. His own voice lowered almost to a whisper. "He was m-m-murdered!"

"By a pack of redskins, way I understand it," Sullivan replied.

"I d-don't know. They were s-s-suspicious."

"That's their job. If they can't find who done it, they'll just have to pin the rap on someone else."

"Y-you d-d-don't mean —"

"I had a word with Mr. Rafferty about this," Sullivan cut in. "We think the smartest thing for you to do, right now, is take yourself a nice vacation. Get away from

Stateline for a while, until this all blows over."

"G-g-get away to where?" asked Fawcett, sounding anxious at the prospect.

"Anywhere you like," said Sullivan. "On Mr. Rafferty, o' course. Stay gone a week or two, at least, till they get fed up lookin' for you. I can tip you when it's safe to double back."

"B-but . . . my d-d-duties . . ."

"Got you covered, Percy. Mr. Rafferty has his own man who can read and send Morse code. No one'll know the difference, and you'll draw your salary the same as always."

"W-well . . . I just d-d-don't know."

"Or you can stick around and see what charge they hang on you. Thing is, in that case, you'd become a liability."

Fawcett looked queasy, staring at the ribs in front of him as if they were his own torn-up remains. "W-when s-s-should I leave?" he asked.

"Tonight," said Sullivan. "Finish your normal shift today, and just play dumb if they come back before you close the office. Give me your address and I'll come by your place, help get you on your way. Say eight o'clock?"

"All r-right." The fat man named a street, added a number. He kept his eyes downcast as Sullivan put money on the table for his ruined meal and left the restaurant.

The Swagger Inn had something like a dozen drinkers lined up at the bar when Slade and Naylor entered, not bad for an early afternoon. A pneumatic player piano tinkled away in one corner, competing with muttered conversation from the bar. One of the joint's soiled doves was sitting at a table by herself, smoking a hand-rolled cigarette and waiting for a customer to notice her. She sized up Slade and Naylor at a glance, dismissing them as soon as she saw their badges.

The barkeep was a redhead, six foot five or six and broad across the chest, whose biceps strained the fabric of his cambric shirt. He frowned at Slade and Naylor as they reached the bar. "I guess you'll want a couple on the house," he said.

"Is that the usual?" asked Naylor.

"Seems like."

"We'll take a minute with your boss, instead."

"He may not have a minute for you."

"Point us toward him," Slade instructed. "We'll find out."

"I'll need to tell him that you're here."

"We'll come along," Slade said and added,

with a side glance at the drinkers who'd gone silent now, "These gentlemen can do without you for a second."

They followed the redhead upstairs, to an office fronting on a gallery that overlooked the barroom. Slade surveyed the layout from that new perspective while the giant knocked and got a call back from within. He ducked inside, closing the door behind him, then emerged a moment later, saying, "Come ahead."

Sean Swagger was a man of average size, whose personality had patently outgrown his body. He wore his black hair long, combed straight back from his suntanned face and brightly oiled, to match his waxed mustache. The vest he wore without a jacket over it had seemingly been fabricated from a Union Jack, made doubly garish by his plain white linen shirt and gray trousers. The ensemble was completed by a small revolver in a shoulder holster, worn beneath his right armpit.

The introductions took no more than twenty seconds. Settled in a reasonably comfortable wooden chair facing the boss man's desk, with Naylor seated to his left, Slade said, "We're running an investigation on the murder of another deputy."

"Bill Tanner."

"So, you knew him?"

"Only from the talk we had while he was here in town. I've got a head for names," said Swagger. "Helps my business if I recognize the customers."

"What did you talk to him about?" asked Naylor.

"Moonshine," Swagger said. "He reckoned someone in the neighborhood was cooking it and selling on the reservations. Figured maybe I'd been offered some, as well."

"And were you?" Slade inquired.

"I wish. The red-eye they ship down to me from Wichita comes dear. I'd like a better profit margin, but alas, no one's come peddling any 'shine my way."

"And what about your opposition there, across the street?" asked Slade.

"Flynn Rafferty? Call him a friendly rival," Swagger said. "I couldn't tell you where he gets his whiskey."

"Even though you're friends? In the same business?" Naylor prodded.

"With the key word being *business*," Swagger answered. "Neither one of us leaks anything to help the other get ahead, you understand."

"But if you knew that he was up to something on the shady side . . ." Slade left it hanging, letting Swagger fill the gap.

"I'm not a nark, and never will be. If you want the dirt on Rafferty, you'll have to dig it somewhere else."

"You think he'll show you the same courtesy?" asked Slade.

"There's only one way to find out. If we're all finished here, I need to buy the house a round. Help prime the pump, you know?"

Grady Sullivan stood in the recessed doorway of O'Malley's barbershop and watched the two new marshals from the Swagger Inn. He'd spotted them by chance, as they went in, and close to twenty minutes had elapsed since then, stalling his plan to tell the big man that their plan for Percy Fawcett was in progress.

Sullivan supposed it made sense for the lawmen to drop in and question Swagger. They were looking into moonshine and he *did* run a saloon. Also, they'd want to check on every step their fellow deputy had made in Stateline, sniffing after leads. The question now was, what had Swagger told them?

Likely nothing, but the big man didn't pay Grady to speculate. When he asked questions, answers were required, not guesswork. A miscalculation could rebound and cost him dearly — at the very least, his job. At worst . . .

He didn't even want to think about it.

On the Oklahoma side of Border Boulevard, the marshals stood and talked together, peering up and down the street suspiciously. Sullivan couldn't hear what they were saying, wished that he could read their lips. Frustration made him raise a hand and gnaw a fingernail before he caught himself and dropped the hand back to his side.

Tim O'Malley came out of his shop, distracted Sullivan by saying, "Grady, you could use a shave." Maybe a joke, or he was trying to drum up some business.

"Not today," said Sullivan, dismissively.

Instead of going back inside, the barber lingered at his elbow, looking off across the street. "More marshals, eh?"

"Looks like."

"First one, now two."

"Don't miss much, do you?" Sullivan replied.

"I keep my eyes open," O'Malley said, missing the jibe.

"And what about your ears?"

"I hear all right," the barber said.

"You still shave Swagger regular?" asked Sullivan.

"Sure do. He's just across the street."

"Same time each day?"

"If nothin' interrupts it."

"And what time would that be?"

"Half past eleven. After he gets up and drinks his breakfast."

"So he's all done for today."

"Slick as a whistle."

Damn it. "Does he talk about his business when you're workin' on him?" Sullivan inquired.

"A bit, sometimes." Suspicious-sounding now. "What are you getting at?"

"I'd like to find out what he talked about with them law dogs. Think you could squeeze that out of him tomorrow?"

"Maybe. I can't promise nothin'." His anxiety gave way to greed, O'Malley asking, "What's it worth?"

"Depends on what you get. Five dollars, maybe ten."

"I'll see what I can do."

Across the street, the objects of his interest were moving, easing off the sidewalk while a buggy passed, then heading toward the Sunflower Saloon.

"Goin' to see your boss, now," said O'Malley.

"Seems so."

And he couldn't even run around the back way with a warning now, for fear of drawing their attention. If he walked and kept it casual, they'd beat him to the big man's office easily.

"Guess you can ask him what they want, yourself," O'Malley kidded him.

Instead of answering, he left the barber standing there and cut across the street, reversing more or less the lawmen's path. Sullivan wasn't headed for the Swagger Inn, however. He had plans to finalize before he hustled Percy Fawcett out of Stateline, helpers to recruit and have on standby when the time came. There was nothing he could do to keep the deputies away from Rafferty, no way to help the big man deal with them. The best thing he could do was follow orders and make certain nothing else went wrong.

The next mistake, he knew, could be his last.

Halfway across the street, between the Swagger Inn and Sunflower Saloon, one ripple of piano music gave way to another. Slade saw a customer emerging from the Sunflower, unsteady on his feet, weaving a little as he turned away from them and tottered east on Border Boulevard.

"No lack of drinkers hereabouts," said

Naylor, as he watched the tipsy man's retreat.

"A good market for whiskey," Slade suggested. "Taxed or otherwise."

"You think Swagger was lying?"

"Couldn't say, unless we check his inventory and supplier."

"Wichita, he said."

"We can go back and get a name, if need be," Slade replied. "Cable up there and save ourselves a hundred miles on horseback."

"Suits me," Naylor said.

The Sunflower was somewhat larger than the Swagger Inn and had a real piano player in the flesh. The rest of it was standard: bar along the back wall of a spacious room with card tables, roulette, and chuck-a-luck. A curved staircase led to the cribs upstairs, but none of the Sunflower's working girls were presently in evidence. Slade counted five men at the bar and three more playing poker at a table to his right.

Whereas the Swagger Inn's bartender was a giant of a man, the Sunflower's was whisper thin and average in height, with jet-black curly hair, clean shaven, scarred along his left jawline as if from dueling with a knife or razor. He was joking with a customer but lost his sense of humor at the sight of badges.

"Help you?" he inquired, not sounding much as if he gave a damn.

"We're looking for the boss," said Naylor.

"He expectin' you?"

"I'll bet he is," Slade said.

The barkeep cracked his knuckles. Said, "I'll have ta check."

"Do that," said Naylor. Then, when he was left alone with Slade, "You think he's heard about us through the grapevine?"

"Stands to reason," Slade replied. "We made a splash with those four stiffs. A town this size, word gets around."

The barkeep was returning, wearing a disgruntled look. "He'll see you. Far end of the bar, the door marked PRIVATE, by the stairs."

They followed his directions, found the door already open to an office with a large desk facing them as they approached. Behind it stood the Sunflower's proprietor, a stocky man with salt-and-pepper hair, dressed all in navy blue. He didn't come around the desk to meet them, but he leaned across to shake their hands.

"Flynn Rafferty," he said, repeating Slade's and Naylor's names in turn as they were given, like a man committing them to memory. "Drag up a couple chairs and rest yourselves."

They found two mismatched chairs and sat, while Rafferty inquired, "How can I help the law today?"

Slade ran it down for Rafferty the way they had for Swagger, starting with the 'shine, then moving on to Tanner's homicide. Rafferty nodded through the recitation, frowning just enough to indicate concern.

"I spoke with your associate when he was here in town, of course," said Rafferty. "Nice man, as far as I could tell."

"He was that," Slade allowed.

"Determined to locate these vermin who've been selling whiskey on the reservations," Rafferty continued.

"It's a problem," Naylor said.

"And tragic, how he met his end. You're thinking redskins are responsible? Maybe he caught some with a load of 'shine?" asked Rafferty.

"That isn't clear," Slade said. "The reason that we're here, it crossed our minds that someone peddling whiskey to the tribes might try his luck with the saloons nearby."

Rafferty raised one eyebrow, kept on nodding. "Wish that I could help you there," he said. "You might check Swagger's place, across the boulevard."

"We did," Naylor replied. "He said he gets

his booze from Wichita."

"Does he? Ours comes in from Joplin."

"In Missouri?" Naylor asked.

Another nod from Rafferty. "It's sixty miles due east, closer than Wichita by half. They have a fine distillery nearby, at Jolly Mill."

"You haven't been approached by anyone with untaxed alcohol to sell?" asked Slade.

"No, sir. I would've sent them packing if I had."

"And turned them in?" asked Naylor.

That received a shrug. "It's not my job," said Rafferty. "I try to live and let live when I can."

"And when you can't?" Slade asked.

"It hasn't come to that, thank goodness." Smiling. "Sorry that I couldn't be more helpful."

"Well, I guess it was a long shot, but we had to ask," Slade said.

"Of course, of course. And while you're here in Stateline, I hope you'll accept our hospitality as time allows."

"That's mighty generous," said Naylor.

"We aim to please."

Outside, Naylor asked Slade, "Did that sound like a bribe to you?"

"Nothing that we could charge him with,"

Slade said. "But that makes four people I'm pretty sure have lied to us so far."

9

On Friday evening Slade and Naylor went to supper at the Lone Star Barbecue. Slade ordered carne asada with an enchilada and frijoles charros on the side, while Naylor ate pork ribs and grilled corn on the cob, washed down with beer. Slade stuck to coffee, strong and black, leaving some room for pie.

"The way I see it," Naylor said, between large bites of pork dripping with sauce, "we need to have a look around Stateline without an audience or anybody offerin' to scout for us. If there's not something fishy goin' on, I'll eat my hat."

"You won't have room, the way you're going," Slade replied. "But I agree with you. I don't trust anyone we've talked to yet."

"Including Marshal Call-Me-Arlo Hickey?"

"Him, for starters. I still think he knew those four we got the drop on, or at least he'd seen them passing through."

"We're on our own, then."

"Way it feels to me," Slade granted.

"Suits me," said Naylor. "Saves a lot of wonderin'."

Dessert was apple pie for Slade, cinnamon cake for Naylor, who'd retired his beer and switched to coffee for the final course. Outside, after they settled up the tab, they lingered on the sidewalk for a moment, in the dusk, deciding where to start their search.

"East side of town," Slade finally suggested. "Check our horses at the livery, if anybody's watching, then work back from there."

"Sly-like," said Naylor. "Think they've put a pair of eyes on us?"

"I haven't spotted any, but I wouldn't put it past them," Slade replied.

"Come out the back way from the livery, I guess, then work out way along behind the shops and all?"

"What I was thinking," Slade agreed. "Get to the other end, then cross without attracting anyone's attention, double back, and do it over on the Kansas side."

"Okay."

There horses seemed content. Slade spent a moment with the hostler, asking if he'd heard of any moonshine operations in the neighborhood, and got a hasty-feeling "No, sir" in return. The fellow watched them exit through the rear, a weakness in their plan if he ran off to warn someone, but it was too late to retract the question.

"So, another liar, do you think?" asked Naylor, when they'd cleared the stable.

"Maybe. Or by now he's heard how Tanner got it, and he doesn't want to take a chance."

"Another way of saying that he might know something," Naylor said.

"I guess that's right."

"Makes me want to grab somebody by the neck and shake 'em till they rattle."

"Still an option," Slade admitted, "if we come up short the other way."

They walked along behind the buildings on the south — or Oklahoma — side of Border Boulevard, full dark overtaking them within a block or so. Slade wasn't sure exactly what to look for, but he'd smelled a whiskey still on several occasions, thinking that the 'shiners couldn't hide that kind of operation from his nose, even if they concealed it from his eyes.

"I've never seen a whole town that could keep a secret," Naylor said, as they were pacing off the fourth block, moving east to west.

"I've seen a couple try," Slade answered, "but they weren't much good at it. Somebody always cracks."

"Nice if we had a way to speed it up."

"Finding the cooker ought to do it," Slade suggested. "Or the place they stash the booze to age it."

"May not age it much," said Naylor. "If it's just your basic popskull, they could sell it raw and let the buyers proof it down."

"Reselling it, you mean."

Luke nodded. "Sure. Stretch the supply and multiply the profit three, four times. Why not."

"Like through saloons," Slade said.

"Best place that I can think of."

"Till somebody checks for tax stamps."

"Make your own. You'd only have to have one honest sample and a printer who can counterfeit them."

"With a label from a recognized distillery," said Slade.

"Whose gonna question it, once you start sellin' in another state?"

"So we don't need to find the still first thing," Slade offered. "Any good-sized cache could do."

"Mount a watch on it. Find out who

comes and goes. I like it," Naylor said.

"Now all we have to do is *find* it," Slade reminded him.

A smile flashed in the night as Naylor said, "What are we waitin' for?"

The knock made Percy Fawcett jump, although he'd been expecting it. Was dreading it, in fact, still not convinced that Grady Sullivan had his best interest in mind. He might be regarded as a danger now, something to be disposed of, and he wasn't taking any chances. Tucked inside his belt, around in back where it was covered by his jacket, Fawcett wore a Colt M1889 revolver chambered for the .38-caliber Short Colt cartridge. In the right-hand pocket of his trousers, he was also carrying a clasp knife with a four-inch blade.

Now, if he only had the nerve to use the weapons, Fawcett thought he should be safe.

Or would he?

Sullivan was known to be a gunman, and the rowdies whom he hung out with were all cut from the same rough cloth. Fair bodyguards, he would imagine, but if they had devilry in mind, he could not hope to best them.

Worried as he was, Fawcett had nearly slipped away from town that afternoon, after his shift was over, but his nerve had failed. He pictured Sullivan and company pursuing him, catching him somewhere on the plains, taking his flight as proof that he'd betrayed them. They would surely kill him then, and no mistake. Playing along with them, at least he had a fighting chance to stay alive.

Now he was answering the door, saw Sullivan and two more men he didn't recognize standing in darkness on his doorstep. Fawcett backed away and beckoned them inside. The little living room of his apartment suddenly felt claustrophobic, redolent of unwashed bodies. He was tempted for a suicidal moment to inquire when they had bathed last, but he bit his tongue instead.

"You packed?" asked Sullivan.

"I am," Fawcett responded, nodding toward a trunk and portmanteau that sat together in the middle of the floor.

"That's ever'thing?"

"It is."

"Go on and shift that to the buggy," Sullivan told his companions. Each man took a handle of the trunk and hauled it out into the night, where Fawcett saw a horse-drawn carriage standing, two more animals secured behind it by their reins. Sullivan took the portmanteau and ordered Fawcett, "Kill the lamps and lock 'er up. You've got a ways to travel."

Fawcett did as he was told, locking the door behind him as he left, and wondered if he'd ever see the place again. He'd grown accustomed to the rooms, but now supposed that even if he managed to survive his trek with Sullivan, it would be hazardous to show his face around Stateline again. After he'd run out on the marshals, they'd be looking for him high and low, assuming he had information they could use.

And they'd be right, of course.

Which made him dangerous — but dangerous enough to kill?

Outside, before he climbed into the carriage, Sullivan told Fawcett, "This is Jeb and Dooley. They'll be takin' you to someplace you'll be safe awhile."

"You won't be coming with us?" Fawcett asked, uncertain whether he should he relieved or worried.

"Not just now," Sullivan said. "I got some things to do for Mr. Rafferty before I come and tuck you in."

"I see." But *did* he? Was the handoff to his cronies simply Grady's way to rid himself of Fawcett while establishing an alibi in town? Did it portend his murder, somewhere in the dark outside of Stateline? And if so, would he be better off with two assassins than with three?

Sullivan helped him up into the buggy, such a gentleman. Once he was seated, Fawcett took advantage of the dark and the distraction of his escorts, reaching underneath his coat to slip the short revolver from his waistband, bringing it around in front where it was easier to reach.

A little life insurance, just in case.

He might not match the speed or skill of Sullivan's companions, but at least he could defend himself and let them know that they'd been in a fight. Whatever happened next, Fawcett would not be led to slaughter like a sheep.

"Hold on. You smell that?" Naylor asked.

"I do," Slade said.

They'd reached the southeast corner of a good-sized building on the Oklahoma side of Border Boulevard, a few doors short of Stateline's western boundary, where the town ran out and open plains began.

"It smell like a saloon to you?" Naylor inquired.

It did, but they were well beyond the Swagger Inn and slightly farther from the Sunflower. There was no breeze to speak of, and the little that Slade felt was blowing from the west, back toward the town's saloons.

"Worth looking into," Slade suggested.

There was nothing painted on the backside of the building to suggest its function or identify its owner. Slade tried the back door and found it locked or bolted from the inside.

"Try around the front?"

"But carefully," Slade answered. "It's not late enough for all the neighbors to be sleeping."

Naylor led the way along a narrow alley set between the aromatic building and a feed store to its right. Their footsteps crunched on dirt and gravel all the way, Slade wincing at the way the alley's confines seemed to magnify the sound. A moment later they were at the alley's mouth, emerging onto Border Boulevard, no street lamps to reveal them, although someone covering the block could see them easily enough.

Turning left, they passed before the building, named up front as Stateline Storage. Sniffing as he passed the padlocked entrance, Slade smelled nothing to provoke suspicion.

"Only round in back," Naylor observed.

"We'd better try to have a look inside," Slade said.

"Suits me."

The problem was legality, of course. Slade hadn't been to law school, but Judge Dennison had quizzed him on the Bill of Rights when he became a marshal and reminded him specifically that searching private property without a proper warrant could result in vital evidence being excluded from a trial. If he and Naylor found a hoard of untaxed whiskey in the warehouse, they could neither confiscate it nor refer to it in any charges later filed against the stockpile's owner — whoever that turned out to be. Still, they were at a dead end as it was, and Slade needed a break to move the case along. Right now, a quiet look-see struck him as the only way to go.

They doubled back along the alley, checked both ways for passersby before they sidled toward the rear approach to Stateline Storage. Naylor tried the door again, as if he thought it might have magically unlocked itself, then raised the right cuff of his pants and drew a long knife from his boot.

"Lucky I brought the key," he said, grinning.

"We're on the wrong side of the law with this, you know," Slade cautioned him.

"The Fourth Amendment, was it?"

"Right."

"You gonna tell on me?"

"I doubt it."

"Well, then." Naylor slipped his blade between the door and jamb, worked it around till something snapped inside, and then withdrew it. When he tried the door again, it opened at his touch. "Easy," he said and tucked his knife away.

Inside the warehouse, there was no denying the pervasive smell of liquor. Slade was cautious as he struck a match and held it high, then found a lamp residing on a shelf beside the door and lit it. With the wick turned down to minimize its glare, he turned to face a wall of barrels. Counted seventeen across the bottom, same across the second tier.

"How far back do they go?" asked Naylor.

Edging to his right, Slade raised the lamp and counted quickly. "Six rows back," he said, "before you hit some other kind of boxes."

"So that's . . . what? Around two hundred?"

"Close. I make it two-oh-four," Slade said, "if all the rows are equal going back."

"And would you call those fifty-gallon kegs?"

"I'd say that's pretty close."

"Over ten thousand gallons, then. You

want to check for tax stamps?"

"Guess we'd better, since we're here," Slade said.

The double row of barrels stood around Slade's six-foot height, too tall for him to simply peer over the top. Naylor produced a short stepladder from a shadowed corner, set it up, and took the lamp from Slade as he ascended. Seconds later he reported back, "No stamps on these, as far as I can see."

"Nothing to say who owns them?"

"Nope."

"All right," Slade said. "Let's clear on out and close it up the best we can. I need to think on this a bit."

Grady Sullivan was passing on his buckskin gelding when the marshals eased out of the alley next to Stateline Storage. Startled as he was, he managed not to gape at them but kept his eyes straight forward, more or less, and rode on by. His stomach churned, though, and he nudged the gelding to a trot, putting more ground between himself and the two lawmen, heading toward the Sunflower Saloon.

Bad news, this was, and the big man would want to hear about it sooner, rather than later. Sullivan hoped that Rafferty was still at the saloon and not in bed with one of his doxies. Interruptions weren't appreciated when the boss was rutting, but he'd have to bust in anyhow if they were on the verge of being raided. More time wasted if the big man had gone back out to his spread, six miles northwest of town, and Sullivan was forced to follow him. Who could predict what damage might be done before they got back into Stateline?

Grady cursed his four men lying stretched out at the undertaker's, waiting for their last trip to the bone orchard. And count Eddie Gillespie with them, planted early in a hole on Rafferty's twelve hundred acres. If they'd done their job correctly in the first place, he'd be sitting down to supper and a few drinks now, instead of rushing to confront the big man with his stomach-churning news.

Goddamn the law dogs, anyhow. If they had found the liquor, he supposed that hustling Percy Fawcett out of town had been another waste of time and effort. Sullivan could just as easily have tracked the marshals, laid an ambush for them in the heart of Stateline, and removed them that way, even if it raised a ruckus. Who among the townspeople was likely to complain — or testify, if it came down to that?

The big man owned this town — well, most of it, at least — but that could change like lightning if the marshals linked him to the moonshine sold to Indians and to the murder of their fellow lawman. One would send him up to Leavenworth; the other would abbreviate his trip and see him hanged in Enid, if convicted.

Either way, what would be left for Grady Sullivan without Flynn Rafferty? More drifting, if he managed to slip through the net and dodge a noose himself. If not . . . well, then his worries would be over, wouldn't they?

Sullivan had given thought to how his life might end, from time to time. He'd never planned on growing old and gray, riding a rocker on a shady porch somewhere. More likely snuffed out by a faster gun one day, or cut down by a coward while his back was turned. That was the life he'd chosen, with the shadow of a gallows always lurking in the background, but it struck him now, riding through darkness, that he didn't want to hang.

Dancing on air and strangling slowly while a crowd of gawkers laughed at him? No, thanks. Given a choice, the lesser of two evils, he'd face down the lawmen on his own and let them finish him.

Or maybe they would die in the attempt.
Why not?

Hell, stranger things had happened.

Sullivan knew that he was reasonably fast.
Not Black Jack Ketchum fast, Wes Hardin
fast, or anything like that. But he was still
alive, and he could name eleven men who
weren't after they'd faced him in a showdown. Plus a few he'd taken care of for the
big man, with the wheat-haired deputy
among them.

Go down fighting if he had to make the
choice, damn right. But in the meantime, if
there was an opportunity to head that off,
he'd risk upsetting Rafferty and his companion for the evening to save them all.

It was the smart thing, and he always tried
to think ahead.

Captain Brody Gallagher was sipping a glass
of whiskey — his third by actual count —
when the Western Union rider found him in
the officers' mess. The young man looked
winded, though Gallagher knew his horse
had done all of the running from Enid to
reach Fort Supply. Traipsing around a
military base had that effect on some civil-
ians, intimidated by the presence of so many
guns and men in uniform.

The rider spent an awkward moment in

the doorway, half a dozen soldiers staring at him while he eyed them one by one, in silence. Gallagher wondered how knowledgeable he might be, concerning officers' insignia, and soon decided that the answer was: not very. Even so, the bars Gallagher wore might not have helped the stranger, since there was another captain in the room, along with three lieutenants and a major.

When the best part of a minute had elapsed, the major — Joseph Nussbaum, often called "Joe Nosey" in his absence — raised his gravel voice to ask, "What brings you here?"

"A cable, sir," the rider answered.

"I'd have guessed it from the cap you're wearing," Nussbaum told him. "Who's it *for*?"

The rider glanced down at the paper in his hand, suggesting he'd forgotten who he came for, then replied, "A Captain Gallagher, if he's available?"

"I am," said Gallagher, not rising from his seat.

The young man hurried over, passed the telegram inside a Western Union envelope with CAPT. GALLAGHER printed in block letters across its front. Job done, the rider stood by for another moment, long enough for Gallagher to think he might be waiting for a tip.

Not likely.

"Well?" Gallagher challenged him, the envelope still resting in his hand unopened.

"I was told to wait for a reply, sir. If there is one."

"Ah." Gallagher tore open the envelope, removed the single flimsy sheet inside, and read the message silently.

NEED HELP WITH UNEXPECTED VISI-
TORS. COME SOONEST WITH APPROPRI-
ATE ASSISTANCE. RR

Gallagher slipped the cable back into its envelope, then tucked the envelope into one of his pockets. "No reply," he told the rider. "You can go."

"Yes, sir."

Was that a look of disappointment? Too damned bad. Gallagher wasn't sending any message back or tipping for delivery of what could only be bad news.

"Another smitten lady?" Nussbaum asked him, fairly leering, as the rider left them.

"You know how it is, sir," Gallagher replied, wearing his best self-deprecating smile. He had something of a reputation as a cocksman, and it served his purpose now to let the others think some damsel pining for his company had wired a plea for some attention.

"Well, let's hear it then?" the other captain in the mess — Dave Thompson — said.

"A gentleman wouldn't respond to that," said Gallagher.

"Since when are *you* a gentleman?" asked Thompson, grinning.

"What I am is tired," Gallagher said, draining his whiskey glass and rising. "With an early start tomorrow."

"The patrol," said Nussbaum.

"Yes, sir."

"Have you picked your men yet?"

"Three or four should do it," Gallagher replied. "I'll pick them in the morning."

But the truth was that he knew which men he needed from among the ranks, had known the minute that he finished reading *RR*'s telegram. A little subterfuge, that sign-off, taken from the big man's spread — the Rocking R — to mask his name. It wasn't all that clever, but at least Enid's telegrapher couldn't identify the sender, even if he must know where the wire had come from.

Stateline. Yet another problem in what seemed to be an endless series of them. "Unexpected visitors," Gallagher muttered to himself. That had to be the law or something like it, but from which side of the border?

He would have to find out for himself, when he arrived. A long day's ride from Fort Supply lay waiting for him in the morning, when he'd been assigned to look for some Cheyenne who'd jumped their reservation earlier that week. They'd have to wait now, and he'd keep his fingers crossed that no white folk were killed while he was off on private business.

Solving one more problem for Flynn Rafferty.

10

For breakfast, Slade and Naylor tried the Borderline Café, already filling up when they arrived at half past six. Slade ordered ham and eggs, with biscuits drenched in gravy on the side. Naylor had skipped the hen fruit, taking bacon and a pile of flapjacks. As whenever he dined out — which came to nearly every meal — Slade made a point of watching people come and go, trying to size them up and guess what they were thinking by the way they acted or conversed with others.

And this morning, nearly everyone who entered the café took care to seem as if they weren't observing Slade and Naylor, shooting sidelong glances toward them on the sly. It nearly worked for some, but others were so clumsy at it that they wound up blushing, losing track of what was being said to them by their breakfast companions. Under other circumstances, Slade supposed he'd find it humorous. But at the moment, he was anxious to be off about their business for the day.

Tracing the ownership of Stateline Storage for a start, then moving on to question the owner about the untaxed liquor stashed away there. That would be a touchy proposition, trying not to give away the fact that they'd already seen the whiskey when, for all intents and purposes, they'd burglarized the warehouse. Any mouthpiece worth his salt could get that evidence thrown out of court in nothing flat, and that would sink their case.

"Best way to do it," Slade suggested, "is to drop in on the mayor and see if he can help us. Tell him that we're following a lead and let it go at that. If he won't spill the name, there has to be a registrar for deeds or something similar."

"That could be in the county seat," Naylor replied, "wherever *that* is. Do we even know which county we're in?"

"Cowley," Slade said. "I looked it up before we left. From what I understand, there's a division of opinion on the county seat. Two towns are claiming it, Cresswell and Winfield. Both are roughly half a day from where we're sitting."

"You did your homework, eh? Too bad we

won't know where to go."

"May not be necessary," Slade remarked, frowning. "Here comes the mayor."

"Oh, goody," Naylor said and stuffed his mouth with pancakes. Mayor Jain entered the restaurant and made a beeline for their table.

"Both of you still hungry, I perceive," he said by way of greeting, standing over them.

"It happens two, three times a day," Naylor informed their uninvited visitor.

Slade wondered whether Jain seemed nervous every day, or if it was their presence in his burg that made him jumpy. It was hard for Slade to picture anyone getting elected, even in a small town, if he couldn't don a steady smile and talk without a tremor in his voice.

"May I sit down?" the mayor inquired, aiming a quick glance at an empty chair standing midway between the two marshals.

"Free country," Slade replied.

"But not the food," said Naylor. "Have to buy your own."

The mayor blinked first, then forced a laugh at that. "Oh, yes. Very amusing. That's a good one."

"Got a million of 'em," Naylor said, before another wedge of syrup-dripping pancakes filled his mouth.

"I was concerned about . . . um, interested in . . . the progress of your ongoing investigation," Jain announced.

"Convenient that you found us then," said Slade. "In fact, there's something that I'm hoping you can help us with?"

"Which is?" asked Jain.

"We'd like to know who owns the warehouse here in town."

"Warehouse?" It wasn't easy, swallowing and frowning at the same time, as he spoke, but Jain managed to do both.

"Stateline Storage," Naylor interjected.

"Ah. It's not quite what I think of as a warehouse."

"Call it what you like," Slade said. "The owner is . . . ?"

"I really couldn't say," the mayor replied.

"Couldn't, or *wouldn't*?" Slade pressed on.

"Well . . . there's an issue, isn't there? I mean, it's private property."

"Set up for business with the public," Slade suggested, "or they likely wouldn't have a sign out front."

"Well, business, yes. I should have said the owner likes his privacy."

"The quiet type," said Naylor.

"Well . . ."

"Where would we go to find those records?" Slade inquired.

"Records?"

"The deeds and such."

"Um . . . well . . ."

"You haven't got a courthouse," Slade reminded him. "I thought maybe the lawyer's office, but a deed has to be filed. They're public records. So, if you could tell us where to go, we'll check it out ourselves and tell the county clerk you sent us. Then come back and see whoever it may be."

"Well, now . . . I wouldn't want to waste your time unnecessarily," said Jain. "It *is* a public record, as you say."

"The name?" Slade prodded.

"I believe that Stateline Storage is an adjunct of the Rocking R."

"Add what?" asked Naylor.

"An extension of," said Jain.

Slade pinned him with a look. "And when you say the Rocking R, you mean . . . ?"

"A ranch outside of town."

"Like pullin' teeth," said Naylor, glaring at the mayor.

"He's asking you who owns the ranch," Slade said.

"Why, Mr. Rafferty. He's big in corn, you know."

"I'll bet he is," Slade said and smiled at Jain across his rising coffee mug.

"Well, if there's nothing else . . ."

"You came lookin' for us, remember?" Naylor asked.

"Oh, yes! But if there's nothing new on your investigation, I suppose . . ."

"You never know," Slade said. "Something could break at any minute."

"Well, I'll keep my fingers crossed," Jain said. "Good day to you."

He rose and hurried out, the lawmen watching him. When he was on the street, Naylor remarked, "Looks like he's in a rush to see somebody."

Slade took another sip of coffee. Said, "I wouldn't be a bit surprised."

Captain Gallagher had picked his troopers carefully, using criteria that suited him but might have raised eyebrows at headquarters. All things considered, though, that was the least of his accumulated problems — or it would be, if he bungled his attempt to help Flynn Rafferty and thereby help himself.

As luck would have it, he'd been scheduled for a routine field patrol that morning, out and back again, but he had told the fort's commander, Colonel Jeroboam Pike, that he — Gallagher — had received a rider from the neighborhood of Stateline, seeking help with renegades who'd jumped one of the nearby reservations. Naturally, his information had been vague. Arapaho, Cheyenne, or Cherokee, how could he tell until the hostiles had been apprehended?

Colonel Pike had nearly sent a dozen men with Gallagher, which would have ruined everything. Some nimble lying was required to narrow down the field, with Gallagher insisting that the raiders number only two or three, at most, maintaining that a five-man squad equipped to travel light and fast would be the best response. It was a tough sale, even so, but he'd prevailed, at least in part due to the colonel's age and evident infirmity. Expected to retire within a year or less, Pike delegated most of his responsibilities to junior officers and soothed his nerves with whiskey from a bottle he kept hidden in his desk.

The men whom Gallagher had chosen for his mission were a crafty lot, drawn to the cavalry after they'd worn out their respective welcomes in a list of cities ranging from New York to Dallas and St. Louis. Sergeant Virgil Bonner was the eldest of them, had served prison time in Arkansas before he joined the army, and was decorated by a pale scar running from his left eyebrow down to the corner of his mouth. The privates serving under him on this detail were Gordon French, a brawler from Missouri; Marlon Wetzel, out of Texas, where he'd killed a man or two as a civilian; and the youngest, Loren Sowder out of Brooklyn or the Bronx — Gallagher got the two mixed up, sometimes — where a creative judge had given him the choice of military service or a two-year stay in jail for burglary. All three had found that army life relieved them of responsibility for making most of life's decisions but did not prevent them from enjoying certain entertainments on the side.

And if they had a chance to supplement their monthly pay of thirteen dollars with whatever private jobs might come their way, they could be trusted to perform and keep their mouths shut afterward. Especially if blabbing meant they'd face a court-martial and firing squad.

Like this time.

Gallagher had spent a restless night considering what might be waiting for them when they got to Stateline. Something Rafferty felt disinclined to handle on his own, that much was obvious. Likely some killing that he didn't wish to be associated with, that might bring lawmen to his neighborhood and cause them to investigate his shady deals.

And if the targets *were* lawmen? What then?

No difference, except that Gallagher would have to make damned sure he was protected from whatever repercussions might arise. It wouldn't be enough to simply gun the targets down and claim that they'd been outlaws on a rampage. They would have to disappear or be disposed of in some way that would divert suspicion from himself and his companions.

Gallagher knew Judge Denison by reputation, though they'd never actually met in person. What he'd learned by word of mouth convinced him that the judge would never rest in his pursuit of anyone who harmed a marshal under his command, and nothing in the military code of justice shielded any officer from prosecution for unlawful homicide. The payoff from his deal with Rafferty would not save Gallagher from dancing at the short end of a rope if anything went wrong.

So nothing must go wrong.

It was, he thought, just as simple as that.

Percy Fawcett knew he should be running for his life, but where was he to go? It was a minor miracle that he'd survived the night, and now, with fresh blood on his hands, he feared that he was running out of time. When Grady Sullivan discovered what he'd done . . .

The escorts Sullivan had picked to sneak him out of Stateline hadn't said a word to Fawcett until they were nearly two miles out of town. At that point, he had asked where they were taking him and one of them — Dooley, the buggy's driver — told him they were headed for a cabin in the Blue Stem Hills where he could lie low for a bit, while Sullivan and Rafferty planned their next moves. It sounded fair enough, but Fawcett was suspicious, noticing a kind of smirk on Dooley's face before he glanced at Jeb, riding a brindle mare beside the carriage.

And from that alone, Fawcett decided that they meant to kill him. How better to silence him for good and leave the marshals back in Stateline searching for a link they'd never find, between Flynn Rafferty and their dead colleague?

They had never reached the cabin last night, if there *was* a cabin. Fawcett had grown deadly nervous, trembling on his wagon seat from fear and chill winds on the prairie, easing one hand underneath his jacket to retrieve the Colt M1889 he'd hidden there. If Dooley noticed, he'd betrayed no sign of it, but when they were a good two hours out of town, he'd reined the buggy to an unexpected stop.

"I need ta piss," he'd said and turned as if to give Fawcett the reins, left-handed, while his right hand shifted toward his holstered pistol. Fawcett saw the move and jammed his .38 against the driver's ribs, triggering a shot that toppled Dooley from the driver's seat and set his shirt on fire.

Beyond the falling gunman, startled Jeb was clawing for his own pistol, cursing a blue streak as his mare shied from the gunshot's echo. Squealing in his own right, Fawcett fired three times and somehow found his mark despite the spastic tremor rippling down his arm. Jeb tumbled from his saddle, hit the ground hard, but he wasn't finished yet. Fawcett was forced to climb down from the buggy and approach him, putting one more shot into his head at point-blank range, before the gunman ceased his thrashing.

Dooley, thank the Lord, was dead before he hit the dirt.

Panic had overtaken Fawcett as he stood beside the bodies of his would-be execution-ers. He was a killer now, with nothing but his word to prove that he had fired in self-defense, if he was apprehended, charged, and held for trial. His more immediate concern was Grady Sullivan, his gunmen, and the man behind them all. Tomorrow or the next day, when the men he'd killed had not returned to Stateline, someone would come looking for them. They would find the bodies — or whatever still remained, after the buzzards and the coyotes ate their fill — and know that he had tricked them. That he had escaped.

From that point onward, he would be a hunted man. The fact that he'd been lucky once was meaningless. Rafferty's men would ultimately find him and eliminate him, likely in the slowest way they could imagine, to repay him for the slaying of their friends.

Where could he hide?

After a cold night sleeping in the wagon, on the open plains, Fawcett awoke to hunger and the knowledge that he likely couldn't find his way to any other town without a guide. The only place that he could locate for a certainty was Stateline, which meant going to his certain death.

Unless . . .

A plan took shape in Fawcett's fevered mind, and awkwardly, he turned the buggy southward.

Warren Jain was nervous as he stepped into

the Sunflower Saloon. He'd let the deputies bamboozle him, intimidate him into saying things he shouldn't have, and now he had to make a clean breast of it. Throw himself upon the big man's mercy while he still had time, before the lawmen came around with questions, maybe mentioning his name.

Surprised as always by the group of breakfast-hour drinkers in the saloon, Jain held himself erect as he approached the bar, hoping the slender thug who doubled as the joint's bartender and his master's gate-keeper wouldn't observe that he was trembling.

"Mornin', Mayor," the barkeep said.

"I need to see him," Jain announced.

"In his office. Don't forget to knock."

In other circumstances, Jain imagined that he might have lanced the barkeep with a glare, or maybe that was wishful thinking. As it was, he bobbed a nod and moved past two determined drinkers caked in trail dust, wondering why alcohol took precedence over a nice hot bath. Reaching the PRIVATE door, he knocked, an almost timid sound. Ten or fifteen seconds passed and he was about to try again, when he heard "Come!"

Jain entered, closed the door behind him, and stood facing Rafferty across the big man's desk. The Sunflower's proprietor was

189

counting cash — his favorite pastime, as far as Jain could tell — but paused to flash a toothy smile.

"Good morning, Mayor. What can I do for you?"

"Well, um, I thought you ought to know," Jain said, then felt the flow of words dry up.

"Know what, pray tell?"

"I ran into those marshals, over at the Borderline Café."

"Oh, yes?"

"Trying to find out what they'd learned so far about . . . you know."

"Do I?"

"Thing is, they started asking questions about Stateline Storage."

"Ah."

"They squeezed me pretty hard. I may have let it slip who owns the place."

"May have?"

"Well, *did.*"

"That's not exactly what I'd call discreet," said Rafferty.

"No, sir. And I apologize for that. But they were going after deeds and records anyway."

"And you just thought you'd make it easy for them. Being neighborly and all."

Jain bit his tongue to keep from saying anything that might rebound against him, make things worse than they already were.

He stuffed his trembling hands into his trouser pockets, then removed them, worried that the pose might seem belligerent.

Rafferty left him sweating for another moment, then told Jain, "It just so happens that I know about their interest in the warehouse. They were seen snooping around the place last night."

"So, then . . . I didn't ruin anything?" asked Jain.

Rafferty frowned at him and said, "It's true I would've liked to keep the ownership a secret from them for at least a little while. But I'll forgive you this time, knowing what a worrier you are."

"I never meant to —"

"Let it go now, Warren, will you? And take extra care to keep your lip buttoned around those fellows in the future, while they're here."

"I will. Yes, sir."

"You still enjoy your job, I take it?"

"Absolutely. Yes."

"And want to keep it?"

"Yes, sir."

"So, be circumspect. Don't volunteer a goddamned thing from here on out. You understand?"

"I do."

"And if they ask you about Percy Fawcett —"

"Fawcett? What about him?"

"*Anything* about him," Rafferty continued. "You just say he had to go and deal with family business back home."

"Where's home?" Jain asked.

"Somewhere back East. That's all you know, because he never shared the details."

"Right. Okay."

"Just stick to that," said Rafferty, "and I suspect you'll be all right."

The Rocking R, Slade learned from Stateline's barber, was located six or seven miles northwest of Stateline, covering twelve hundred acres more or less, and most of it in corn. That ought to keep a good-sized still in business, but the supposition wasn't evidence. So far, Slade knew Flynn Rafferty was storing untaxed whiskey in his warehouse, but he couldn't use the evidence of his own eyes in court. And it was still a leap from stashing liquor to distilling it. There was a chance, however slim, that Rafferty was just a middleman.

But either way, regardless of his status in the operation, he was still a suspect in Bill Tanner's death. Slade now supposed that Tanner must have followed the same leads as he and Naylor had, then wired his vague report back to Judge Dennison and thereby sealed his fate.

They checked the Western Union office on their way down to the livery, but found it closed, no sign of the telegrapher. "Look for him when we get back, then," Naylor suggested, and they passed on to the stable for their animals.

Passing down Border Boulevard, they got the same looks they'd received on Friday riding into town. A few townsfolk seemed curious, but most took pains to keep their faces blank, some seeking refuge from eye contact with a sudden interest in the windows of whatever shop was handy.

"Not exactly what I'd call a warm town," Naylor said. "You think they're in on it?"

"The 'shine? I doubt it," Slade replied. "Least not directly. Sharing profits with a whole town makes no sense. Whether they know about it is another question."

"Or about Bill Tanner."

"That's a harder thing to live with," Slade suggested, "but I wouldn't rule it out."

"I hate to think about a whole town helping killers," Naylor said.

"Fear might be part of it."

"Still no excuse. A town this size, how many people would it take to scare them?"

"All depends," Slade said.

"On what?"

"How much they stand to lose by speaking out."

"I guess. You need to have some self-respect, though. Am I right?"

"No telling what they went through, coming out here," Slade replied. "Or what they've sacrificed to stay."

"Maybe. But anyone that I can prove is covering for Tanner's killers, I intend to take them in."

"Let's find the killers first and deal with them," Slade said. "The rest may take care of itself."

"You don't shy from a fight, the way I hear it," Naylor said.

"Not so far."

"Then you're with me if we need to charge a mess of people with obstructing justice?"

"If it comes to that," Slade said. "And if it fits the facts."

"About this Rocking R," said Naylor. "What is it you hope to find besides a lot of corn?"

"A cooker maybe," Slade replied. "Something that we can use, connecting Rafferty to that stockpile of whiskey."

"And to Tanner."

"First and foremost on my mind," Slade said.

"He'll likely have some guns around the place."

"I'd say it's more than likely."

"And we're trespassin' again," Naylor reminded him.

"Having a look around," Slade said. "Going to see the man in charge."

"Who's back in town right now."

"Nobody told me that. The only thing I've heard this morning," Slade replied, "is that he's got a spread outside of Stateline. Where else would we go to find a fellow, but at home?"

"You think the judge will buy that?"

"Maybe wrapped up with a ribbon on it," Slade suggested. "If we find a nice, big still."

11

A decent wagon road led north from State-line over flat, clear land, aimed more or less toward Garnett, Kansas City, and the border with Missouri. Naylor and Slade weren't traveling that far, however. When they reached a Y fork in the road, about four miles from town, they veered off to the west and slowed their pace. Another half mile on, they stopped and Slade took out his spyglass, peering farther down the track. He saw the kind of gate some ranchers liked to put up at the entrance to their property, even without a fence or wall attached to it. Tall timbers with a crossbar at the top, and standing proud atop that bar, a rocking *R*.

"That's it," he said. "You ready?"

"As I'll ever be," Naylor replied.

They had talked about the best approach, deciding they should play a stealthy hand. Approach Rafferty's spread as unobtrusively as possible and have a look around. If they were intercepted on the way, it was a simple matter to explain that they'd come out to see the boss and might have wandered off the beaten track by accident. It might be thin, and Naylor had expressed concern over the possibility they'd both be shot for trespassing, but the alternative — riding direct to Rafferty's front door — promised to yield nothing.

Hedging his bets, Slade had prepared his two long guns for rapid action, each one with a live round in its chamber and the hammers down, requiring only pressure from his thumb to cock them. Any challenge from a distance, he could answer with his rifle. Closer in, he had the shotgun and his Colt.

Assuming that the first shots didn't take him down.

They turned off-road and passed the gate, two hundred yards northward. Slade could track the road from that distance, ride parallel and watch for any traffic heading back toward Stateline, hopefully in time to keep from being spotted. It was risky here, with so much open land. The nearest halfway decent cover Slade could see lay north and farther west, a wooded rise at least three-quarters of a mile away.

Then, there was corn.

A sea of it, it seemed, stretching away to the horizon, leafy stalks approaching seven feet in height, marching in rows that stood about three feet apart. Slade paused with Naylor at the edge of it, imagining how early pioneers had felt upon encountering a trackless forest, but the maze before them was man-made.

"Seems like the rows run more or less in the direction of the road," Naylor observed.

"Let's hope so," Slade replied.

"We doing it?"

Slade nodded, said, "We're doing it," and nudged his roan into the rustling vastness of the field.

They followed two parallel rows, green stalks with good-sized tasseled ears of corn brushing against their legs and horses' flanks. The field smelled dusty, making Slade's nose twitch. He tried to watch the road, past Naylor riding to his right, imagining what they might look like to a passerby, their disembodied heads bobbing along above the stalks. The very opposite of headless horsemen, something that a drunk might see and blather to his friends about.

Or something a sniper might decide to fire at for the hell of it.

And if they met somebody coming through the corn on foot? What then?

See what he does, Slade thought, *and go from there.*

A long, slow hour later he picked out a smudge of wood smoke rising from what had to be a chimney, then the roofline of a house. Naylor had seen it, too, glancing at Slade across the stalks that separated them, reining his Appaloosa to an even slower walk. Before they reached the last fringe of the cornfield, Slade could see a barn and other outbuildings arrayed to either side of Flynn Rafferty's home.

"I'm walking in from here," he said, keeping his voice low-pitched despite their distance from the buildings and the muffling effect of all that corn.

"Sounds good," Naylor replied. Not quite a whisper.

They dismounted, led their horses by the reins, and tied them loosely to a pair of corn stalks fifty feet or so inside the field, before they reached clear ground. From there, the lawmen walked on, hats removed and shoulders hunched to keep from letting anybody in the barnyard spot them. It was shady in among the rows, which also helped.

"Now what?" asked Naylor when they'd found a vantage point.

"Now," Slade replied, "we wait and see what we can see."

■ ■ ■ ■

Percy Fawcett entered Stateline from the north, on foot, avoiding Border Boulevard. He'd stopped the buggy two miles out from town, released its horse to run at liberty, and walked the final distance with his portmanteau, leaving the trunk behind. It would, he thought, present a mystery for Sullivan and Rafferty to solve. And if his luck held, it might buy Fawcett himself some breathing room.

For what?

First thing, a hasty meal, something to drink, before a washup and a change of clothes. When all of that was done, he planned to wait for nightfall, then sneak out and find the U.S. marshals who'd been sent to follow up the last one's murder. In the meantime, he would keep his door locked and his pistol handy, making no unnecessary noise to let the neighbors know he was at home.

If Grady Sullivan came looking for him . . . well, Fawcett would deal with that threat if and when it happened. He'd become a killer overnight, relieved and sickened in approximately equal measure by the double slaying, and he thought he'd have no trouble shooting Sullivan or anyone whom Rafferty dispatched to find him.

Not unless they saw him first.

But Fawcett hoped that wouldn't happen. First, he thought, Rafferty's men would go off northward, looking for the pair who hadn't made it home last night. Whether they found the buggy first or missed it altogether, riding on until a flock of buzzards led them to the bodies, that would take some time. They'd likely search for Fawcett then, unwilling to believe he'd turn around and run back toward the lion's den in Stateline. Every hour wasted brought him closer to the night, when he could move about more safely, seeking help.

What could the marshals do for him?

They already suspected his involvement in the slaying of their friend. He'd be confessing to complicity once he admitted showing Sullivan the other lawman's telegram, which might mean prison time, but that still beat the death sentence imposed on him by Rafferty. If he agreed to testify in court, they would be duty bound to keep him safe. And if that meant a cell in Enid while he waited for the trial, so be it.

Returning from his interrupted journey overnight, Fawcett had grappled with a nagging strain of doubt. Part of his mind suggested that the men he'd shot — Dooley and Jeb — had not intended to eliminate him after all. If they had simply been escorting him to hiding, at a cabin in the hills, that made Fawcett a murderer. And even if they'd planned to kill him, Sullivan and Rafferty could spin the tale another way at trial, to help themselves or simply get revenge.

To have him join them on the gallows.

"Never mind," he muttered to the silent room. Fawcett believed his life had been in danger on the prairie, that he'd fired in self-defense, and he could sell that story to a jury any day, once they were privy to the other crimes of Rafferty and Sullivan. Who would believe the claims of two moonshiners who had killed a deputy — and God alone knew how many others?

No one.

Fawcett's challenge now was to survive and find the marshals, tell his story, throw himself upon their mercy. Sell them on the idea that they needed him to make their case and net the bigger fish.

They wouldn't let him keep his Colt, of course, but he'd be safer in their custody than wandering around all by himself, armed to the teeth. Marshals were man-hunters, by definition. He would trust his fate to them and pray that if that choice was a mistake, the men who came to kill him would be quick about it.

Quick and clean, to send him on his way.

Lying on their bellies at the edge of the cornfield, Slade and Naylor eyed the house and outbuildings a quarter mile due west. Slade used his spyglass, passing it to Naylor for a look around, then used it to sweep the grounds again.

"Not what I'd call a busy place," Naylor observed, as two men strolled across the yard and went into the house.

"There must not be a lot to do with corn," Slade said. "Plant it, wait for the rain, pick it."

"No animals around except the chickens. Like to get a look inside that barn."

"We'd have to wait for that till after dark. You want to hang around that long?" Slade asked.

"Can't say I would. The other way's to ride down there and tell 'em that we've come to see the boss. One of us does the talkin', while the other drifts around a bit and tries to spot something. Or smell it, either one."

"And when they say the boss is back in town, then what?" asked Slade.

"We leave, nice and polite-like," Naylor

answered. "Maybe with enough to tell the judge and get ourselves a warrant."

"Maybe."

Slade had counted seven men drifting around the property, performing minor chores, together with an eighth one going to the privy from the house, then back again. He didn't like the odds, if shooting started, and was not inclined to spark a skirmish if he could avoid it.

He rooted for his pocket watch, retrieved it, and opened it. "Five minutes to eleven," he announced. "We have to sneak down there, I'd rather wait until they're sitting down to lunch."

"At least another hour, then," said Naylor, slapping at some kind of insect on his neck.

"We'll see." Slade cautioned him, "You know, we creep around and spot something, we still can't use it, since we haven't got a warrant."

"Or the evidence is lying in plain sight," Naylor replied.

"It's not," Slade said. "We both know that."

"It would be their word against ours."

"Until Judge Dennison inquires why we were on the property to start with, nobody around."

"Just lucky," Naylor said. "We rode in toward the house and caught a whiff of something from the barn. Rode over there — the doors were standing open — and we saw the cooker."

"If there *is* a cooker."

"Where else would it be?"

He had a point. "So, if it *is,*" Slade said, "then what?"

"We up stakes, get a wiggle on, and tell the judge. Come back with reinforcements for a raid."

"Might work," Slade granted. "But we —"

"Wait a second! What are those guys doing?"

Through his telescope, Slade watched two of the ranch hands leading horses toward a nearby empty wagon. Teaming up, they got the animals in harness, led them to the barn, then got the wagon backed around so that its tailgate faced the open doors.

"Looks like they plan on loadin' something," Naylor said.

"I'd say."

When the wagon was positioned to their liking, with the tailgate down, one man climbed up into its empty bed. The other went into the barn, and came back moments later with a third ranch hand, both of them lugging wooden crates. Each placed his in the wagon, then retreated to the barn, leaving their helper to arrange the boxes in the wagon's bed.

"I've got a dollar says there's whiskey bottles in those crates," said Naylor.

"No bet," Slade replied.

"So, what now?"

Slade considered it and said, "I always like the easy way, myself. They load it, we hang back and follow. Find out where they're headed. We can always stop them on the road and have a word. Maybe convince them we should have a look inside one of the boxes."

"Well off from the rest of them," said Naylor.

"That's my thought."

"Sounds good to me."

"Rate they're going, if they fill the wagon, they'll be done in . . . what, an hour?"

"Pretty close."

"Then maybe have some lunch before they leave," said Naylor.

"We can wait them out."

Naylor slapped at another bug and said, "I reckon so."

Grady Sullivan was getting itchy, his frustration turning into anger as he walked the streets of Stateline, looking high and low for

Jeb and Dooley. They were meant to meet him back in town after they'd taken care of Percy Fawcett, but they hadn't shown up yet. Sullivan's first thought was that they had come in late, had a few drinks, and settled in with whores to spend the night, be he'd already checked the Sunflower and Swagger Inn without success. The barkeeps hadn't seen his men, and there was no one sleeping over with the girls.

Now what?

He wondered if, between them, they were dumb enough to get his orders backward and return Rafferty's buggy to the Rocking R. One thing that Sullivan had learned, bossing the other hands around for Rafferty, was that you never knew how stupid some of them could be. A couple of them, he supposed, wouldn't know how to pour piss from a boot with the instructions printed on the heel.

But Jeb and Dooley, now, they should be able to remember simple orders. Meeting Sullivan in town when they were finished meant exactly that, and nothing else. He hadn't picked the crew's worst dummies; quite the opposite, in fact.

So where in hell were they?

After the two saloons, he checked the Stateline Arms and came up empty.

Next, he made a pass by each of the three restaurants in town. More nothing for his trouble.

He was passing by the barber's shop when Tim O'Malley cracked the door and made a sound like "Psssst!"

Sullivan doubled back, eyeing the street in both directions, passing on into the shop.

"I've been looking for you," said the barber. "Did you hear about those marshals?"

"What about them?"

"They came by this morning."

"Came by *here*?"

"The very place," O'Malley said.

"So, did you shave 'em up, or what?"

"It wasn't shaves they wanted. Asked some questions, though."

"What kind of questions?"

"One that sticks in mind was how to find the Rocking R," O'Malley said. "Well . . . I told 'em. Couldn't very well pretend I never heard of it, could I? Being the biggest spread around, and all."

"You get the feeling they were headed out there?" Sullivan inquired.

"Not just a feeling. Saw 'em head down to the livery and ride out, pretty soon after we talked."

Goddamn it!

"And what time was that?" asked Sullivan.

"A couple hours ago."

"The other questions they were askin'. You remember any of 'em?"

"There was something about Stateline Storage, up the street," O'Malley said. "Who owns it, this and that. I didn't help 'em, there."

"Awright, then. If they come back in —"

"I don't know nothin' more," O'Malley said.

"Let's keep it that way."

Back on Border Boulevard, Sullivan knew he had a choice to make. Stop by the Sunflower and tell the big man that the marshals had gone out to see the Rocking R, or just ride after them without consulting Rafferty. A two-hour head start placed Grady well behind the lawmen, and the time he'd waste with Rafferty would make it even worse. He knew the boss would send him out to see what they were doing, maybe get them off the spread without a fuss or deal with any problems they'd created. Whether he'd give Sullivan the go-ahead to kill them was another question, but sometimes you had to make those calls without submitting them to anybody higher up.

Get moving, then, he thought, and started down the street. Not running, which would draw undue attention to himself, but walking fast enough to shave a minute off the trip to fetch his horse — and warn other pedestrians to get the hell out of his way.

His mind was churning by the time he reached his buckskin gelding, tied outside the Sunflower Saloon. He thought once more of going in, advising Rafferty of what had happened, then dismissed the thought.

No time to waste.

Slade and Naylor watched the wagon leave with two men on its high seat, one handling the reins, the other with a shotgun in his lap. They gave the team a good head start, then crept back to their horses in the cornfield, mounted up, and followed on a course that paralleled the access road. Slade worried more than ever now about a ranch hand intercepting them, since it would likely mean a shootout *and* losing the wagon after they'd waited so long to see it loaded.

Luck was with them, though, and no one spotted them as they retreated from the house, back toward the county road where their intended quarry would be forced to choose a turning, north or south. Both marshals made a point of hunching in their saddles, as they had on their approach, to keep the teamster and his guard from catching sight of them if either chanced to gaze off through the corn. They passed along without a spoken word between them, hoping any sounds they made would be attributed to wind among the stalks.

The wagon had a lead of some five hundred yards when it passed through the tall gate with the Rocking R on top. Behind it, shaded by the corn, Slade tracked it with his spyglass, waiting for the man who held the reins to make his choice.

"South takes 'em back to Stateline," Naylor said. "You figure that's another warehouse load?"

"Crates mean they've bottled up the 'shine," Slade said. "It could be stock for one of the saloons in town."

"Or both," Naylor replied. "I didn't trust that Swagger fella any more than Rafferty."

Another moment, and the wagon reached the county road, paused there a moment, then turned left.

"Stateline it is," said Naylor.

"Or someplace beyond it," Slade suggested. "This could be another shipment for the reservations, or it could be going farther south. For all we know, they might be heading for Eufala, maybe even Oklahoma City."

"Maybe Enid," Naylor said, half smiling.

"That'd frost the judge."

"I guess we'd better ask them," Slade replied.

Emerging from the cornfield at a trot, then galloping, they overtook the slower-moving wagon in about four minutes, reining back when they were thirty yards or so behind it.

"Shotgun rider's mine," said Naylor, palm resting atop the curved grip of his right-hand Colt.

Slade swung out to the driver's side, his roan mare cantering, and called out to the wagon, "U.S. marshals! Hold up there!"

Two startled, scowling faces turned to face the lawmen. Slade suspected that the driver might try running for it, but he hauled back on the reins instead and slowed his team, then brought it to a halt. Up close, the sound of bottles rattling in wooden crates was clearly audible.

Slade rode up on the left, the driver's side, while Naylor eased around the right, his Colt half drawn. "Be smart and lay that shotgun by your feet," Naylor advised the guard. Reluctantly, the shooter did as he was told.

"How come you're stoppin' us?" the wagon's driver asked.

"It just so happens that we're on a moonshine hunt," Slade said. "You wouldn't know of any in the neighborhood, by chance?"

"Why should we?"

"Call me the suspicious sort," Slade said. "I hear those bottles clanking in your wagon and I get an itch to know what's in them."

"Sarsaparilla," said the guard. "What of it?"

"Last I heard," said Naylor, "sarsaparilla comes from berries off a vine, not corn."

"Listen," the driver said, "you don't know who you're mussing with."

"Enlighten us," Slade said.

The driver spat tobacco juice into the road, seemed on the verge of answering, when suddenly the right side of his face imploded, spraying blood. Slade heard the echo of a distant gunshot half a second later, when the shotgun guard was cursing, diving for his weapon.

"Hold it!" Naylor shouted, but the guard was long past listening. He turned, raising the double barrel, angling it toward Naylor, thumbing back twin hammers as he turned.

Naylor and Slade fired simultaneously, drilled the gunman front and back, pitching him sidelong from his seat and down between the horses harnessed to the wagon. Whether they were used to shooting, or the driver's dead weight on their reins restrained them, neither of the horses bolted.

"Where'd that first shot come from?" Naylor asked, sweeping his Colt in search of other targets.

Slade's gaze swept the skyline, picking out the small form of a rider fleeing southward.

"There!" he said, pointing, and nudged his roan to forward motion.

"What about the wagon?" Naylor asked him.

"They aren't going anywhere," Slade said and charged off in pursuit.

12

Slade heard Naylor's snowflake Appaloosa gaining on him as he trailed the distant gunman, trying hard to close the gap between them. They had been a quarter mile or so apart when the sniper's shot killed the wagon driver, firing from the saddle and retreating hell-for-leather after squeezing off a single round. The shooter had a good horse under him, and he was obviously skilled in handling it, hunched low over his saddle horn and riding like a jockey in a race. Slade did his best to match that pace, reached back to slap his roan's flank with an open hand and shout encouragement, but even as he ate the sniper's dust his mind was racing faster than his animal.

Drilling a man-sized target at a quarter mile was certainly possible, say with the .45-70 Government cartridge used in the Winchester Model 1886 rifle. A skilled hand with assistance from a telescopic sight could kill with that gun at a thousand yards, and consistent hits at six hundred yards were required to earn an army marksman's medal. Nothing special in itself about the shot, then — but who was the actual target?

Suppose that the sniper had *missed* from that range. Was he shooting at Slade or at Naylor? Had he plugged the driver accidentally, then panicked? If he'd meant to drop the driver and could kill reliably at that range, why stop with a single shot?

Too many questions, none that Slade could answer if the shooter got away from him or died resisting capture.

Clinging to the mare's reins, Slade called back over his shoulder, "Luke! We need this one alive!"

And Naylor's wind-whipped voice came back to him: "Let's catch the bastard first!"

Ahead of them, three-quarters of a mile away but drawing closer by the second, Slade made out a line of trees atop a rise. They hadn't passed that way, riding from Stateline to the Rocking R, but they were off the main road now and moving farther from it all the time. A sniper in those trees could pick them off or pin them down till nightfall, make his getaway in darkness if he hadn't killed them outright to begin with.

It was no good warning Naylor. Slade assumed that he could see the wooded ridge and grasp its import as they galloped toward it, horses fighting for the next breath to propel them onward. Slade prayed that the grassy land in front of them concealed no tunnels dug by prairie dogs to snap a fetlock, no gullies to send him tumbling with a broken neck or back.

They still weren't close enough to risk a pistol shot that likely would have missed their prey entirely but could just as easily have killed the fugitive before they had a chance to question him. At least their breakneck speed prevented any aimed fire from the fleeing rifleman, but he had nearly reached the trees now, still four hundred yards or so ahead of Slade and Naylor.

"Faster, damn it!" Slade exhorted, but the roan was giving everything she had. A moment later, Slade cursed bitterly, watching his adversary vanish in among the shady trees.

What now?

A rifle spoke in answer to his silent question, its location indicated by a puff of gun smoke. Slade braced for the killing impact, but the bullet missed him, whistling past what felt like mere inches from his face. Instinctively, he veered off course, looking for cover of his own and hoped Naylor was smart enough to do the same.

And once Slade swung away, there *was* a gully, running roughly parallel to the direction he'd been traveling. Once into it, he found that it was deep enough to hide him once he'd leaped down from his saddle. Naylor tumbled into the ravine a moment later, as another shot cracked overhead.

"I think he clipped my sleeve with that one," said the younger marshal, grinning with excitement.

Slade, rifle in hand, replied, "I plan to creep in toward him, if this gully doesn't peter out. See if there's any chance to get the drop on him."

"Sounds good." Naylor drew both Colts, looking eager.

"I'd prefer it if you covered me from here," Slade said. "Keep him distracted while I try to work around behind him."

"Okay. Sure," said Naylor, clearly disappointed.

Slade took off without debating it, hearing Naylor open up behind him, firing well-spaced shots. The gully led him more or less directly where he hoped to go, but only time would tell if that was good or bad. Whether he rushed toward the solution of a mystery or to his death.

■ ■ ■ ■

Grady Sullivan fired one last shot to keep the lawmen under cover, then hauled on his horse's reins and steered the buckskin gelding southward, back toward Stateline. He was galloping away and out of range when someone fired a pistol shot behind him, wasted. Glancing back, he saw one of the marshals there between the trees, his six-gun dangling, and imagined the frustration he must feel.

Goddamn, but that was close!

Sullivan hadn't been exactly sure how he should deal with the two officers when he left town, riding to intercept them at the Rocking R. He'd hoped to get there and discover that the other hands on duty had prevented any search that would reveal their giant whiskey still. Sullivan understood the basic rule of warrants, but he thought that if the cops got close enough to smell 'shine cooking, that might grant them leave to snoop around. In which case, he supposed he'd have to deal with them, whether the big man finally approved or not.

The last thing Sullivan expected was to find the marshals holding up a whiskey wagon on the county road. He'd felt a spark of panic then, knowing that they were bound to open up one of the crates and find the bottled liquor, whereupon the driver and his guard would likely squeal to save themselves from doing time. A heartbeat later, Sullivan had found the rifle in his hands and fired almost without conscious volition, taking down the driver — and all hell broke loose.

What was he thinking? Should his shot have been directed at a marshal, followed by a second round to drop the other one? Whatever hindsight told him would have been the wisest course, he couldn't turn back time and do it over. Anyhow, the main thing was that he'd escaped, while keeping space enough between himself and the two lawmen to prevent them from identifying him by sight.

So far, so good.

But now he had to break the news to Mr. Rafferty, admit that he'd gone off half-cocked and kicked a hornets' nest. The marshals were alive, they had a wagonload of whiskey from the Rocking R, and if that wasn't evidence enough to hurt the big man . . . well, what was?

It wasn't over yet, though. Even in his frazzled state, Sullivan thought there might be hope. With Percy Fawcett missing, any message that the lawmen tried to send from Stateline to their boss would have to wait. They might decide to pass on through and take the wagon back to Enid on their own, but that meant camping overnight, somewhere along the way. And Sullivan had learned his lesson about sending others out to do a job he should've done himself.

With or without the 'shine, they'd never make it back to tell Judge Dennison what they had found. Sullivan was prepared to bet his life on that.

In fact, he'd placed the bet already.

He would beat them back to town, brief Mr. Rafferty on what had happened, and explain his plan for cleaning up the mess. Whether the marshals stayed in Stateline overnight or pushed on through, he had them covered.

Now he only had to sweat the big man's anger, hoping he wouldn't fly off the handle and do something lethal. Like killing the messenger, say. If Sullivan could make it through their meeting with his skin intact, he thought the other pieces should fall neatly into place all right.

And if they didn't . . . well, he'd think about that when he had no other choice.

Disgruntled at losing the sniper, Slade hiked

back to Naylor and the horses, tersely reporting his failure. Naylor seemed to take the news in stride, asking, "But he was heading back to Stateline, though?"

"The last I saw of him," Slade said. "Might be a false lead, though. He could be anywhere by now."

"Back at the Rocking R?"

Slade shrugged. "I wouldn't know him if he met us on the porch. Besides, I wouldn't want to take the whiskey wagon back there with their two dead pals."

"I'm thinking," Naylor said, once he was settled on his Appaloosa's saddle, "we should make sure that it *is* a whiskey wagon."

"Right," Slade said and mounted up.

That would be the last straw, he decided, if they killed one man and nearly got shot themselves for something other than the moonshine they were after. Feeling sour all the way back to the wagon with its load of crates and dead men, Slade sat back and watched while Naylor dropped the wagon's tailgate, used his knife to open up the nearest crate, and lifted out a bottle filled with amber-colored liquid. Prying out the cork, he sniffed, then took a healthy swig.

"I'd say that's pretty close to eighty proof," he said. "You want a shot?"

"No, thanks," Slade answered, satisfied with the relief he felt just then.

They hoisted the two corpses back into the wagon's bed, no tarpaulin to cover them, and Naylor used a rag he found beneath the driver's seat to wipe most of the blood away. Unsatisfied with the result, he stripped the lifeless driver's jacket off and draped it on the seat to hide the stains.

"Who drives?" he asked.

"I may as well," said Slade.

He led his mare around behind the wagon and secured her reins to the tailgate, then mounted to the driver's seat and settled on the dead man's denim jacket. It had been a while since Slade had driven any kind of team, but it came back to him, the docile horses helping out. Naylor rode point, his rifle out and ready, just in case the long-range killer doubled back to try his luck a second time.

He didn't, though, and they reached Stateline without further incident. Towns-people on the street made no pretense of looking through them this time, as they brought the wagon and its corpses creaking down the length of Border Boulevard, to stop outside the marshal's office. Arlo Hickey was already on the sidewalk, thick arms folded, watching them approach.

"More dead men," he observed.

"And a wagon full of moonshine that you'll need to keep an eye on, overnight," Slade said.

"Want me to test it for you, while I'm at it?"

"Won't be necessary."

"Pity." Hickey stepped into the street and walked around to get a better look at the two corpses. Blinking at their faces, he said, "Hey, these boys are from the Rockin' R."

"Is that right?" Naylor asked.

"Sure is. I know 'em both. Mike Embry and Tom Logan. They're in town a lot. What happened?"

"We were asking them about their cargo," Slade replied, "when someone shot the driver from a distance. After that, the guard thought maybe he should take a shot at us."

"We didn't feel like sittin' still for it," said Naylor.

"Jesus. What about the other shooter?"

"He was faster off the mark than I was," Slade allowed. "I lost him."

Hickey spat into the dust and said, "I'll go'n fetch the undertaker. Wouldn't be surprised if he's the best friend you two have in town."

"We aim to please," Naylor remarked.

"About this liquor, now . . ."

"Just keep it safe and sound tonight," Slade said. "We'll start for Enid with it in the morning."

"You'll wanna talk to Mr. Rafferty about it, I suppose," said Hickey.

"We already did that," Slade replied.

"He never heard of anybody cookin' 'shine around these parts," Naylor chimed in.

"I just meant, since these were his boys and all . . ."

"You want to break it to him, be our guest," said Naylor.

"Not my business," Hickey said and moved off down the street.

"So, how about it?" Naylor asked. "You want to have another word with Rafferty before we go?"

"I thought we'd wait," Slade said. "See if he has a word for us."

From the undertaker's parlor, Arlo Hickey scuttled on to the Sunflower, dreading what he had to tell the big man. Rafferty was unpredictable, where bad news was concerned, and there'd been nothing else to tell him since the new lawmen hit town.

The bartender saw Hickey coming, read his somber face, and nodded him on back. Rafferty's voice boomed out almost before the marshal's knuckles tapped his office door.

"Enter!"

Hickey went in and shut the door behind him, found the big man pacing back and forth behind his desk. Before he had a chance to speak, Rafferty said, "I understand we have a problem, Arlo."

"Yes, sir."

"Mike and Tom have gone to their reward."

"Whatever that might be," said Hickey.

"Fruitless speculation. And the shipment?"

"Sittin' in a wagon right outside my office. I'm supposed to watch it overnight and see 'em off to Enid with it in the morning."

"Ah."

"I asked 'em if they meant to speak with you about it," Hickey said, hating the way his voice cracked as his throat began to tighten.

"And?"

"They didn't seem too interested. Said they had a talk with you already and you couldn't tell 'em anything."

"I'd say we're in a pickle, then," said Rafferty.

You're in a pickle, Hickey thought, then cleared his throat and said, "I mighta let it slip to 'em Tom 'n' Mike were from the Rockin' R."

"How thoughtful of you, Marshal."

"Thing is, Mr. Rafferty, they didn't seem to care."

"Oh, no?"

"See, I was thinkin' —"

"That's a bad start, Arlo. Say no more."

"Yes, sir."

"It's evident our uninvited visitors know where the whiskey came from. They were at the Rocking R and trailed it back toward town."

"How'd you know that?"

"Let's say I heard it from a little bird."

It clicked. "They said somebody shot Joe from afar off," Hickey said. "I get it now."

"Get what?" Rafferty challenged him.

"Um, well. Nothin', I guess."

"Nothing is right. The only thing you need to know is that a court will see that wagon-load of 'shine and grant search warrants. After that, well . . . surely I don't need to tell you, Arlo, that if *I* go down, some others will be going with me."

Hickey didn't like the sound of that. He had no dealings with the 'shine racket himself, except to play blind, deaf, and dumb. He'd absolutely had no part in killing the last U.S. marshal who had passed through Stateline, but Judge Dennison might see it otherwise, once he got in a hanging mood.

"What should I do?" he asked.

"For now," said Rafferty, "just what they've told you. Keep the whiskey safe and sound until I send someone to deal with it. If there's no evidence, they've got no case."

"We still expectin' soldiers?" Hickey asked.

"We are, indeed. Early tomorrow, I would say."

"You figure they'll go up against the lawmen?"

"I believe they'll do their duty to the best of their ability."

Hickey supposed it would be pushing things to ask what duty that might be. Instead, he told the big man, "If you need some help . . . um, well . . . you know."

"I will not hesitate to call on you. Good day, Marshal."

Officially dismissed, Hickey retreated from the office, out through the saloon, with bright piano music sounding off-key to his ears. Outside, he felt an urge to stride on past his office, pick his horse up from the livery, and ride like hell away from Stateline toward whatever compass point seemed promising. How far would anybody chase him if he ran right now, leaving the big man and his shooters to their fate?

Not far, perhaps, but he was old for starting over, nothing to his name except a horse, a pistol, and a couple of dollars in his pocket. Hickey knew for damn sure that he couldn't count on any reference from Mr. Rafferty. In fact, he might not want to use his own name if he started fresh, in case it showed up on a poster somewhere down the line.

The more he thought about it, though, escaping seemed like too much work. If he stayed put and waited out the storm, he still might be all right.

Maybe.

Back at his office, Hickey passed the whiskey wagon — horses gone now, taken to the livery or back out to the Rocking R, he hoped — and went inside. It felt like time to double-check his stock of guns.

Lord knew he had all night.

I've got all night, thought Percy Fawcett, sitting at the table in his small apartment where he ate most of his frugal meals. In front of him, two fried eggs and some beans lay cooling on a plate, half eaten. Fawcett had laid down his knife and fork, resting his right hand on the Colt that lay beside his plate.

A noise outside. Footsteps. Just someone passing by, he figured now, since they'd kept going without pause. He had the heavy curtain drawn over his one small window, leaking daylight at the edges, but the quality of light had lately changed. A glance at Fawcett's watch, open beside the pistol, told him it was five minutes past six o'clock.

Another hour, more or less, would cloak Stateline in darkness. He could slip out then and try to find the marshals. One or both, it didn't matter. Either one of them could help him, but the pair of them together offered more protection than a single gun.

He didn't fancy creeping through the streets and alleyways of Stateline like a thief or rodent, but he had no choice. He might be shot on sight by Grady Sullivan or any of his men, if Fawcett showed his face on Border Boulevard. Whether they'd turned up Jeb and Dooley yet or not, Sullivan and Rafferty must know he'd given them the slip. They wouldn't take it lightly, and he guessed that there would be no second try at taking him away without a fuss.

It all comes down to this, thought Fawcett, feeling as if his whole life had been a waste, in fact. He'd never married, had no one to mourn him when he croaked, and nothing much to leave them if they had existed, but a memory of what a spineless sheep he'd been. Going along to get along had always been his style, and look where it had gotten him.

For half a second, maybe less, Fawcett considered walking out on Border Boulevard where everyone could see him. Picking out a corner where he could regale them with his knowledge of Flynn Rafferty and all he'd done to make Stateline a place of dirty secrets. Not that anyone with half a brain would be surprised at anything he said. The so-called mayor and marshal were neck-deep in Rafferty's corruption, and the shopkeepers in town existed by the big man's sufferance.

The only thing a public rant would get him was a bullet in the gut. But if he went down fighting, could he salvage something of his reputation, poor as it might be? Could he at least die like a man?

No. Not tonight.

He'd take the Colt revolver with him when he went out, naturally, but with no view toward using it unless his adversaries cornered him. In which case, he would have to choose his targets wisely. Would he shoot them, or himself?

Rafferty had too many gunmen on his payroll for a single man, regardless of his skill, to stop them all. Fawcett's hope was that the U.S. marshals, once they heard his story, would see fit to spirit him away from Stateline, back to Enid or wherever they could hold him in protective custody. He didn't think there was a fee for testifying against criminals, but maybe he could beg a stipend from the court to help him relocate — to California, say, or maybe Oregon.

Maybe run all the way to Canada if he could hide there, safe at last.

A little longer. Just until the sun went down.

Fawcett compelled himself to eat the food remaining on his plate. He would need energy tonight and didn't want his stomach growling at him while he told his story to the lawmen.

If they'd listen, after he had lied to them before.

Would they?

He grimaced, told himself they *had* to listen.

Otherwise, he was as good as dead.

13

Slade and Naylor went back to the Border-line Café for supper, even though they'd eaten breakfast there. Pork chops, a baked potato, and some greens for Slade, while Naylor had beef stew with biscuits on the side. Slade felt the other diners shooting surreptitious glances toward their table, eyes quickly averted when he raised his own, and guessed that half the whispered conversations in the restaurant revolved around the bodies they'd delivered to the marshal's office earlier.

Why not? Two days, and they had ridden in with six dead men plus thirty crates of moonshine in a wagon from the Rocking R. It would've been surprising if the townsfolk *weren't* discussing what had happened, wondering what it could mean for Stateline and Flynn Rafferty.

"You think we've got him, then?" asked Naylor, seemingly attuned to Slade's own silent thoughts.

"We've got his whiskey, anyway," Slade answered. "We can link it to his ranch, which ought to justify a warrant. Come back with some extra hands and check the barn, *then* I would say we've got him."

"If he doesn't run by then. Or have his men break down the still and move it."

"It's a possibility," Slade granted. "Nothing we can do about it, though. If Rafferty takes off, we print the posters up and keep him running. Make him someone else's problem for a while."

"And what about Bill Tanner?" Naylor asked.

"When we come back, if we find any evidence of 'shining, we'll arrest whoever's still hanging around the Rocking R. My guess would be that some of them will talk to make it easy on themselves. Pile up the evidence on Rafferty, and when he's finally arrested, bring him back to hang."

"*If* he's arrested." Naylor sounded skeptical.

"What's the alternative? Take him to Enid now and risk having the case thrown out? That happens, we may never get another crack at him."

"I know, damn it. It frustrates me, is all."

"Get used to that," Slade said, "on this job."

"Do you trust that half-baked marshal with the 'shine?" asked Naylor, when he downed another mouthful of his stew.

"I think he's spooked right now, and leery of what might befall him if he messes up."

"You know he's talked to Rafferty by now, or someone working for him. Probably the mayor, as well."

"The whole town knows we brought the whiskey in," Slade said. "Nothing that we can do about it now, unless you want to sit up with it overnight."

"And leave tomorrow at the crack of dawn? No, thanks," Naylor replied.

"The crack it is, then," Slade agreed. "Let's finish up and hit the hay."

"Think I might have a drink first, if it's all the same to you."

"Feel free, as long as you don't spoil your beauty sleep."

"I'll be bright-eyed and bushy-tailed," said Naylor. Scraping up the last dregs of his stew, he left coins on the table for his tab and rose. "See you tomorrow, then."

"See you," Slade said and took his time clearing the plate in front of him.

Six forty by his watch, and he'd decided on another look around Stateline before he went to bed. Check on the whiskey wagon one more time, most definitely, just to re-assure himself that Marshal Hickey wasn't being lax, and then he'd head back to the Stateline Arms. He'd need his wits about him in the morning for the long ride back to Enid with their evidence, when anything might happen on the trail.

More bodies for the undertaker, if it came to that.

But whose?

Standing in the alley next to Benteen's Hardware, Percy Fawcett watched the marshals talking at their table in the Border-line Café. It hadn't been much trouble find-ing them at supper time, only three restau-rants in town, but creeping in the shadows had played havoc with his nerves. Now that he'd found the lawmen, Fawcett felt an urge to rush across the street and join them, make them take him into custody that very moment, but his fear of being spotted held him back.

Even remaining where he was put strain on Fawcett, knowing any passerby might turn in to the alley on a whim, taking a shortcut home from shopping, and discover him. He didn't fear the ordinary townsfolk, but if one of them remarked on seeing him, however casual the comment, it might reach the wrong ears and betray him. Grady Sullivan was likely hunting him by now, which meant the rest of Rafferty's hired hands would also be involved.

How many men? He wasn't sure and didn't care. A mental image of them scouring the countryside made Fawcett's knees go weak. He leaned against the wall immediately to his left, one hand inside his jacket, drawing strength from contact with the checkered grip of his revolver.

This time yesterday, he'd been a frightened rabbit, nearly certain that his life was over. He was still frightened today — more so, if anything — but having proved that he could kill in self-defense, the fear seemed slightly more remote, somehow. Or maybe he'd been scared for so long he was simply going numb.

Across the street, the younger of the marshals rose, put money on the table, then went out and left the other one to finish eating on his own. Fawcett edged closer to the street, a cautious step or two, and watched the lawman pass down Border Boulevard in the direction of the Sunflower Saloon. Going to visit Rafferty, or just to have a drink?

One thing was certain: trailing him to Rafferty's establishment was tantamount to suicide. It would be quicker and more merciful if Fawcett used his own Colt on himself. Cut out the middleman and spare himself from any inquisition Grady Sullivan might have in mind.

The other marshal sat and ate methodically, cleaning his plate, in no apparent rush. The café's waitress, Rosie Hammond, brought more coffee to his table and the lawman nodded thanks, then sipped it gingerly, testing its heat. What was his name? Naylor or Slade? Fawcett couldn't remember which was which, after they'd spooked him with their first appearance at his office. Now, he wished that he could shout across the street and rush the man along, but settled for a muted curse instead.

Two horsemen clip-clopped past the ally where he stood, and Fawcett edged back farther into darkness. Were they some of Rafferty's hired guns? He couldn't tell, had never met them all, but from their attitude it didn't seem that they were searching. Fawcett tracked them until they passed out of sight, relieved that neither one had glanced in his direction.

Now the second marshal rose, set money by his plate, made some remark to Rosie as he left and got a smile back for his effort. Fawcett saw him leave the restaurant, praying he wouldn't head for either one of the saloons, and almost whooped aloud when this one turned back toward the Stateline Arms. Another moment made it certain, as he saw the marshal reach the hotel's entry-way and step inside.

Feeling his pulse throb in his temples, Percy Fawcett started off on the roundabout path that would place him behind the hotel. If he could reach the back door without be-ing spotted, maybe he would make it through the night alive.

The Sunflower Saloon had thirty-five to forty drinkers getting down to business by the time Luke Naylor pushed his way in through the bat-wing doors. One of the working girls was singing, more or less, while the pianist played a song that had begun to make the rounds, "The Cat Came Back." She flashed a smile at Naylor when he passed and got a nod back in return, her off-key voice trailing him to the bar.

He found a space and got one boot up on the rail between a smelly teamster and a man dressed like a storekeeper. It struck him odd that neither one of them spared him a glance, but Naylor guessed they may have seen him coming in the back-bar mir-ror and decided it was unwise to acknowledge him. That or the whiskey they were slugging down demanded all of the attention they could muster.

Maybe moonshine?

When the barkeep made his way around, Naylor ordered a beer and got a mug brimming with foam. It wasn't ice-cold, but it wasn't watered, either, so he figured it would do. When he was halfway through the mug, Flynn Rafferty came by, working the room, and stopped to pass the time.

"Marshal, is everybody treating you all right?" he asked.

"I can't complain," Naylor replied.

"I understand you had a look around the countryside today," Rafferty said.

Wanting to spar a little, Naylor thought. And said, "A bit of it. I'm sure there's lots we didn't see."

"And any progress on your quest?"

Naylor allowed himself a shrug. "It's hard to say."

"Well, if there's anything that I can do to help . . ."

The Sunflower's proprietor was leaving as he spoke, his smile directed toward the players in a nearby poker game. Naylor was tempted to pursue and question him, but Slade was adamant about tipping their hand before they had a warrant from Judge

Dennison. Give Rafferty some time to sweat, see what his next move was, and go from there.

He took advantage of the back-bar mirror, tracking Rafferty across the room until he stopped by the piano, bent his head and told the singer something. Naylor saw her glance his way, over the boss's shoulder, nodding as she answered back. When the pianist started up another tune, she left him to it, winding through the tables toward the spot where Naylor stood before the bar.

A moment later, with a warm hand on his arm, he heard her say, "You're new in town."

He turned to face her. Answered, "That I am."

"I would've noticed you, if you'd been through before."

Her face beneath a spill of auburn hair wasn't as hard as some he'd seen working saloons. Naylor decided she was probably nineteen or twenty, put together well enough inside a purple satin dress, some kind of corset thing on top that emphasized her breasts, puffed sleeves, and a black velvet choker wrapped around her neck. The beauty mark on her left cheek was something she had pasted on.

"I came in yesterday," he said. "You weren't around."

"Day off," she told him. "But we're both here now."

"Looks like it," Naylor said. "Something to drink?"

"I don't mind if I do." She stepped in closer, nuzzling his right arm with a breast. "You want to take that drink upstairs?"

He felt a smile twitch at the corners of his mouth, knowing that she was bait, wondering how and when the trap would spring. Resolved to keep his twin Colts close at hand.

And said, "I might, at that."

Sullivan entered through the back door of the marshal's office; there was no one in the cells tonight for Arlo to concern himself about. The confiscated whiskey wagon sat out back, its crates of bottled moonshine covered with a tarp that Hickey must have found somewhere.

"I wasn't sure you'd make it," said the marshal, slouched behind his cluttered desk.

"Told you I'd be here, didn't I?"

"People tell me all kinds of things." Hickey stood up and moved around the desk toward Sullivan. "You know I can't be held responsible for this. I want to help and all, but if it comes to doin' time . . ."

"You can't be trusted not to squeal," said

Sullivan. "We all know that, Arlo."

"Hey, wait a second, now! I never said —"
He saw Sullivan draw his six-gun, blanching at the sight of it. "Now, Grady . . . just hold on there! You and Mr. Rafferty should know I'd never carry tales. For Christ's sake, I'm in this as much as any one of you!"

"That's right," said Sullivan. "You are. But we still want this lookin' realistic, don't we? For the other law dogs?"

"Well . . . I mean . . . What have you got in mind?"

"Brave man like you," Sullivan answered with a crooked smile, "wouldn't just let somebody walk in here and do away with evidence. You'd do your duty, eh? Put up a fight?"

"I'm not about to draw on you, Grady. You think I'm crazy?"

"Nope. Just yellow."

As he spoke, Sullivan closed the gap between them, swung his pistol in a flashing arc, and smashed it into Arlo's cheek. The marshal staggered backward, crying out, and fell against his desk, one arm outflung, his papers scattering. He spat blood, sobbing out, "Hold on, now!"

Sullivan lashed out again, a backhand this time, catching Hickey on the right side of his face and opening a gash beside his nose.

The marshal folded, slipping off the desk and dropping to all fours, blood dribbling from his face onto the floor.

"Them U.S. marshals see you," Sullivan advised, "they're gonna know you fought real hard to save that 'shine. Be proud of you, I bet."

His boot caught Hickey in the ribs with force enough to lift him off the floor and drop him on his side, groaning, knees rising to protect his groin and stomach. Something came out of the marshal's bloody mouth that sounded like a plea for mercy, falling on deaf ears.

"Don't want 'em claimin' you're a faker, do we, Arlo? Wouldn't set right."

Grady stepped around his fallen victim, raised one foot, and drove his boot heel down into the lawman's ribs. Hickey convulsed, squealing in pain, tears mingling with the blood that smeared his cheeks.

"Reckon that oughta do it," Sullivan announced. He looked around the small office and spotted two lamps burning, one on each side of the room. Stepping around the desk to reach the nearest of them, he asked, "You don't mind if I borrow this? Okay, I didn't think so."

Out the back door with the lamp in hand, feeling its heat, Sullivan stood beside the whiskey wagon's tailgate, checking both directions in the night. He saw no sign of anybody watching him.

"Seems like an awful waste," he muttered, then reared back and pitched the lamp into the wagon's bed, where it exploded into leaping flames.

The rapping on Slade's door was muffled, tentative, as if his caller might be having second thoughts — or didn't want to rouse the occupants of nearby rooms. Slade drew his Peacemaker and cocked it as he crossed the hotel room in stocking feet to reach the door. He stood aside from it with his left shoulder to the wall, his pistol raised.

"Who's that?" he asked.

A soft voice answered, "P-P-Percy Fawcett."

Lowering the Colt around waist level, Slade opened the door with his left hand, peered through the three-inch crack, and verified that Fawcett was alone. "What can I do for you?"

"We should talk," said the telegrapher. "I have some information that can help you."

Slade stepped back, opened the door for Fawcett, then spotted the bulge beneath his coat and jammed the muzzle of his Colt against his visitor's rib cage. "You won't be needing this," he said and pulled the short-barreled revolver out of Fawcett's belt.

"That's for my own p-p-protection," Fawcett said, but made no move to take the weapon back.

Slade shut and latched the door behind him, nodding Fawcett toward a nearby chair. "You'll get it back on your way out," he said.

"I c-c-can't go back out there," said the telegrapher. "They're after me!"

"Who is?"

"Rafferty's men. They've tried to k-k-kill me once, already."

"When was this?" Slade asked.

"Last night. G-G-Grady Sullivan pretended we were going somewhere s-s-safe, outside of town, but I could tell that he was l-l-lying. Jeb and Dooley . . . when they t-t-tried . . . I shot them."

"Here in town?"

The nervous caller shook his head. "A couple miles off toward the B-B-Blue Stem Hills."

"Why would they want to kill you?" Slade inquired.

"To s-s-shut me up," said Fawcett. "I . . . I lied to you about the other marshal's telegram."

"You let somebody see it."

"Sullivan."

"And what is he to Rafferty, exactly?"

"He does all the d-d-dirty work," Fawcett replied.

"And he's afraid you'll talk."

A jerky nod. Fawcett's hands lay twisting in his lap.

"Are you prepared to testify in court?" asked Slade.

"I'll d-d-do whatever's necessary," Fawcett said. "To stay alive."

"Showing the telegram's not criminal," Slade said, "but you can kiss your job good-bye."

"L-l-least of my worries, isn't it?"

"If you come with us back to Enid, you can tell your story to Judge Dennison. For full cooperation, I suspect he'll let you off the hook as an accessory."

"Accessory to w-w-what?"

"Conspiracy to kill a U.S. marshal," Slade replied. "You wouldn't hang for that, I guess. Ten years at Leavenworth is probably more like it."

"But I didn't *know*!"

"Just stick to that and tell the judge what happened, any thing this Grady told you at the time or afterward. My guess is that —"

Outside, from Border Boulevard, a man's voice shouted, "Fire!" Another picked it up, farther away, and by the time Slade reached his window, he saw half a dozen figures running past, in the direction of the marshal's office.

Where the yellow light of flames was visible behind the row of buildings, leaping high.

Slade took the hotel stairs three at a time, buckling his gunbelt as he went, out past the worried-looking clerk and onto Border Boulevard. Townsfolk were out in force now, answering the cry of "Fire" that ranked among a frontier town's worst nightmares. Slade could smell wood smoke and something else, sharp in his nostrils as he struck off toward the marshal's office.

Whiskey burning?

Damn it!

By the time he got to Hickey's office, two men were emerging with the marshal slung between them, arms across their shoulders, toes dragging across the sidewalk. Slade glimpsed Hickey's swollen, bloody face and ran on past him, down the nearest alley toward the heat and crackling sound of fire. Already there ahead of him were eight or nine townsmen with buckets, throwing water on the rear wall of the nearest building while the whiskey-wagon bonfire blazed away.

Priorities. Of course, they'd let the wagon burn and concentrate on saving Stateline from a fire that might take down the whole north side of Border Boulevard. Why not? Some of the first men on the scene had pulled the wagon slightly farther from the marshal's office, braving heat intense enough to blister skin while they were at it, but the load of moonshine wasn't going any farther.

Not unless you counted going up in smoke.

"What happened?" someone asked, behind him.

Turning, Slade saw Naylor standing with his gunbelt slung over one shoulder and his shirt unbuttoned, with its tails outside his pants. "I just got here," he said. "Looks like you found yourself a party."

Naylor let that pass. Replied, instead, "I saw the constable out front. Looks like somebody thumped him pretty good."

"We'll need to see if he can tell us who that was," Slade said.

"Need something, that's for sure," said Naylor. "We just lost our evidence."

"Some of it," Slade replied. "We've got another angle, though."

"Which is?"

"Somebody waiting back at the hotel you need to see."

"Oh yeah? You gonna tease me with it?"

"Fawcett. The telegrapher," Slade said.

"He came to you?"

"Claims someone tried to kill him, but he got the drop on them instead. Come on. Let's have a word with Hickey, then go back and you can hear his story for yourself."

One of the men who'd carried Arlo Hickey from his office still remained beside the marshal when they reached him, making sure he didn't topple over in the dirt. The other one had gone in search of Stateline's doctor, due back anytime. Hickey was barely conscious, drooling blood, and muttered incoherently when Slade asked who had beaten him.

"What say we try him in the morning," Naylor offered. "We can see about that other thing, meanwhile."

Slade rose from where he'd knelt beside the battered lawman, turned back toward the Stateline Arms, and froze at sight of Percy Fawcett leaning up against one of the wooden pillars out in front of the hotel.

"Damn it, I told him not to leave the room," Slade said.

"Too much excitement for him," Naylor

said, crossing the street with Slade. "He didn't want to miss the show."

Frowning, Slade asked, "He look all right to you?"

Now that he focused on it, the telegrapher was standing with one arm around the pillar, and his free hand raised to cup his chin. No, he was clutching at his throat, with crimson spilling through his fingers now.

"Jesus!"

Slade ran the final thirty yards or so but missed his chance at catching Fawcett when the man pitched forward, landing facedown in the street. They turned him over, saw the gaping slash across his throat, and knew that he was gone when one last bubble burst there, with a liquid wheezing sound.

"I'll go and fetch the undertaker," Naylor said. "He'll likely want to set us up a running tab."

14

Stiff from sleeping on the ground and bleary-eyed from rising with the sun, Captain Brody Gallagher reflected that his youth had passed him by and he was not the soldier that he used to be. No great surprise on either count, of course, but facing up to one's mortality was never pleasant, and the bitter aftertaste of breakfast — fatty bacon and some beans, washed down with lousy campfire coffee — only made it worse.

He was relieved, therefore, to see the smudge of Stateline when it finally showed up on the horizon, Sunday morning, gradually taking shape into the town that Gallagher remembered from his prior excursions there. Most of his business with the man in charge could not be safely carried out by telegraph, their thoughts and schemes reduced to writing anyone might see, and so he'd come to know the strange divided settlement quite well over the past twelve months or so.

Not *like* it, necessarily. Just *know* it.

Only one of his companions on this journey had been with him previously. Sergeant Bonner knew enough about Gallagher's business to be helpful — or, if viewed another way, to make him dangerous. The rest were just along to do some dirty work for money, having proved that they could keep their mouths shut about violations of the law. Later, when he'd retired, Gallagher thought they might continue in his service, do for him what Grady Sullivan and others did for Rafferty. Or, if their presence in his life proved troublesome, well, they could simply disappear.

That was the wonder of America. A vast land filled with promise and with scavengers.

Three hours after spotting Stateline, they were riding into town on Border Boulevard, dusty and weary from the trail but still in some kind of formation. Men and women on the sidewalks stopped to eye the bluecoats passing by, some of them doubtless recognizing Gallagher, although he'd never cared enough to memorize their names or faces. In his way of thinking, they were little more than peasants. Serfs to Rafferty in fact, whether they recognized that fact or not.

It would be bad form, making straight for Rafferty's saloon. Instead, Gallagher nosed his palomino stallion toward the marshal's office, followed by his troops. Before he could dismount, a lawman that he'd never seen before emerged onto the sidewalk, thumbs hooked underneath his gunbelt, studying the soldiers with a curious expression on his youthful face.

"I need to see the marshal," Gallagher informed him.

"He's to home, sir. Got hisself beat up last night," the young man said. Up close, his badge read DEPUTY. "I'm Jared Wilkes. Just fillin' in for him, till he's back on his feet an' all."

"I see. Was his assailant captured?"

"How's that?"

"Did you catch the man who did it?" Gallagher translated.

"Oh. No, sir. Arlo — that's Marshal Hickey — says he didn't get a look at 'em. Reckon they wanted him outta the way before they burnt the moonshine."

"So, you had a fire as well?" asked Gallagher. It was a labor not to glance at Stateline Storage, down the street.

"Well, just a wagon out in back." Wilkes

cocked a thumb in that direction. "Nothin' the bucket brigade couldn't handle."

"Thank the Lord for that."

"Amen, sir."

"Now, if you could tell me where to find the mayor . . ."

Wilkes peered along the street, eastward, and cracked a smile, pointing. "Right there he goes, into the Sunflower. Can't miss that bowler hat."

The Sunflower. *Two birds, one stone,* thought Rafferty, and he turned his stallion off toward the saloon.

Arlo Hickey's house was small and pink. Slade guessed it had been red at one time, but the elements had faded it and no one was concerned enough to freshen up its paint. A woman answered Naylor's knock and peered at them suspiciously through her screen door. Slade placed her age somewhere in the mid-forties, guessing from the furrows bracketing her mouth that she was used to frowning at the world.

"Good morning, ma'am," he said. "We're here to see the marshal."

"Marshal isn't well," she answered.

"No, ma'am. We're aware of that. There's just a couple questions that we need to ask, about last night."

"He isn't well," she said again, louder, as if suspecting Slade were deaf.

"I understand that, ma'am. But —"

"Missus," she corrected him. "It's *Missus* Hickey."

"Missus Hickey, we're investigating the attack against your husband. Now that he's had some time to rest —"

"He. Isn't. Well," she interrupted Slade.

"And every minute wasted now helps those responsible for hurting him escape their rightful punishment."

She spent another of those minutes glaring at the two of them, then grudgingly unlatched the screen door, giving it a shove in Slade's direction. "All right, then," she said. "If you can't leave an ailing man in peace, come in and ask your questions."

Arlo Hickey was reclining on a chintzy sofa in the small home's parlor, by a window with the curtains drawn against daylight. His face was swollen and discolored, with a line of sutures holding his left cheek together.

"Whadda you two want?" he asked, lips barely moving as he spoke.

"We didn't have a chance to talk last night," Slade said.

"Nothin' to say," Hickey replied.

"We're looking for the man or men who

did this to you and destroyed our evidence," Slade said.

"Worried about your 'shine? I hear it's gone."

"The whiskey *and* a criminal attack against the law," Slade said.

"Doc says I'll be awright, given some time."

"I'm glad to hear it. But the folks responsible —"

"Already got away with it," said Hickey.

"And you're satisfied with that?" asked Naylor.

"Satisfied? Do I look *satisfied* to you, sonny? What's done is done, that's all."

"And if they'd gone a little further? Made your wife a widow?" Slade asked.

"Well, they didn't. This time, anyway."

"But you're afraid they might, is that it? If you talk?"

"Listen, I didn't see who done it. Took the first hit from behind, then all the rest of it's just blurry. I can't help you none."

"You sure that's how you want to play it?" Naylor asked.

"You may've missed it, boy," Hickey replied, "but this ain't playin'. This shit's life and death."

Naylor seemed on the verge of making some reply when Slade cut in, saying, "We'll let you rest, then. If you change your mind and want to talk . . ."

"Can't change what happened," Hickey said. "Ain't gonna say I seen things that I didn't."

Hickey's wife said nothing as she showed them out, just latched the screen behind them, using extra force to shut the inner door. Slade scanned the part of Border Boulevard that he could see from where they stood and wondered whether anyone was watching them.

"He knows whoever worked him over," Naylor said.

"Bet on it," Slade replied. "They've got him scared."

"And got us stymied, eh? We're right back where we started."

"If we let it go at that."

"And what's the other choice?" Naylor inquired.

"I'm giving that some thought," Slade said.

Captain Gallagher entered the Sunflower Saloon with his soldiers trailing behind him. Sergeant Bonner led the others toward the bar while Gallagher proceeded toward the office where he knew he'd find Flynn Rafferty with Stateline's mayor. Arriving at the door marked PRIVATE, he knocked sharply, waited for the summons, then went in.

"Ah, Captain!" Rafferty was on his feet and circling around the desk to greet him, while the mayor — *what was his name, again?* — stayed seated, derby planted on his lap, and peered at Gallagher with anxious eyes.

Gallagher shook Rafferty's hand and nodded to the mayor, whose name came back to him just in the nick of time. "Mayor Jain," he said. "A fellow at the marshal's office told me that I'd find you here."

"Well . . ."

"As I understand it, you've endured some difficulty."

"You could say that," Jain replied.

"He's still a little shaken by it all," said Rafferty. "Captain, please have a seat — and can I tempt you with a whiskey?"

"I could use one," Gallagher agreed.

Rafferty poured a double Scotch from one of several bottles standing on a sideboard, handed it to Gallagher, then went back to his place behind the spacious desk. Gallagher noted that Mayor Jain had not received a glass.

"I'm not sure what you've heard," said Rafferty, "but we're relieved to have you here. Lord knows we need the help, with this attack on Marshal Hickey and the fire last night. Add in the death of that poor deputy from Enid who was here last week, and we've been sorely tested. Would you say so, Warren?"

"Sorely," Jain conceded. "Tested."

Gallagher nodded, wearing an expression that he hoped was sympathetic. "I'm available to offer you whatever aid may be appropriate," he said. "While recognizing the authority of your civilian government, of course."

"I have some thoughts on that, myself," said Rafferty. "Mayor Jain was just expressing his desire to check on Marshal Hickey, weren't you, Warren?"

Jain blinked at the question, caught off guard, then nodded. "Right. Somebody ought to do that."

"We won't keep you, then," said Rafferty.

The mayor put on his derby, rose and started for the door, then doubled back to pump Gallagher's hand before departing. "Captain, thanks for everything," he said, eyes dodging Gallagher's, and took his leave.

"You've got a sharp one there," said Gallagher, when they were finally alone.

"He has his uses," Rafferty replied. "You obviously got my wire."

Gallagher sipped his whiskey. Nodded.

"Unexpected visitors, you said."

"Two marshals, this time," Rafferty explained.

"You had to know they'd be around, after the last one."

"Truth be told," said Rafferty, "I hoped they'd blame it on the redskins. Grady seemed to have it pretty well thought out."

"It still might fly," said Gallagher.

Rafferty shook his head, frowning. "Too late for that. They know about the whiskey."

"Oh?"

"Sullivan saw them snooping at the warehouse, night before last. They've connected me to that and stopped one of my wagons headed south, just yesterday. I couldn't wait for you to get here, or they would've had it halfway back to Enid now. That load's gone up in smoke now, but they won't quit trying."

"I suppose they've tipped Judge Dennison," said Gallagher.

"No, we had some luck there," Rafferty replied, "but it was close. They spoke to our telegrapher first thing, about the last deputy's wire. He put them off at first, then Grady tried to deal with him before he changed his mind. That went awry, it seems, and he came back to tip them off."

"You call that luck?"

"The lucky part was that he only came around last night," said Rafferty. "He met one of the marshals, but we had the fire and all. Grady was able to slip in and take him down in the confusion."

"Jesus, Flynn! If he already spilled it —"

"It's been handled," Flynn assured him. "I need you to get these two out of my hair before they dig up something else to hang us with."

Gallagher drained his whiskey glass. "I'll see what I can do. What's going on with Berringer?"

"No problem there," said Rafferty. "Another incident or two and he's convinced that he can get approval for a clearance of the reservation's eastern half. We'll have first bid, at bargain rates."

"Well, then," Gallagher said, "I guess there's nothing left for me to do but make your marshals disappear."

Grady Sullivan was waiting when the captain left Rafferty's office. Sitting at a table by himself, he waited for the bluecoats to clear out before he rose and made his way back to the big man's lair and knocked.

"Enter!"

Sullivan closed the door securely before speaking. "Did you get it sorted out?"

"Gallagher's motivated," Rafferty replied. "He has my every confidence."

"Still say I coulda handled it myself."

"No pouting, Grady. You've done everything I asked of you and cleaned up that mistake with Fawcett, too."

"Not *my* mistake," said Sullivan.

"Let's not split hairs. You chose the men to deal with him. They failed. I'm not assigning blame for that. Who would've thought that milksop could've got the drop on Jeb and Dooley, anyhow?"

"Still haven't found 'em," Sullivan replied.

"Forget those idjits. If they aren't dead, after letting Fawcett slip, they should be smart enough to keep on running. Focus on what matters now."

"You think the army needs my help?"

"I think we need better security around the Rocking R," said Rafferty. "It's plain to me these marshals must've paid a visit to the spread with no one noticing. I can't believe they happened on our shipment just by serendipity. Can you?"

The hell is serendipity? thought Sullivan. "I reckon not."

"Well, then. Rather than pull up stakes and find a new home for the still, we need to make sure that our people keep their damned eyes open, eh? No more careless mistakes. I don't intend to kick wind just because some lazy bastard's sleeping on the job. Do you?"

"No, sir." Sullivan didn't fancy hanging, no matter whose fault it was.

"Then we're agreed. We need guards posted day and night, watching the road and property. No more intruders slipping through."

"I hear you, Boss."

"Perfect. I'll leave you to it, then, while Captain Gallagher deals with our other problem."

"And what happens if he can't?"

"Why, then, you'll get your chance. And if it serves our purpose, you can deal with him, as well."

Sullivan nearly smiled at that but didn't want to press his luck. Instead, he left the big man's office and the Sunflower Saloon, bound for the Rocking R. To kick some ass and make damn sure things didn't fall apart.

Or if they *did,* make sure he'd have ample time to get the hell away.

The burned-out whiskey wagon was a mess, its form unrecognizable beyond the rims of its four wheels, their axles, and its metal tongue protruding from a heap of ashes. Mixed up in the ash, Slade spotted small nails from the former crates and shards of blackened glass from bottles that had burst with the ignition of their volatile contents. Whatever might have passed for evidence was well and truly gone.

Like Percy Fawcett, lying over at the undertaker's parlor with his throat stitched back together for his funeral. Who would attend the send-off? Stopping by that morning, after breakfast at the Grub Stake, Slade was told that no one had come forward, yet, to claim the body or arrange for any kind of service. Fawcett's religious leanings, if he'd had any, meant nothing with no minister or church in town, but one more unclaimed body meant another grave in potter's field.

And once again, no evidence for Slade to use against Flynn Rafferty.

So far, he had his word and Naylor's that they'd seen the whiskey wagon leave the Rocking R — an observation rendered inadmissible since they'd been trespassing without a warrant. Same thing with the whiskey stashed at Stateline Storage. As for Fawcett's claim that he had shown Bill Tanner's telegram to Rafferty's head shooter, only Slade's word would support it now. The latest victim hadn't lasted long enough to share the tale with Naylor.

Leaving them with nada. Nothing.

Slade was on his way to rendezvous with Naylor at the dry goods store and make their way around the local shops with questions about Rafferty, for what it might be worth, when someone called out "Marshal!" from behind him. He turned back to find a captain of the cavalry approaching, four more soldiers grouped a half-block farther east, just idling.

"So, the army's in," Slade said.

"A few of us. I'm Captain Gallagher."

Slade shook the officer's extended hand. "Jack Slade. What brings you up to Stateline?"

"We got word one of your colleagues may have run afoul of hostiles," Gallagher replied.

"Who told you that?"

"It was reported back to Fort Supply. His injuries —"

"We now believe were meant to look like Indians had killed him," Slade cut in. "And who'd you say reported it, again?"

The captain frowned. "I can't be sure," he said. "Maybe the reservation agent? I get orders and I go where I've been told to go. You say the injuries were *faked*?"

"Oh, they were real enough to kill him," Slade confirmed. "We just don't think that it was done by Indians."

"I see." The captain's frown gave him an almost mournful look. "You won't mind if I still pursue the other angle, just in case you're wrong?"

"Feel free. You won't be in our way."

"You have another marshal with you, I believe."

"Around here somewhere," Slade agreed.

"Perhaps I'll meet him later on?"

"I wouldn't be surprised."

"We'll leave you to it, then."

Slade watched the officer rejoin his men, a couple of the others sliding glances toward him while their leader spoke. The huddle hadn't broken up when Slade moved on, crossing the street and angling toward the dry goods store, with Naylor waiting for him on the sidewalk.

"Reinforcements?" Luke inquired, as Slade approached.

"They reckon Indians killed Tanner," Slade replied.

"Who sent 'em?"

"Funny you should ask. The captain didn't seem too sure of that, himself."

"Trouble?"

"I wouldn't like to think so," Slade replied. "But keep your eyes peeled, anyway."

Their canvass of the town's shopkeepers

267

yielded nothing. Everyone in Stateline knew Flynn Rafferty, of course, though some only admitted knowing him by sight and seemed evasive while confessing that. Others were quick to sing his praises, but their comments struck Slade as repetitive, almost rehearsed, as if they'd been presented with a script to follow if and when a stranger raised Rafferty's name in conversation. Wariness appeared to be the rule of thumb, with two of those they spoke to — O'Malley, the barber, and a lawyer named Coltrane — going overboard in listing the saloon proprietor's outstanding qualities.

"Salt of the earth," said Naylor, as they left the lawyer's office. "Did he really say that?"

"Nothing wrong with your ears," Slade confirmed.

"You get the feeling certain folks in town are scared of Rafferty?"

"I'd say they should be, after last night's work."

"And we can't touch him," Naylor said.

"Not legally. Not yet."

"Sounds like you've got something in mind, Jack."

"We know where he cooks his 'shine, right?" Slade pressed on, not waiting for an answer. "And we know he'll have another

268

shipment moving out, sooner or later."

"Sounds like we'll be camping out."

"Unless you've got another thought on how to pin him down."

"Can't say I do," Naylor admitted. "But you have to figure they'll be watching for us."

"Doesn't mean they'll see us," Slade replied.

"It's chancy."

"Granted."

"Say we grab another wagon. What's the plan to keep from losing it?"

"First thing, we try to keep the crew alive. Then head straight back to Enid, without stopping off in Stateline."

"With the whole bunch after us."

"Could be. Or we give up for now, go back, and tell Judge Dennison what's happened. See what he thinks should be done to put it right."

"I'd hate to stand before him empty-handed," Naylor said.

"Well, then."

"We'll need food to tide us over. Something we don't have to cook, so there's no fire."

"Three restaurants in town," Slade said. "They must have something we can carry out."

"And we could use a couple more canteens," said Naylor.

"Saw some at the hardware store," Slade said.

"You want to tip the soldiers where we're going?"

"Rather not," said Slade.

"So it's like that?"

"Let's say I'd like to play it safe."

"One way to check on them would be to telegraph the fort," Naylor suggested.

"Right. Except the town's telegrapher is laid out waiting for his funeral."

"Somebody else in town might have the knack."

"One of the people we've been talking to?"

"Guess not. I thought about learning the Morse code once," said Naylor. "Never got around to it."

"I'd say it's too late now."

"You think the judge will reimburse us for the new canteens?"

"Can't hurt to ask. You want to get them?"

"Might as well," said Naylor.

"Fine. I'll get the food."

"No hardtack, though. It hurts my teeth."

They separated, moving off in opposite directions on their errands. Slade felt energized once more, after a night of pondering a new approach to Rafferty's arrest.

The course they'd mapped was hazardous, but nothing else had yet occurred to him.

Nothing to do but play it out, he thought. *And hope to still be breathing when tomorrow comes.*

15

Captain Gallagher stood on the shaded sidewalk with his men, watching the marshals take their leave of Stateline. He already had a fair idea where they were going, back out to the Rocking R, and there was nothing he could do about it.

Nothing *legal,* anyhow.

That hadn't been the plan, of course, when Rafferty had called him from his post at Fort Supply. Legality had never been an issue. Gallagher was needed to resolve a problem quickly, for the big man's benefit and for his own.

It rankled, summoned and commanded by a mere civilian, but he'd cast his lot with Rafferty, for better or for worse. Retirement on a soldier's pension didn't suit him when there was a fortune to be made and shared among a few bold men of vision. Rafferty had hatched the plan with Berringer, the agent reaching out to Gallagher because, it seemed, he was a savvy judge of character. Together, with a friend or two in Washington, their dream would soon be realized.

Some redskins would be pushed aside, of course. So what? They should be used to it by now. Four hundred years since they had first been rousted by the Spanish, nearly three since English colonists had staked their claim back East, and every day since then the native tribes had been propelled steadily westward. If they weren't accustomed to it yet, to hell with them.

"We gonna trail 'em, Captain?" Sergeant Bonner asked him.

"That's the plan. Give them a lead, so they don't feel us breathing down their necks, then catch up with them on the way."

"You think they's any good?" asked Private French, of no one in particular.

"They're U.S. marshals," Private Sowder answered.

"Don't prove nothin'," Private Wetzel offered, "till you've seen 'em shoot."

"Won't need to see it, if we do this right," said Bonner.

"You have a plan, Sergeant?" asked Gallagher.

"Two ways to do it, sir. Come up behind 'em, actin' friendly-like, then all cut loose," Bonner explained. "Or ride around and get in front of 'em. Set up an ambush."

"Flat country," Gallagher reminded him. "To get ahead, we'd have to circle wide out of our way, and still we might not find a decent place to wait. Might even lose them if they try a shortcut."

"Only leaves one way to go, then," Bonner said.

"Agreed."

The two lawmen had passed from sight now, turning north once they were clear of Border Boulevard. They'd still be visible to someone watching from the eastern edge of town, though. The captain was in no great hurry as he led his soldiers toward the livery.

From this day forward, Gallagher was bound to Bonner and the others by the crime they were about to carry out. He didn't like it — hadn't planned on taking anybody with him when he left the army to retire in luxury — but there were ways around that, too.

No end of ways to cut the ties that bind.

"You think they'll ship another batch of 'shine right off?" asked Naylor when they were a mile or so from town.

"Can't guarantee it," Slade replied, "but Rafferty most likely has a list of buyers waiting for the shipment that we intercepted.

He's a businessman, which means he won't like disappointing customers."

"Makes sense. But if he knows we're watching him, he might try sending it around some other way."

Slade had considered that. The land around the Rocking R was flat enough to let a wagon pass, once it had cleared the sea of corn, but travel overland would still present its share of difficulties and require more time than traveling along established roads. Unless a route was charted in advance, a shipment might be stopped by obstacles that forced the driver to retreat and start afresh, uncertain when or how he'd make it through at last.

Bad business, all around.

"Let's give the road another chance," Slade said. "I can't help thinking time is on our side."

"See if you feel that way after a couple nights of sleepin' on the ground."

"Won't be the first time," Slade replied.

And suddenly, for no good reason he could name, his thoughts went back to Faith. Slade wondered how her plans for moving had progressed, if she would find a buyer for her ranch before she left. They hadn't spoken since the afternoon she'd told him she was leaving Enid, but the town was small enough that Slade knew he'd have heard about a pending sale. With people being what they were, the gossip would've reached him soon enough.

He didn't think she'd wait, though. Having made her choice, he couldn't picture Faith postponing her departure any longer than was absolutely necessary. Not unless . . .

He'd seen her at the doctor's office. Not a social call, Slade figured. Was she suffering some kind of relapse from the injuries inflicted on what should have been their wedding day? Faith hadn't looked sick, standing with Doc Abernathy on the street, but who was Slade to say? He didn't have a medical degree, couldn't pretend to diagnose an illness passing on the street.

If he could just —

"Marshals!"

A voice behind them, small with distance. Slade and Naylor turned as one, to see the bluecoats trailing them.

"What'n hell do they want?" Naylor asked.

"One way to find out," Slade replied, reining his mare back to a halt.

"Strike you as odd, them coming after us?"

"It doesn't fit with what their captain told me," Slade replied. "About them hunting

Indians."

"No reservation hereabouts," said Naylor.

"No."

Slade freed the hammer thong that kept his Peacemaker secure inside its holster, seeing Naylor do the same, times two. He thought about the shotgun in its saddle scabbard but decided drawing it right now would be a bit too much.

The captain — Gallagher — was smiling as he led his little troop toward Slade and Naylor at a walk. The sergeant wore a poker face, the others looking vaguely sullen and disgruntled. As they closed the distance down to thirty feet or so, Gallagher said, "I'm glad we caught you."

"Didn't know that you were chasing us," the younger of the marshals said.

He had a wary look, it seemed to Virgil Bonner, sitting with his right hand near a holstered Colt, his left hand filled with reins. Both men were on guard, but still outnumbered more than two to one.

"Not chasing," Captain Gallagher replied, "but when I saw you leaving town I had a thought."

"Which was?" the older marshal asked.

"I wondered if you might be onto something after all," said Gallagher. "About the renegades."

Bonner wished they could just be done with it. He felt the others getting twitchy, wasn't sure that he could count on them to keep their pistols holstered if the captain dragged the conversation out too long. They'd ridden out of town to do a job, and stalling only raised the tension level. Sowder, French, and Wetzel weren't the most reliable of men under the best conditions. Twiddling their thumbs when they expected action only made them more unstable.

"Thing is," the younger lawman said, "we're workin' on a lead here. It's a two-man job."

"More hands make lighter work," said Gallagher.

"In this case," said the older of the pair, "five extra men in uniform make it impossible."

That stalled the captain for a second, working on the next thing he should say, still not giving the signal to get on with business. Why in hell was he still talking, anyway?

No guts, thought Bonner, as his right hand came to rest atop his thigh, edging a little closer to his holster. Army fashion dictated a holster on the right hip, with the pistol placed butt-forward for a kind of backward draw. The style had started with some fuddy-duddy who believed a mounted soldier's foremost weapon was his saber, wielded in the right hand, while a pistol — being secondary — could be drawn if absolutely necessary with the left hand. As it happened, though, the holster's placement proved ideal for right-handed drawing when a man was sitting down, if he had practiced and was smart enough to leave his holster flap unbuttoned.

Sergeant Bonner *was* a practiced shooter with his Colt Single-Action Army, and his holster flap *was* open. All he needed was the signal from his captain, or a false move from the lawmen they had ridden out from town to murder.

Any second now . . .

But Gallagher kept droning on. "I'm sorry, gentlemen," he said. "We didn't mean to inconvenience you, of course. But since we're here —"

Bonner glimpsed sudden movement on his left, French going for his pistol, sick of waiting, and there wasn't any way to stop him. As the younger lawman shifted toward him, right hand dropping toward his own Colt, Bonner gave it up and made his move.

The crack of gunfire stung Slade's ears, then he was adding to it with his own Peacemaker, drawing as the first two shots ripped out, Naylor and one of the blue-coated privates firing almost simultaneously. Slade had seen it coming, Naylor just a hair-breadth faster in responding, and the soldier toppling over from his saddle with a kind of gasping, snarling sound that may have come from his constricted throat or from a bullet-punctured lung.

A couple of the army horses reared, and Slade's mare shied a little as he got a shot off toward the scruffy-looking sergeant who was next in line. It was a hasty shot. Slade winged him, saw a puff of scarlet mist above one shoulder, but it didn't slow the sergeant's aim enough to matter. He returned Slade's fire, a slug from the long-barreled Colt Army fanning the air beside Slade's cheek, and then all hell broke loose.

There was no time to think, with six guns blasting back and forth from thirty feet or so, a couple of the horses making sounds like women screaming. A part of Slade's mind was surprised, expecting army horses to be better trained for battle, but another part was grateful that it spoiled his adversaries' aim.

Slade's mare was cutting didoes of her own, a kind of hopping, prancing circle to the left that saved the wounded sergeant from his second shot. Slade's bullet flew somewhere between the sergeant and a red-faced private to his right, whose Colt was blazing off a round toward Naylor. Naylor cursed, returned fire, as the roan's quick circling motion brought Slade back around to face the firing line.

Enough!

Slade knew he would be quicker, maybe safer, on his own two feet. With that in mind, he kicked free of his stirrups, vaulted from the saddle, snatching at his lever-action shotgun in its scabbard as he dropped. Got off another wild shot from his Colt as he touched down and rolled, guessing the round was wasted since none of the men intent on killing him went down.

The shotgun's eight-pound weight was reassuring in Slade's hands. A second after he'd returned his six-gun to its holster, he squeezed off a blast in the direction of the sergeant he had winged, absorbed the recoil with his hip, and saw the storm of buckshot strike his target's chest. No flesh wound this time, as the heavy buckshot pellets shattered ribs and breastbone, punching Slade's target backward from his saddle, airborne and ass over teakettle.

The shotgun blast provoked more squealing from a couple of the army horses, two already breaking formation, riderless. That left three mounted bluecoats firing, Naylor still astride his gelding too but saddle-slumped as if to make himself a smaller target for the enemy. Slade saw his partner fire a shot across the Appaloosa's arching neck and heard one of the soldiers gasp a curse as he was hit, then Slade himself was dodging as the captain brought him under fire.

Gallagher saw the grounded marshal — Slade, his name was — swing the lever-action shotgun back around in his direction, lining up a shot. The captain fired instinctively, guessing the round was wasted, hoping it would make the lawman duck and miss, at least. Even while firing, Gallagher was hauling on his palomino's reins, swinging the stallion hard around and out of line, prepared to run. A shotgun blast behind him gave the horse momentum and it bolted, rump-stung by a buckshot pellet, charging off to southward.

Running for its life, and Gallagher along with it, praying that he could hang on for the ride.

And what in hell was he supposed to do *but* run, for Christ's sake? French and Bonner down already, dead or dying, and he'd never been a brave man, really. West Point had prepared him for command, but all the action Gallagher had ever seen was routing Indians from villages when they'd been ordered to move out, not even skirmishes in the accepted sense, although he'd killed a brave or two along the way, proving he had the stomach for it. And if they had been unarmed, what of it? Most of those the army killed were women, children, or the elderly. There hadn't been a battle worthy of the name since Gallagher was sent to Fort Supply.

But he was in one now — or running from it — and as he put space between himself and the ongoing gunfire, Gallagher began to think about how he'd explain it all to Colonel Pike. Much would depend upon the outcome, granted, and it suddenly occurred to Gallagher that bolting was a bad idea. By giving in to panic and escaping from the action, he'd created further problems for himself.

For one, he wouldn't know the outcome of the fight until survivors straggled back to Stateline. If the lawmen made it back, he'd have no recourse but to run and keep on running, looking for a hideout where the army and the U.S. Marshals Service couldn't find him. If a remnant of his troop returned, Gallagher would be faced with trouble of another sort.

They would be furious at him for running off, of course, but he could work that out. Bribe them to keep their mouths shut and concoct a story about hostiles who had jumped them on the trail, eliminating Bonner, French, and anybody else the marshals killed. He would go back with the survivors, make damned sure the lawmen's corpses disappeared, use whatever remained of his authority and Rafferty's cold cash to keep the men in line.

Or better yet, borrow a few of Rafferty's hard cases from the Rocking R to finish off his squad. Let death ensure their silence while he staged the scene and spun a fable of miraculous escape from overwhelming odds. He even had the rump graze on his mount to make the story credible, and once the two lawmen had disappeared without a trace, who'd doubt that they had fallen prey to the same renegades?

With any luck at all, he just might pull it off.

Slade saw the captain bolt and chased him with a twelve-gauge blast, then had to focus on the bluecoats who had stayed behind to fight it out. One spurred his mount toward

Naylor, trading close-range shots and doubling over as a bullet drilled his abdomen. Slade swung around to face the other, found the soldier bearing down on him, and squeezed off from the hip without a chance to aim.

It didn't matter with the target looming over him, a stocky soldier leaning right across his saddle for a better shot at Slade. The buckshot barely had a chance to spread before it turned the shooter's face and brains across his horse's croup. The chestnut gelding bucked and sent its nearly headless rider flopping from his saddle to the ground, landing with all the grace of dirty laundry in a canvas bag.

Which still left one.

Slade pumped the shotgun's lever action, spinning back toward Naylor and his gut-shot adversary, just in time to see a bullet strike the younger marshal's chest. Naylor lurched sideways, spilling toward the earth, while Slade lined up the wounded private in his sights and blasted him from life into oblivion.

Four down, and as he ran toward Naylor, Slade had no view left of the retreating officer in charge. Dismissing Gallagher from conscious thought, a job to handle later when he had the time, Slade knelt at Naylor's side and found the younger marshal laboring to breathe. A punctured lung and sucking chest wound made it doubly difficult, painting the lower half of Naylor's face with blood. A darker stain, spreading across Luke's shirt, told Slade one of the slugs had pierced his liver.

"Guess you'll . . . have to . . . finish . . . this job . . . on your own," said Naylor, laboring to force the words out of his throat.

"Hang on," Slade said. "I'll get you back to town. The doctor —"

Even as he spoke, Naylor convulsed and coughed a small geyser of blood. As he slumped back to earth, his eyes were dim, unfocused, staring off somewhere beyond the morning's scattered clouds.

Slade still went through the motions, feeling for a pulse he knew he wouldn't find, then rose and looked around the battleground. Aside from Luke, four bodies lay in twisted attitudes of death, their faces slack, blood soaking through the tunics of their uniforms. Their horses hadn't run far, once the shooting stopped, but Slade was damned if he would spend the whole day hauling corpses onto saddles single-handed.

One was quite enough.

The horses he could handle, though, once he had Naylor draped across his patient Appaloosa, standing still as if it understood the situation, maybe even felt a certain sense of loss. The other animals responded to his call, offered him no resistance as he linked their reins, forming a small remuda that would trail him back to town.

Another customer for Stateline's undertaker, and if anybody wanted to retrieve the fallen soldiers, they were free to do so. Bill the army for their burial, or plant them with the other stiffs in potter's field, Slade didn't give a damn.

He had a date with Brody Gallagher, no matter where the captain tried to hide.

"And your bright idea was running straight back here?" asked Rafferty, sounding bemused.

"Where else?" Gallagher's face was mottled, sickly looking. Shallow breathing made it sound as if he'd done the running back to Stateline, rather than his winded, wounded horse.

"Try *anyplace*," Rafferty answered. "Christ, man! Did you have to lead them back to me?"

"You don't know that I've led them anywhere," said Gallagher. "Or that there's anyone to lead."

"That's right. I don't know, since you ran

and left your men to do the dirty work. But if you thought that they were *winning,* you'd have stuck with them to finish it."

Gallagher drained the glass of whiskey that he'd poured himself while giving Rafferty a sketchy version of the fight. When Gallagher could speak again, he said, "You weren't there, Flynn. You didn't see. I panicked, damn it! I'll admit that."

"It's a harder job than shooting squaws and their papooses, I suppose," Rafferty sneered.

"You go to Hell! Suppose I hadn't come back. You'd be sitting here and thinking everything was rosy till the marshals walked in and arrested you."

"Or," Rafferty replied, "you might've done the job you were assigned by staying with your men. An extra gun to make the difference. Who knows?"

"I think you'd rather I was dead!" said Gallagher.

"Than bawling in my office? Why not? Either way, you're useless to me now."

"Goddamn you!"

"Think about it, *Captain,*" Rafferty bored in. "You can't go back to Fort Supply without your men, now, can you? Who'd believe that redskins killed the rest and let you go? Worse yet, if either one of those damned marshals is alive, you'll be a hunted man. And anyone associated with you will be hunted, too."

"You're all heart, Rafferty." The captain's dour expression would have fit a sulky child.

"I hope you didn't walk in here expecting sympathy," said the saloon proprietor. "Your only hope is that your men got lucky with the marshals. Better yet, if *all* of them are dead."

"You mean — ?"

"The only thing you've said this morning that makes sense. If everybody's dead, we make the lawmen disappear and claim that renegades wiped out your squad. It would be better if you had an honorable wound to sell the story. Maybe if a bullet creased your head and knocked you out. They might've figured you were done for."

Gallagher was frowning now, shaking his head.

"Your other choice is lighting out and see how far you get. Between the army and the marshals, I don't like your chances much."

"Head wound," said Gallagher. "Can't say I like the sound of that."

"Your other choice, the way it looks to me, would be head in a noose. And I don't plan to stand beside you on the scaffold."

"I have to go back, then."

"But not alone," said Rafferty. "It wouldn't do for you to soil your drawers. I'll talk to Sullivan."

"I wish I'd never gotten into this," said Gallagher.

"Next time around, think twice," said Rafferty. "Right now, shut up and let me try to save your ass."

16

Stateline's undertaker was a chubby, round-faced man named Abberline, who combed his thinning sandy hair across a bald spot on his crown. He seemed to be a relatively jolly sort, for one in his profession, but his face fell when he saw Luke Naylor draped across the saddle of his Appaloosa, spectators already gathering from shops along the street.

"Oh, my," he said. "This is . . . this is . . ." He gave it up and settled for the old standby. "Marshal, I'm sorry for your loss."

"He's not alone," Slade said and nodded toward the horses he'd led into town behind the Appaloosa. "Four more waiting for you on the north road, three miles out of town. I didn't feel like packing them."

"Those look like army saddles," Abberline observed, sounding concerned.

Ignoring that, Slade walked around toward Naylor's head and said, "You want to help me carry him inside?"

The undertaker would have liked to wait, Slade guessed, and have his flunkies do the job, but Slade was tired of people gawking at the body, muttering among themselves. Together, he and Abberline hauled Luke down from his blood-smeared saddle, got him slung between them, Slade taking the head end, and hauled him down an alley to a side door of the undertaker's parlor. Once inside, they got him situated on a table in the middle of the room and Abberline stepped back to catch his breath.

"I'll handle everything from here," the undertaker said, when he could speak again, dabbing his sweaty forehead with a handkerchief. "And bill the court in Enid, shall I?"

Slade peered at him, asking, "What's your normal practice?"

"With a law enforcement officer," said Abberline, "it's common for the service or department that employed him to assume responsibility. Of course, if family prefer to make some alternate arrangement, we accommodate their needs, as well."

"I don't know if there's any family," Slade said. "We never talked about it."

"In that case, I'll wire Judge Dennison with an inquiry."

"And you'd do that how, again?" asked Slade.

"I beg your pardon?"

"With your town's telegrapher already here, I mean."

"Ah, yes. I see your point. Well . . . I suppose Mayor Jain might know of someone else who's qualified. Or Marshal Hickey, if he's up to talking yet."

Slade frowned and said, "So there's been no communication in or out of Stateline by the telegraph since . . . when? Sometime on Friday afternoon, when Fawcett first dropped out of sight?"

The undertaker pondered that and finally replied, "You know, I couldn't say. It's been a few weeks since I had to send a wire, myself."

"But if a telegram was sent to Fort Supply on Friday evening, say . . . who would've handled that?"

Abberline shrugged. "If Mr. Fawcett didn't send it, I have no idea."

Something to think about. Rafferty must have known he could reach out for help, even if Fawcett was removed from circulation. What did it take, besides a knowledge of Morse code? Minimal training on the telegraph itself, learning to tap the key. It wouldn't take a genius. Slade supposed that anyone of average intelligence could master it with practice.

Wishing that he knew the code himself, he turned to leave. Pausing at the exit, he told Abberline, "If you have any trouble reaching Enid, let me know. I'll see what I can do."

"Of course, Marshal."

"And have your helpers standing by," Slade said. "You've got more business coming pretty soon."

Rafferty knew that Stateline's mayor was agitated from the way he held his bowler hat in front of him, shield-like, kneading its brim with nervous hands so that the hat rotated counterclockwise in his grip.

"What has you troubled, Warren?" he inquired.

"Those marshals," said the mayor.

"In what respect?"

"You haven't heard? Well, let me tell you. One just brought the other in to Abberline's, stone dead. And he was leading army horses. Four of them. No riders."

So, thought Rafferty, *I guess we won't be blaming this on redskins, after all.*

"They've just arrived?" he asked.

"Five minutes, give or take," said Jain. "I should go speak to him, but what on earth am I supposed to say?"

"Good question," Rafferty acknowledged. "When you go — and I agree you should — be sure and take Arlo's replacement with you. What's his name?"

"Wilkes. Jared Wilkes."

"All right. Take Marshal Wilkes along with you to see — which one is it who's still alive?"

"The older one. Jack Slade."

"Stress your concern for law and order here in Stateline. Ask about the soldiers. Find out anything you can."

"One thing I know already," Jain replied. "Five bluecoats came to town this morning, now there's four who won't be going home. What happened to the fifth?"

"You're asking me?" Rafferty frowned.

"It was rhetorical."

"Best save your rhetoric for the election stump there, Warren. What we need right now is solid information. First, what happened. Second, what the marshal who's still breathing plans to do about it."

"Not much that he can do, is there, but send out for reinforcements? Old Judge Dennison won't take a second marshal's murder lying down."

Rafferty felt his anger simmering. "You worked that out all by yourself?" he asked.

"Well, I —"

"Do us both a favor, Warren. Put that silly hat back on your head, get out of here, and do as you've been told. All right?"

Face flushing crimson, Jain put on his bowler hat and left without another word. When he was gone, Rafferty poured himself a double shot of whiskey, threw it down in one gulp, and stood waiting for the alcohol to calm him.

Reinforcements. *Damn it!*

He'd been trusting Brody Gallagher to make his latest problem go away, but now Rafferty knew his trust had been misplaced. The captain was a coward who'd say anything to save himself if he was charged with murder, and the men he'd brought along to help him were a pack of bunglers.

Make that *had been* bunglers. Dead now, they at least could pose no further threat to Rafferty. Only their captain still remained to be eliminated. Rafferty could pass that job to Grady Sullivan or deal with it himself, as long as it was handled soon.

Meanwhile, this Marshal Slade would try to reach his boss in Enid and report the loss of yet another deputy. Grady had done a service there, eliminating Percy Fawcett, but for all Rafferty knew the marshal might be skilled enough to send a wire himself. If not, he'd scour the town until he found someone who was. Rafferty had his own key tapper at the Rocking R, but Slade might turn up someone else if he was diligent.

If he lived long enough.

In for a dime, in for a dollar, he decided. Killing one more lawman hardly mattered at this point. Judge Dennison could only hang him once, and getting rid of Slade would buy more time for Rafferty to cover his own tracks. He had no major fear of anyone in town betraying him, at least until an army of police showed up to put the squeeze on them. If Rafferty could put his house in order first, convince the townspeople who mattered that he had it all under control, there was a chance he'd still slip through the net. And Berringer could help him sell the redskin angle if it came to that.

Get busy then, he thought. *You're wasting precious time.*

Slade was halfway to the Stateline Arms when he saw Mayor Jain and the young deputy marshal up ahead, crossing the street to intercept him. Warily, he stopped and waited for them on the sidewalk, near the barber's shop.

"Oh, Marshal, there you are!" said Jain, as he approached.

"Looks like it," Slade replied.

"There's been more trouble, it appears."

"No shortage of it, Mayor."

"Since you hit town, at least," said Jain.

Slade's eyes narrowed to slits. "You're blaming *me* for this?"

"Well —"

"You recollect another marshal who was murdered after passing through, before I ever saw this place?"

"That was unfortunate, but —"

"And the men who tried to kill me and my partner on the trail before we got here? Men no one in town admits to knowing."

"Sir, I —"

"Now the army gets a call to come and help. Nobody knows who sent for them, I guess."

"Not me," said Jain. "I can assure you that —"

"And then *they* kill my partner, try and kill me, too, before they've been in town two hours. How am I to blame for that, again?"

"Marshal, I didn't mean to say that —"

"What you've got here," Slade pressed on, "as far as I can see, would be a town built on a lie. Somebody hereabouts is cooking moonshine, selling it to Indians and anybody else who'll buy it, cheating Uncle Sam out of the tax. You know the man responsible and take no steps against him. As the man supposedly in charge of Stateline, that makes you a criminal accomplice. And your marshal, too, unless I miss my guess."

"Now, hold on," said the deputy. "You've got no call —"

"Not you," Slade cut him off. "Hickey. I'd bet you next month's pay that he arranged to have our evidence go up in smoke, then somebody surprised him with a beating just to sell it."

When neither man replied, both gaping at him in surprise, Slade asked the mayor, "Who have you got in town that knows the telegraph, with Fawcett gone?"

"Well, um . . ."

"I know Morse code," said Jared Wilkes. "I've never used the key, though."

"Anybody else?" Slade asked.

"There might be someone at the Rocking R," Jain said, reluctantly.

"No help to me, then." Slade turned back to Wilkes and said, "You're it, then, Deputy. I'll be in touch. Make sure you don't get lost."

"Don't worry," Wilkes replied. "I won't be goin' anywhere."

"That's what my partner thought, this morning," Slade informed him. "And some soldiers, too, I bet."

With that, he left them standing open-mouthed and passed on down the street to his hotel. It may have been Slade's own imagination that the desk clerk seemed surprised to see him.

Getting edgy there, Slade warned himself. *Calm down and take it one step at a time.*

As long as those steps led him to Flynn Rafferty.

"Did you hear all that?" asked Rafferty.

Emerging from the office closet where he'd hastily concealed himself upon Mayor Jain's arrival, Captain Gallagher brushed off one tunic sleeve and nodded. "I could hear you."

"It appears your days in uniform are coming to an end. Once Marshal Slade reports back to Judge Dennison, it won't take long for word to reach your colonel."

"What's your point?" Gallagher asked, while pouring out a double whiskey for himself.

"Isn't it obvious? You were an asset as a captain in the U.S. Army. Now, you're nothing but a liability. A fugitive. I can't be seen with you or recognized as giving you a lick of help. I'm sorry to be blunt here, Brody, but you're worse than useless to me now."

"Listen, you bastard! I've done everything you asked me, right along. I've kept my mouth shut and I'll *keep* it shut from here on, but you have to help me get away."

"Where would you go?" asked Rafferty.

"I haven't worked that out. First thing I need is money for the road. A lot of money."

"That could be arranged, I think," said Rafferty. He slipped a hand into a pocket of his coat, as if to palm a roll of bills right then and there. Instead, his fingers closed around the weight of his Apache pistol, folded small enough to fit inside his palm.

"I'd likely need a couple thousand, anyway, to get me started," Gallagher suggested.

"Not unreasonable, when I think about the help you've given us," Rafferty said. "Perhaps friend Berringer would add a little something on his own account."

"He should, you know," said Gallagher. "He damn well should."

"I would suggest you stop and see him when you leave here, but I guess that won't be feasible."

"Can't show my face around the rez with soldiers looking for me," Gallagher agreed.

"I wonder if there's still a way to salvage your career, though," Rafferty replied.

A sudden hopeful glint shone in the

captain's eye. "What do you mean?"

Rafferty rose and moved around his desk, hand still inside his pocket, fingers tucked inside the steel rings of his pistol's knuckle-duster grip. His thumb pressed flat against the little weapon's folded bayonet-style blade.

"Well, think about it," he replied, moving to stand at Gallagher's right side. "Slade hasn't wired his news to Enid yet. He'll have to root around for someone who can operate the telegraph. I'd say that gives you time and opportunity to shut him up before he ruins you."

"He could've told the undertaker —"

"Let me worry about that. Fred Abberline knows when to play along."

"If we got rid of Slade —"

"If *you* got rid of him."

"— I still might have a chance to sell the story my way!"

"Now you're talking," Rafferty agreed.

And as he spoke, he withdrew the pistol from his pocket, thumbed its blade erect, and drove the three-inch knife into Gallagher's throat. A rip and twist severed the artery feeding the captain's brain, blood spouting from the wound as Rafferty withdrew his blade. Gallagher gasped and raised a hand to close the wound, but Rafferty was faster, swinging a steel-knuckled haymaker into the captain's right temple.

Gallagher dropped like a poleaxed steer, twitching in his death throes as blood pumped from his ravaged neck, soaking through the woven rug beneath him. That would have to go, together with his corpse, and Rafferty would need a mop to clear away the rest.

"Damned fool," he told the dying man. "Why couldn't you just do your job?"

"What happened?" Grady Sullivan inquired, standing above the bloody corpse.

"I cut my losses," Rafferty replied. "We need to get him out of here, discreetly."

"Be a two-man job, at least," said Sullivan. "Best if we wait for dark."

"See to it, then. I have some business to take care of at the Rocking R."

"You're going now?"

"If I can leave this in your hands," the big man said.

"Sure, I'll take care of it," said Sullivan. Thinking, *Same way I always do.*

"You need an extra hand?"

"I've got a couple of the boys in town already."

"Perfect, then."

Rafferty left him with the stiff, taking a

satchel from beneath his desk and going out as if he didn't have a trouble in the world. Which was an easy way to be, if someone else always took care of problems for you like a servant.

Get on with it, he thought and knelt to wrap the captain's corpse up in the bloody rug he'd sprawled across as he was dying. That would be the easy part, just rolling him like he was the tobacco in a giant cigarette, while making sure none of his blood marked Grady's faded jeans. His hands were smeared with it, but that would wash right off.

When Gallagher was wrapped, Sullivan checked and saw where blood had soaked right through the rug to smear the floorboards. They were varnished, though, and he was confident a wet mop would remove the stains. Once it was dark, he'd send one of his hands to fetch a buckboard and they'd take their package out the back way, off into the night, to plant it somewhere safe. Retrieve the other soldiers' bodies, set the scene just right . . .

And that left only Marshal Slade.

If Sullivan could deal with him, where Gallagher had failed, they still might salvage something from the captain's mess. And if they couldn't . . . well, how much did Sullivan really owe the big man, after all? Not his life. Not his neck in a noose, when he'd only been following orders.

There was a big country outside of Oklahoma Territory, easy to get lost in. If it worried him too much, the U.S. marshals tracking him, then there was always Mexico. One extra gringo wouldn't draw attention if he watched his manners, did his best to fit in with the easy life.

Why not?

One final dirty job for Rafferty, and if it didn't bring the payoff they were hoping for, then Sullivan would hit the trail. He'd been a drifter off and on, throughout his life, and didn't mind the traveling. Never got homesick. Never pined away for someone he could talk to. Solitude had always suited him just fine.

And if he heard someday, somewhere, that Rafferty was hanged for what they'd done, so what?

The feeling Sullivan expected on that day would be relief he'd escaped the day of reckoning. Let lawmen hunt him till the end of time, as long as he could stay one jump ahead of them.

And Mexico was sounding better all the time.

Sullivan spoke some Spanish and could

learn more in a hurry, if he had to. He could take siestas with the best of them, eat beans, and drink tequila. Make a new life for himself a thousand miles away from anyone who still remembered him or gave a damn what had become of him.

It sounded like a slice of Heaven — or, at least, his personal reprieve from Hell.

"I need to speak with Mr. Rafferty," Slade said.

The barkeep shook his head. Replied, "You missed him, Marshal. He's already gone."

"Gone where?"

A shrug. "Back home, I guess."

"Meaning the Rocking R."

"Best guess. He sleeps there two, three nights a week."

Slade considered going back to check Rafferty's office, but the barkeep didn't strike him as a liar — at the moment, anyway — and he'd gain nothing from a fracas with the Sunflower's employees if their boss was off the premises. He had no present grounds for an arrest of anyone but Captain Gallagher, if he could find the man.

Where would a fugitive from military *and* civilian justice go to hide? First thing, he'd have to trade his uniform for normal clothing that would let him pass without a second glance while traveling. He would need money to support himself, a means of transportation, and at least some vestige of a long-range plan. Dodging from town to town without a destination would defeat him in the end. Once posters were in circulation, he would have to go to ground.

If their positions were reversed, Slade thought he would be making tracks for Mexico. Or, then again, since that was obvious, maybe the longer run to Canada would be his choice, instead. A country larger than the States, from what he'd heard, and while the winters could be killing cold, there was no extradition once you crossed the border.

Perfect.

In the meantime, Slade decided, Gallagher was likely to find sanctuary with Flynn Rafferty. The Rocking R would make a decent starting point for any getaway. Stock up on food and other necessaries for the trip, leave after dark, and by the time Slade started looking for him, he could be long miles away.

Unless Slade made the Rocking R his next stop, without wasting any further time.

So be it.

Slade surprised the hotel clerk again, leaving within ten minutes of returning to his room. The young man didn't ask where he was going, made believe Slade was invisible as he passed through the lobby, out to Border Boulevard. His roan was barely settled at the livery, but she'd had time to eat some oats and drink some water. Slade allowed himself a brief conceit, imagining the mare shared the immediacy of his need to reach the Rocking R before his quarry slipped away.

If he could just take Gallagher alive, Slade thought the officer would spill more than he needed to hang Rafferty. Already proved a coward by his own reaction to the afternoon's gunplay, Gallagher struck him as the sort who'd crack when any kind of pressure was applied to him. And once he started talking, there would be no problem justifying Rafferty's arrest, the seizure of his still and moonshine cache. The whole damned gang could swing, unless Judge Dennison took pity on the small fry.

Either way, it would mean justice for Bill Tanner. For Luke Naylor. Percy Fawcett. For whoever else the whiskey ring had trampled on, whether or not Slade ever learned their names.

Slade knew he'd have to watch his step. The cavalry was out, but Rafferty still had his private army standing by to guard the

Rocking R. Nightfall would cover him to some extent, but one false move could get him killed.

Or someone else, if they were standing in his way.

17

"Now listen up, the lot of you," Flynn Rafferty commanded. His assembled men, an even dozen with a handful left in town, stood in the dooryard of his ranch house at the Rocking R. "We may have company tonight, and no one — I mean *no one* — has permission to be prowling on the property. You find a trespasser, bring him to me. Alive if possible, but if he gives you any trouble, kill him."

"S'pose it's more'n one?" a voice asked from the semidarkness, somewhere near the back.

"Same thing," said Rafferty. "Tonight, tomorrow, and until I tell you otherwise, outsider visits to the Rocking R will be by invitation only. And that means a *written* invitation, signed by yours truly."

Or a warrant, he amended silently, keeping the notion to himself. Slade obviously couldn't get a warrant for the Rocking R unless he first communicated with Judge Dennison, and even then the paperwork would have to reach Stateline before he served it. Two days minimum, if he found someone who could operate the telegraph in Percy Fawcett's place. Meanwhile, if he showed up again it would be trespassing — a fatal error, most especially at night, when it was difficult to spot a badge.

Rafferty thought his men could handle Slade all right, but he still wished that Grady and the rest were with him, rather than in Stateline. Then again, there was a chance that Sullivan would deal with Slade in town and save them all the bother. Earn a bonus for himself and solve Rafferty's problem — for the moment, anyway.

They'd still be forced to make some changes in their operation, though. He'd have to move the whiskey cache from Stateline Storage, maybe even think about relocating the still. It hadn't taken Slade and his dead partner long to sniff out Rafferty's supply and trace it to the source, which was a lesson for him in itself. Maybe he'd grown complacent, even arrogant. With so much more at stake than just the booze, he'd have to reevaluate his methods, guard against discovery until the plan he'd hatched with Berringer paid off.

Nearly quadrupling the acreage he owned already, Rafferty would rank among the greatest landowners in Oklahoma Territory. That meant vastly greater profits from his crops — and better still, when friends in Washington confirmed approval for a railroad meant to carve its way across the land once promised to the Indians forever, now earmarked for Rafferty's expanded Rocking R. All things considered, he was ready to become a millionaire.

But first, he had to deal with Slade, and then clean house to ward off any problems with the marshals who were sure to follow him, investigating how and why so many lawmen died or disappeared around Stateline. Suspicion, Rafferty could live with. It was part of doing business on the shady side. But prison wasn't part of any plan he'd laid out for himself. Being caged was unacceptable.

In fact, he'd rather die first. And if it came down to that, he didn't plan to go alone.

Part of becoming rich was learning to defend what you'd accumulated from a world of people bent on taking it away. Flynn Rafferty had learned to fight around the same time that he'd learned to walk, and he'd been fighting ever since, for one thing or another. Only difference now was that he hired professionals to do his fighting for him.

But he still knew how, as Brody Gallagher had learned.

And Marshal Slade was next.

Slade took his time finding a way onto the Rocking R. He left the access road well short of Rafferty's freestanding gate and traveled overland, staying alert for lookouts until he was in the corn, dismounting then and walking his mare between tall rows of stalks that rustled with a night wind passing through. The field managed to smell both green and dusty, all at once.

Slade knew approximately where the house and other buildings were, although he wasn't following the same path that he'd taken with Luke Naylor — was it only yesterday? So much had happened since the first time they had spied on Rafferty's employees, eight more deaths including Naylor, and no end to it in sight. There was a chance, Slade knew, that he would join the growing list tonight.

That took his thoughts back once again to Faith, but Slade couldn't afford distractions at the moment. Every step he took toward Rafferty, his men, and the distillery they had committed murder to conceal was one

313

more step toward danger and away from what he'd come to think of as his home, the place where he'd built a new life for himself.

Almost.

With Faith, he feared, there was no going back. She'd made that plain enough by now.

A sudden rustling sound in front of him made Slade freeze in his tracks. It had been louder than the breeze and moving toward him, though the wind was at his back. An animal should smell him coming and retreat, but this noise kept advancing at a steady pace.

Maybe a lookout, then.

Slade gripped his lever-action shotgun, chosen as a better close-range weapon in the dark, and hoped he wouldn't have to fire when he was still at least a half mile from the house. Giving himself away that early in the game would ruin any chance of reaching Rafferty, much less mounting surveillance on the place. But if he kept his wits about him, found another way to handle it . . .

Slade had a knife, but springing out and stabbing one of Rafferty's employees would be murder, plain and simple. If he'd had a warrant, it would be a different story, but the legal paper would've granted him a front-door entry without asking anyone's permission, much less jumping them in darkness, slitting throats.

Another way, then.

Slade stood waiting while the new arrival in the cornfield neared him, traveling along the next row to his right. His ears picked out the sound of horse's hooves on soil now, and he craned his neck to spot the shadow of a mounted rider drawing nearer. As the gap between them closed, Slade braced himself, shotgun reversed and held to serve him as a quarterstaff.

A final nervous moment, and he leaped from hiding, crashing through the stalks of corn and striking at his faceless adversary in the dark. Slade's first blow struck the startled rider's chest, unseating him. He landed hard, fighting to catch his breath and reach his six-gun all at once, but Slade was faster, swinging once more with the shotgun's butt to render his opponent limp and senseless.

Through it all, the rider's horse stood by and waited without bolting. Slade removed a coil of rope from his unconscious adversary's saddle, cut enough to hogtie him, and got it done in seconds flat. The lookout's neckerchief served as a gag to silence him when he awoke. Slade planned on being finished with his business long before the shooter could undo the knots securing his arms and legs, but took his Colt and rifle, just in case.

He moved on through the darkness toward his goal.

Rafferty paced his study in the ranch house, whiskey glass in hand, restless, unable to sit still. He had removed a Winchester Model 1892 rifle from the study's gun cabinet, confirmed that its magazine held fifteen .44-40 rounds plus one in the chamber, and left the weapon lying handy on his desk. Beside the rifle, ready to be tucked inside his belt as needed, lay a .38-caliber Colt M1892 revolver, commonly called the new Army and Navy model. With the Apache pistol in his pocket, Rafferty believed he was prepared for anything.

So, why was he afraid?

He didn't like admitting that, not even silently to himself. It set a precedent that might betray him, when a situation called for special strength. If anyone suspected that he had a yellow streak, however well concealed, it might turn out to be a fatal flaw.

A dozen men and guns galore should be enough to rid him of a single lawman who had overstepped his bounds. If not, perhaps he ought to take the Colt and and use it on himself, bring all the anxious waiting to an end.

Disgusted by the thought, Rafferty drained his whiskey, moved to pour another, then stopped short at the sound of shouting from the yard outside. A heartbeat later, gunfire echoed from the darkness and he dropped his glass, which rebounded from the woven rug beneath his feet. More shots exploded as he rushed back toward the desk, snatching his weapons, conscious of a tremor in his hands.

One of his gunmen burst into the study without knocking, hesitated as if bracing for a tongue-lashing at the intrusion, then told Rafferty, "There's somebody outside, Boss! Somebody who don't belong, I mean."

"You've seen him?" Rafferty demanded.

"Me? Uh, no sir. Couple of the others seen him though and started shootin'. That's what all the racket is about."

"Show me!"

All thought of hiding, giving up, was driven from his thoughts by the invasion of his property. Raw anger made Rafferty's pulse throb in his ears, and if his fear still lingered, nagging at him from a corner of his mind, at least he had it mastered for the moment.

Slade had come for him — who else

would dare? — and now he could eliminate the lawman, just as he would dump a sharp stone from his boot. Get rid of him, and then be on about the business of preparing for the next lot, and the ones who'd follow after that.

For just a moment, rushing off to battle, Rafferty imagined that he was invincible.

He lost that feeling in a hurry, once he left the house and darkness lowered over him, reducing vision and reminding him how small he really was, how vulnerable to a stray shot in the night. Rafferty edged along the porch, staying away from lighted windows, flinching each time that a shot rang out, a muzzle-flash sparking in shadows.

"Where in hell is he?" Rafferty demanded of the hand who'd fetched him.

"Over by the barn, I think. Leastways, that what they said."

"Who's *they*?"

"Whoever seen him. Wanna come and look, Boss?"

"You go on," said Rafferty. "I'll circle round the back."

"You want me to come with you?"

"Won't be necessary. Just do like I told you."

"Sure. Okay."

Alone once more, Rafferty turned and started for the stable he'd had built at the same time the barn had been converted into a distillery. The only thought remaining to him now was saddling the fastest horse he had and getting back to town.

Slade wasn't sure exactly where the first shot came from. He'd left his mare in the cornfield, proceeding on foot toward the barn with a quarter moon overhead screened by thin clouds. When he had almost reached the hulking structure, someone shouted from the shadows, "Hey! Somebody's over there!"

The rifle shot came close behind that warning, launching Slade into a sprint that let him reach the barn before one shot became a crackle of incoming fire. He knelt and risked a low-down glance around the corner that concealed him, spotted half a dozen muzzle flashes in the dark all aimed in his direction, and retreated out of range.

Not what he'd had in mind at all, hoping to get a closer look around the place without sparking a fight. He hadn't seen the still yet, much less got a line on Rafferty, and now the hunters stalking him made both prospects unlikely.

They had been expecting him, that much

was clear. Or, rather, they had been expecting *someone*. In the dark, Slade knew no one had seen his face yet, or his badge. Even the lookout he'd left tied up in the cornfield had been taken by surprise, with no chance to identify his ambusher. Slade felt a sudden kind of freedom, knowing he could get away with damn near anything, as long as no one made him for a lawman.

He could even up the score for Tanner and Luke Naylor. He could lay waste to the moonshine ring without a second thought to following procedure. Who would ever know, besides himself?

But first, he had to stay alive. Survival, always, was the top priority.

Slade moved along the west wall of the barn, smelling the mash cooking inside, and found a side door with a simple latch but no padlock. He slipped inside, gunshots still peppering the corner where his enemies had seen him last, the shooters working up their nerve to rush him. Standing in the barn, the giant still in front of him, Slade saw its copper mass burnished by lamplight. Unattended at the moment, still it cooked around the clock, turning out liquid gold for Rafferty.

Poison for reservation dwellers. Death for lawmen who investigated.

Slade took the nearest of two lamps, left burning in the barn, and placed it near the metal drum set up to catch Rafferty's 'shine as it came dripping from the coil. Retreating half a dozen paces then, he raised his shotgun, aimed, and fired.

Slade's buckshot pellets smashed the lamp, punctured the drum of alcohol, and in a fraction of a second sent a fireball wafting toward the high-peaked ceiling of the barn. He was already at the exit when the drum of alcohol exploded, spraying liquid fire around the walls and floor, prompting more shouts from Rafferty's collected gunmen in the yard outside.

Trying to save the barn and still should keep most of them busy while he ran through darkness toward the ranch house, seeking Rafferty. With any luck, the shooters might believe he was inside and frying, maybe even blame themselves for sparking the inferno with a careless shot.

Stick to the fire, he thought.

But if they followed him, they would regret it. Some unto their dying day.

Rafferty buckled the flank cinch on his saddle, gave the rig a tug, then hauled himself aboard the restless grullo stallion, reaching back to double-check his rifle in

321

its scabbard. One more second to adjust the Colt revolver tucked beneath his belt, to stop its muzzle jabbing at his groin, and Rafferty was off, spurring the animal around behind his house and toward the road that would eventually take him back to Stateline.

His home had turned into a battleground, and he was glad to let his hired hands do the fighting. Why risk his life to stick around and watch it, when the men he paid to take risks for him were already on the job?

He'd covered thirty yards or so when an explosion rocked the property and made him rein in, looking back in the direction of his house and barn. It only took a second for the flames inside the barn to catch, their harsh light plainly visible around the large front door and through the loft's wide-open loading bay. Outside the burning structure, men were running every which way in the yard, shouting to one another, pausing here and there to fire a shot at God knew what or whom.

Gripped by a sudden rush of panic, Rafferty faced back into the dark and snapped his grullo's reins to get the stallion galloping along the access road and back to town. His mind was in chaotic turmoil, part of it intensely focused on escape, the rest reeling from shock of grim disaster ravaging his master plan. Wind in his face chilled Rafferty without refreshing him or cutting through the haze of dread that kept pace with his running animal.

All right, the still was gone, but he could always have a new one built. Same with the barn. The first priority was getting out from under federal scrutiny, wiping the slate and buying time to put his house in order, be prepared for when Judge Dennison dispatched another team of snoops to nose around.

And if he couldn't manage that?

Then racing through the night to Stateline wouldn't be the end of running, only the beginning. With a stack of murder warrants haunting him, there'd be no safe place left for Rafferty to hide. His hard work and the blood he'd shed would all have been for nothing. Wasted.

But he wouldn't go without a fight. Whatever happened at the ranch, he still had Grady Sullivan and more men waiting for him back in town. A last chance to prevent the loss he'd suffered at the Rocking R tonight from overwhelming him.

A chance. But it would only work on one condition. Rafferty was sure of that, if nothing else.

Jack Slade would have to die.

The barn was burning fiercely now, its light revealing Flynn Rafferty's gunmen as they tried to duck and hide, their giant shadows stretching out behind them. Slade crouched at the northwest corner of the ranch house, watching them run helter-skelter through the yard, firing at random when they spotted a suspected target. Any minute now, he thought they might start shooting one another, and he left them to it.

Rafferty was not among the shooters Slade had seen so far, which likely meant that he was still inside the house, letting his hirelings fight his battle for him. Rather than attempt to enter through the front door, bathed in firelight from the yard and likely covered from inside, Slade jogged around behind the rambling structure, looking for another entrance. He found a door that granted access to the kitchen, and was pleased to feel the knob turn in his hand.

Slade entered cautiously, closing the door softly behind him so it wouldn't draw attention from the circling gunmen, standing open. He considered latching it, as well, then changed his mind as he envisioned being trapped inside, denied a swift retreat by something he had done himself. Moving as quietly as possible, trusting the racket from outside to cover any passing noise he made, he crossed the kitchen, cleared a spacious formal dining room, and pressed on through the house, seeking its owner.

Slade was ready with the twelve-gauge when he left the dining room and stepped into a hallway running north-south through the center of the house. In front of him, a slender man stood frozen in surprise. Chinese, maybe the cook, since he was clutching a meat cleaver in one hand.

"You'll want to drop that," Slade suggested and relaxed a little as the cleaver hit the floor, piercing one of the boards and standing upright, quivering from impact.

"No shoot, please!"

"I don't plan on it. Where's your boss?" Slade asked.

"Gone off on horse, good-bye!"

"And when was this?"

"Five minutes, maybe."

"Going where?" asked Slade.

A shrug. "He don't tell me."

Stateline. It had to be, unless . . .

"If I find out you're lying to me —"

"Not lying! Check all house, you want to see."

The cook's apparent indignation sold it. Slade retreated, covering him just in case he made a lunge to reach the cleaver, then ran back the way he'd come, through the dining room and kitchen, out into the night.

Rafferty's men had given up on hunting him, it seemed. Slade saw a couple of them standing guard, the others trying futilely to fight the fire with buckets full of water, flinging them against a solid wall of flame that mocked their puny efforts with its roar. He left them to it, ran around the house to keep its bulk between him and the shooters, trusting luck at last to cover him when he was in the open, dashing for the cornfield.

And his luck was holding — anyway, enough to keep from being shot down in the yard. The other side of that was missing Rafferty at home and maybe losing him completely. If his guess was wrong, and Rafferty didn't return to Stateline, Slade would guarantee his getaway by riding back to town. That was a long shot, though, logic dictating that the fugitive would try to salvage what he could from this night's loss, maybe hole up at the Sunflower overnight, or at the very least retrieve cash for the road from his saloon.

Slade found his roan, ignored the moaning lookout he'd left trussed up in the corn nearby, and saddled up. Five minutes later he was on the road, nearing the gate that advertised the Rocking R. When he reached the county highway, Slade turned south toward Stateline, hoping that he hadn't thrown away his last, best chance to overtake his quarry.

Grim-faced in the night, he galloped back toward town.

18

"So, is he coming after you or not?" asked Grady Sullivan.

"The hell should I know?" Rafferty snapped back at him. "I'm *here*. He's *there*, or somewhere in between."

Sullivan knew better than to insult his boss by calling him a yellow dog. Instead, he nodded understanding. Said, "You got a dozen men out there. Maybe they've finished him by now."

"Maybe." Rafferty drank the whiskey Sullivan had poured him. Not his first tonight, by any means, the way he'd smelled when he came barging in. "You didn't see them mill around like goddamn chickens with their heads cut off."

"Trying to save the barn and still, you said."

"Too late! The place went up in nothing flat. They gave up hunting Slade the minute that they saw the fire."

"If it *was* Slade," said Sullivan.

Rafferty stopped his pacing, glared at him. "Who else?"

Sullivan shrugged. "Maybe the judge sent other deputies to help him out by now."

"Why would he? Do you know something?"

"No, Boss. I —"

"Did he find someone to help him use the goddamn telegraph?"

"Not that I know of."

Rafferty sneered, moving to pour himself another drink. "I wonder sometimes what you know," he said.

"What's that supposed to mean?"

"It *means* that for my second in command, you seem to let things get away from you."

"Your second in command? Since when?" asked Sullivan, feeling the rise of anger warm his cheeks.

"Well, who else is there?"

"Cap'n Gallagher, until you slit his throat. And Berringer."

"A damn bookkeeper, counting redskins on the reservation. Christ, he wouldn't know a pistol from a piss pot."

"I can tell the difference," said Sullivan. "But I can't shoot what I can't see."

"He'll be here," Rafferty insisted. "If he

makes it off the Rocking R alive, he'll come for me."

"And if he don't? How long are we supposed to wait around?"

"Daylight. If there's no sign of him by then, we'll send one of the men out for a look around the place. How many do you have in town?"

"Still five," said Sullivan. Thinking, *Same as the last two times you asked.*

"We need to get them spotted, watching out for Slade."

"Already done. I told you that."

"You did?"

"Yes, sir."

"All right." The big man slugged his liquor down, then laid the glass aside. "We'll hole up here and wait till someone spots him. If he makes it."

"What about the warehouse?" Sullivan inquired.

"It's safe enough for now. Six men should be enough to stop him," Rafferty replied.

Meaning I'm in it, too, thought Sullivan. *About damn time.*

And said, "Six here, if he already got away from twelve."

"Their hearts weren't in it, Grady. If you could've seen them . . ."

"Headless chickens. Got it."

"Show him to me dead, and there's a thousand-dollar bonus in it for you."

"It'll be my pleasure, Boss."

"And no mistakes this time."

"I'll see to it myself." Thinking, *The way I should've done, first thing.*

"You'd better make the rounds and keep them sharp," said Rafferty.

"Just thinkin' that, myself."

"Oh, what about the captain?" Rafferty inquired, as Sullivan was leaving.

"Got him tucked away, together with his soldier boys. After we finish up with Slade, I'll take 'em out and set up somethin' for the law to find."

Rafferty nodded and turned back to the whiskey bottle. Sullivan was glad to get away from him and out into the night. Hoping Slade *was* alive, and that he'd turn up soon.

This time, he thought, *we do it right.*

Slade circled wide around Stateline to enter from the east. It cost him time, but there were hours yet till daylight, and he knew that any lookouts Rafferty had posted would expect him to be coming from the north or west. Making his way back into town unseen might not be half the battle, but it was a decent start.

It would have helped to know how many

guns were waiting for him, but he'd never got a final tally on how many Rafferty employed. Whatever, they'd been whittled down by six before tonight, not counting bluecoats, and he'd left at least a dozen at the Rocking R, trying to keep the barn fire from expanding to consume the house and other outbuildings.

How many more were waiting for him now, he only needed to uncover one of them.

Flynn Rafferty.

And then what? Play the cards as they were dealt, and see what happened next.

There was no outcry and no shooting as he left his roan behind the Stateline Arms, untied and free to run away if anything went wrong. Not safe, exactly, but it was the best that he could do under the circumstances. Leaving her, he took both long guns with him — one for range, the other for its close-up stopping power.

Ready for the worst Stateline and Rafferty could throw at him.

The only foot traffic that Slade could see on Border Boulevard consisted of a few men passing in and out of each saloon, down-range. The Sunflower and Swagger Inn were making money, making noise, while the remainder of their neighbors slept, or tried to. Slade stood peering from an alleyway beside the barber's shop, watching for any sign of lookouts on the street, but couldn't spot them. Either they were hidden well, or Rafferty had posted them at vantage points where they could scan the road and prairie north of town.

Too late for that, since he was on the inside now and drawing closer to his quarry.

Rafferty would be inside the Sunflower, Slade reasoned. All he had to do was cross the street and work his way around behind the shops on Border Boulevard's north side, find the saloon's back door, and drop into surprise its owner. The Sunflower was a public place, no warrant needed for a visit to the premises, and if someone sprang an ambush on him, Slade would naturally have to act in self-defense.

Of course, if Rafferty experienced an unexpected impulse to surrender and confess his crimes, Slade would be pleased to listen and arrest him. There'd already been enough blood spilled — too much, in fact — for one investigation.

Slade stepped from the alley, glanced both ways along the street once more, then started for the other side. An easy jog, nothing to draw attention from the drinkers down the street, but neither did he want to linger in the open any longer than required.

Halfway across, something buzzed past his face, an angry wasp's sound, then he heard the sharp crack of a rifle shot from somewhere to his right. In the direction of the Sunflower Saloon. Instead of looking for the shooter, trying to return fire, Slade kicked into top speed, sprinting for the far side of the street. He made it as a second shot rang out and struck one of the posts holding an awning up in front of lawyer Coltrane's office.

Then another alley swallowed Slade, and he was on his way.

Surrender, hell. The fight was on.

Grady Sullivan cursed his wasted shot and shook his Winchester, as if it were the rifle's fault. In fact, he knew he'd been too hasty on the first one, jerked the trigger when he should've squeezed it gently, and the second had been close to hopeless once his target started sprinting through the shadows.

"Shit fire!"

Now he had to scramble like a madman, out of Rosy Harrow's little room, located at the southeast corner of the second floor, and back downstairs to meet Slade if he tried to get inside the Sunflower. The echo of his rifle shots had spoiled the party going on downstairs, dried up the jangling piano music and Rosy's off-key voice trying to sing along.

To hell with it. If Rafferty lost money getting rid of Slade, whose fault was that? Sullivan thought they should've killed both marshals on the same day they arrived in Stateline, but his boss had called for caution, prudence, all of it a goddamn waste of time. Now they were sunk unless he dealt with Slade immediately, and the boss was out God only knew how many thousands of his hard-earned dollars anyhow.

Sullivan hammered down the stairs, some of the lushes from the barroom drifting back to meet him, asking stupid questions, getting in his way. He shouldered past them, hit one in the belly with his rifle butt for grabbing at his sleeve, and left the idjit puking on the floor as Sullivan moved on.

He'd locked the back door personally, double-checking it before he went upstairs to watch the street from Rosy's crib. They had a spare room in the upstairs brothel at the moment, so his presence wouldn't hamper business if she caught herself a paying customer. Meanwhile, her window had the best view of the eastern end of Border Boulevard, and Grady's other men were concentrated to the west.

The way Slade should have come to town, but hadn't. Getting tricky, thinking he could slip in unobserved to do his dirty work. The lawman's first mistake might also prove to be his last.

Wishing he could call the others in from where he'd posted them, Sullivan hoped his wasted shots would serve to summon them. If the remaining hands showed up to find their enemy already dead, so much the better. The could cart him off, along with his dead partner and the soldiers Sullivan had kept on hand as props for the persuasive scene he planned to stage on Rafferty's behalf.

One marshal scalped and butchered hadn't been enough to sell Judge Dennison on hostile redskins. How about an army squad and two more deputies slaughtered together, maybe with some arrows added for effect to set the stage. Dump all of them together, near the rez where Agent Berringer could do his part in building up the story, and they'd be a long way toward their goal of booting useless Indians off land they'd never managed to develop anyway.

A winning situation all the way around.

Sullivan raced along the hallway toward the back door, voices calling after him, demanding that he tell them what in hell was going on. He reached the door, found it secure, and reached out to unlock it, balancing his Winchester one-handed. He threw the door wide open and plunged through it in a rush, turning to an enemy approaching from the east.

A voice behind him asked, "Looking for me?"

The shooter hesitated for a second, maybe calculating odds, then spun around toward Slade, his rifle rising to his shoulder. Slade was ready with the shotgun, squeezing off from ten feet with no possibility of missing. Barely spreading at that range, his buckshot tore a gaping hole in the unlucky gunman's chest and hurled him backward through a sloppy somersault that left him facedown in the dust.

Slade pumped the shotgun's lever action, rifle in his left hand as he charged the Sunflower's back door. Some eight or ten spectators watched him from the far end of a hallway leading to the barroom, none holding a weapon, though a couple of the men were obviously heeled. They didn't try to draw on Slade, instead retreating hastily as he approached.

The hallway was clear by the time Slade reached Rafferty's office. He didn't bother knocking, just gave the door a kick and followed through to find the chamber empty. There was no way to determine when the Sunflower's proprietor had left — or if, in fact, he'd even stopped there after fleeing from the Rocking R. A side trip to the barroom found the customers evacuating, while the girls in residence were crouched with the piano player, down behind his instrument. The bartender showed Slade a blank face and his empty hands.

"Where's Rafferty?" asked Slade.

"Beats me," the barkeep said. "He came in looking spooked, maybe an hour back. I didn't see him leave."

Slade backed into the corridor, considered scouring the place from top to bottom. It could be a waste of time, but if he didn't check . . .

Before he could decide, two gunmen barged in through the back door he'd left standing open, pistols drawn. Their faces told him they'd already seen their friend lying outside and didn't feel like joining him if they could help it. Six-guns barked at Slade, as he lunged headlong to the floor, dropping his rifle for the moment, freeing both hands for the shotgun.

There was no time to aim precisely, so he picked a spot *between* his two assailants, waist-high on the taller of the pair, and let a charge of buckshot do the rest. They spun in opposite directions, both men crying out in shock and pain as leaden pellets ripped through flesh and shattered bone on impact. Scrambling to his feet, Slade swapped out guns and caught the shooter on his left trying to rise, his pistol still in hand, slamming a .44-40 Winchester round through his chest.

The other guy had drawn himself into a fetal curl, clutching his punctured abdomen and sobbing from the pain that wracked him. Slade passed by and left him to it, after kicking both men's pistols down the hall and out of reach. Whether the wounded gunman lived or died was someone else's problem now.

Slade guessed that there were others still outside, prepared to take him down if they could manage it. He'd deal with them the best he could, as they appeared, but his priority was still Flynn Rafferty. Where would the fleeing fugitive have gone, if he was flushed out of the Sunflower, still looking for a way to cut his losses?

Maybe Stateline Storage and the bootleg whiskey cache?

Slade reckoned it was worth a try, as he ducked back into the night.

In fact, Flynn Rafferty had given up on saving anything except himself. The sounds of gunfire from the Sunflower Saloon told him that Marshal Slade was both alive and stalking him in Stateline. Grady Sullivan might slow the lawman down — might even kill him with a lucky shot — but Rafferty had already decided it was too damn late to salvage anything from the chaotic shambles of his enterprise.

Escape was now his only option, leaving no hard evidence behind him.

Grady and his other men would go down fighting, if they didn't cut and run. Whichever way it went, they wouldn't be around to testify if Rafferty was ultimately found, arrested, and returned for trial. Not one of them would put his own head in a noose by telling tales. Likewise, the court would wring no damning testimony out of Brody Gallagher or his pathetic troop of soldiers, silenced now for good. Investigators might make something of the burned-out still, but how much of it would survive in recognizable condition from the hellish blaze he'd witnessed at the Rocking R?

Only his warehouse stock remained to link

him positively with the racket that had wound up spilling so much blood. And he could solve that problem with a kitchen match.

Fearful as he was of being spotted on the street, Rafferty did not run directly down to Stateline Storage. First, he found the darkest spot he could for crossing Border Boulevard, well clear of the saloon lights and the fools who milled around outside them. By the time the shooting started, drawing customers out of the Swagger Inn, he'd covered half the length of town in fits and starts, reaching his destination in a final rush along a pitch-black alleyway. He stumbled once, flaying his palms on grit and gravel, but the pain seemed insignificant beside his fear.

Rafferty used his key to open the back door, closed it behind him, struck one of his matches to locate a lamp and light it. Working with the wick turned low, he found a hammer in the box of tools that stood against one wall and used its claw-end to open one of the whiskey crates, casting the wooden lid aside. Eight bottles nestled in the crate, surrounded by excelsior for padding.

Perfect.

Rafferty removed two of the bottles,

smashing off their tall necks with the hammer, using one to drench the contents of the open crate. He splashed the other's pungent liquor over other boxes in the pile, drenching the raw unpainted wood with alcohol. Fumes filled his nostrils, threatening to make him sneeze, but Rafferty controlled it, stepping back a pace to strike another match and toss it down into the open whiskey crate.

The burst of flame surprised him, drove him back with eyebrows singed. He stepped on the discarded hammer, lost his footing, and went down, *woof*ing in startled pain before the open crate of booze exploded, spewing fiery streamers all around like something from a celebration staged on Independence Day. The next thing that the big man knew, his pants cuffs were on fire and he was screaming.

Rafferty scrambled to his feet, bending to slap at burning ankles with his bloodied palms, to no effect. The flames were at his knees before he bolted toward the back door. He had almost cleared it when the pile of whiskey crates exploded with a sound like thunder, hurling him into the night, a screaming comet with a fiery tail.

Slade was two blocks from the warehouse

when a gunshot from behind him made him stop and dive for cover in the recessed doorway of a dry goods store. The slug had missed him, and it brought to mind a saying that he must have heard two dozen times, over the years. *You never hear the shot that kills you.*

Wrong.

He'd seen enough men gut-shot, bleeding out in agony, to know that wasn't true. But this time he'd been lucky — so far, anyway.

Slade risked a look around the corner and saw three men moving toward him, fanning out, all clutching pistols and the nearest of them holding two. It looked like shotgun work, if he could let them come a little closer. Maybe manage to surprise them, even though they'd seen where he had gone to ground.

Slade did a quick count of the rounds remaining in the shotgun. He had started out with one shell in the chamber, five more in the weapon's magazine. Two shots fired at the Sunflower left him with four — enough to do the job if none were wasted spraying empty air. It all came down to timing, decent aim, and holding steady once his targets had begun returning fire.

Do it! he thought and leaned around the corner, lining up his shot. Slade squeezed the shotgun's trigger, rode its recoil as the shooter with the pair of Colts went down, and then the night exploded at his back. A wave of heat rushed down the length of Border Boulevard, while sudden firelight made the street as bright as day. Slade hesitated, almost turning, and his two surviving adversaries bolted, running for their lives as if he'd opened up on them with field artillery.

When they were safely out of range, Slade rose and faced the blazing wreck of Stateline Storage. He was moving out in that direction when a fiery scarecrow burst out of the alley on the near side of the warehouse, lurching toward the middle of the street and shrieking in a high-pitched, barely human voice. Arms flailing, smoke and sparks trailing behind, the doomed man staggered on a dead-end run to nowhere.

Slade was on him in another second, sweeping the runner off his feet and crouching near him, scooping up handfuls of dirt from the street and pitching them onto the scorched figure writing in front of him, dousing the fire by degrees. Other townsmen soon joined him, one detouring from a charge toward the warehouse and dumping his bucket of water on top of the badly burned man.

At last, Slade rolled the smoking figure over on its back, not quite surprised to recognize Flynn Rafferty, blistered and blackened where the flames had licked his face. Most of his hair was gone, leaving a grotesque caricature of the man Slade had been hunting all night long. Rafferty's lips were moving, voice too faint for Slade to understand amidst the chaos that enveloped Border Boulevard.

He leaned in close. Told Rafferty, "You're dying. Is there anything you want to say?"

The burned man tried to raise his head, wearing a grimace like a ghoulish smile. "Get Berringer," he gasped. "All his idea . . . run drunken redskins off the rez . . . railroad . . . big money . . . bastard sitting pretty . . ."

"Not for long," Slade promised him, but Rafferty was long past hearing now. His last breath was a wisp of smoke from seared lungs, snaking from his blistered lips and gone wherever damned souls go.

19

"I'm sorry about Naylor," said Judge Dennison.

"Me, too. He did a good job while he lasted," Slade replied.

"I won't say that I'm shocked about the soldiers, but it's definitely . . . disappointing."

"Way it seems to me," Slade answered, "Rafferty and Berringer required some muscle for their plan to shift the trip, and that was Captain Brody. I don't know about the others. Maybe they were rotten apples that he picked out of the barrel."

"Pity none of them survived to help us understand the whole arrangement," Dennison observed.

"My guess would be they didn't want to face a firing squad."

Slade and the judge faced one another with the judge's desk between them, bathed in midmorning light from tall windows facing the courtyard and gallows below. So far, on this job, Slade had brought the judge no one to hang.

"And you think Rafferty disposed of Brody?"

"Must have," Slade agreed. "I found him with the others at the undertaker's parlor, stacked up in the back like cord wood. Someone cut the captain's throat."

"He could have filled us in, I'd wager."

"Likely why he got the chop," Slade said. "Rafferty wasn't leaving any witnesses."

"There'll be some from his ranch, I guess," said Dennison. "But scattered to the winds."

"I got some names before I left, but putting them with faces . . . well, we weren't exactly introduced."

"I'm more concerned about the town's officials," Dennison replied. "The mayor, the marshal."

"And the undertaker," Slade amended. "I've got all three waiting for a pickup. Or, I should say, the new marshal has. A kid named Wilkes. He's done all right so far. Might even fit if you're replacing Luke."

"Somebody has to," Dennison agreed. "And Tanner, too."

Bill Tanner, who had died and started all of it. Slade was embarrassed that the first murder had slipped his mind.

347

"Just one job left," he said.

Dennison pushed a folded paper toward him, settled back into his high-backed chair, and said, "You have your warrant, Jack. But put the kid gloves on for this one. Berringer has friends in Washington."

"In spite of all he's done?"

"The word won't reach them until he's in custody, but when you're talking Congress . . . well, you never know how some of those folk may react."

"Or whether they're involved," Slade added.

"That, we'll likely never know," said Dennison. "Unless friend Berringer decides to bargain for his life. In which case, can we even trust him?"

"Wouldn't hurt to ask."

"But *only* ask," the jurist emphasized. "No undue zeal."

"Define *undue*," Slade said.

"I'm serious," Judge Dennison replied. "If he resists arrest and suffers injury as a result, I'll need statements from witnesses."

Slade had a thought. "Tribal police?" he asked.

"That could be interesting," Dennison allowed. "But watch your back."

"I will."

"You still don't want assistance?"

"It's one man," Slade said. "He's not Wes Hardin."

"Just a cornered rat. They're known to fight."

"Don't get my hopes up," Slade replied. He took the warrant with him as he left.

It seemed to be a slow day at the courthouse. Leaving, squinting into sudden sunlight, Slade almost collided with a woman on the sidewalk. Stepping back, he saw that it was Faith and instantly forgot whatever he had been about to say, in terms of an apology. She looked surprised, a little flustered, and he was afraid she wouldn't speak.

"Jack."

"Faith."

"I heard about your friends. I'm sorry."

Luke and Tanner, she must mean. He shrugged. "I hardly knew them, really."

"Still."

"You're looking well," he said and hated how it sounded in the open air.

"I've meant to visit you."

"We've both been busy."

"Yes."

"In fact, I'm off to serve a warrant. Wrap this up, I hope."

"Be careful, will you?"

"Sure. Good seeing you," he said and

moved off toward the livery, half strangled by the hard lump in his throat.

Slade didn't rush his ride out to the reservation. He'd be satisfied to lose a little sleep and bring his prisoner back into Enid after nightfall, if it came to that.

Dead or alive, he thought, but he didn't want to disappoint Judge Dennison if he could help it.

Some of that might still depend on the reservation's tribal police. As stoic as they were, in his experience, Slade couldn't say how any of them felt about Frank Berringer. On one hand, he was just another white man sent from Washington or somewhere else back East, to keep the so-called savages in line. Conversely, he'd promoted them to jobs that must have had some privileges attached. And if they chose to stand with him against a solitary U.S. marshal, then what?

Slade smiled at the irony of being forced to call the troops at Fort Supply for help, if Cherokee police defended Berringer. That ought to go down well, after he'd killed four of the outpost's troopers personally and disgraced a captain who was later slain by one of his accomplices in crime.

But, then again, it might be someone else calling for troops, if Slade came up against it on the rez and found himself outgunned. Somebody else's problem, evening the score and carting Slade to Holland Mattson's funeral parlor, back in Enid.

It was a trip that everybody took, sooner or later, but Slade wasn't in a hurry for his turn. One thing he had decided, beyond any doubt: if it came down to do or die, he didn't plan to croak before he got a shot at Berringer. The two of them could go together, and the army or whoever could sort out the rest of it.

"Or maybe no one has to die at all," Slade told his mare.

She snorted in reply, not overly concerned.

Another mile or so, before he crossed onto the rez. Slade had prepared himself in every way he could, face freshly shaved, guns oiled and fully loaded, breakfast settled in his belly — though the last part might turn out to be a handicap, if he was gut-shot later on. The warrant in his pocket seemed to weigh more than it should, a trick of the imagination, keeping Slade in mind of his responsibility and promise to Judge Dennison.

He thought of Faith no more than half a dozen times during his ride, wondering if her attitude that morning indicated any kind of thaw in their relationship. There was no reason to believe so, but he guessed that hope would linger till she finally sold up and left the territory, headed back wherever she was bound. Slade had no reason to expect that she would take him back, no prospect that she would forget — much less forgive. He hadn't prayed in years and reckoned it would be the ultimate hypocrisy to start up now, begging a favor for himself.

And all distractions were forgotten in an instant when he saw the riders ranged in front of him. Four Cherokees, with sunlight glinting on the metal badges that they wore.

The tribal officers waited for Slade, not riding out to meet him. All of them were armed, but none had guns in hand, which Slade took as a hopeful sign. He told them he had business with their BIA administrator and they fell in line around him for the ride back to the agency. One thing about the Cherokees in general, and their policemen in particular: they didn't waste a lot of time or energy on small talk.

Half a silent hour later, Slade picked out the buildings clustered around Berringer's office and residence. When they had closed the half mile remaining to a hundred yards or so, the leader of Slade's escorts said, "You were a friend of Little Wolf."

Not asking him.

Slade caught the past tense, worried by it. He replied, "I *am* his friend."

"Dead men do not have friends," the Cherokee informed him.

Something tightened in Slade's gut. "You're telling me that Little Wolf is dead?"

"His pony came without him to the village. Searching for him, we find nothing, but he did not leave on foot."

"What are you telling me?" asked Slade.

"Last time you came, it was about the whiskey being smuggled in by whites."

"That's right. It's taken care of," Slade informed him. Thinking, *This time, anyway.*

"Before he disappeared," the leader told Slade, "Little Wolf was looking for the men smugglers. He believed they had a friend here, and perhaps where you come from."

"In Enid?"

"Someone to pass messages," the Cherokee explained.

That made good sense to Slade. Rafferty would have wanted someone who could warn him if Judge Dennison caught wind of anything affecting liquor traffic in the territory. Someone who could tip him off when marshals were en route to Stateline, for example, helping Rafferty arrange an ambush for them on the trail.

"I'll check that, when I get back home," Slade said.

"Maybe ask Agent Berringer," his escort said, and then stopped talking as they neared the agency.

Where Berringer stood waiting to receive them once again. *Just like old times,* Slade thought. *Except this time, you're leaving with me.*

"Marshal Slade, we meet again," said Berringer, half smiling from the porch.

"Can't tear myself away," Slade said. No smile on his side.

"You're alone this time."

"Looks like it."

"How goes your investigation of the whiskey running?"

"Pretty well wrapped up," Slade said. "A couple of loose ends to tie up, still, but I'm about to top it off."

"We should enjoy some peace and quiet, then," said Berringer.

"At least until the trial," Slade said.

"You've made arrests, then?" Berringer had lost a little of the color from his face.

"Just one or two to go."

"I call that a success. And I appreciate you coming out to share the news."

"Figured you ought to be the first to know," Slade said, "about a warrant with your name on it."

"Is that supposed to be a joke, Marshal?"

"You see me laughing, Mr. Berringer?"

The agent stared at Slade a moment longer, then ducked back inside his house and slammed the door behind him, shooting bolts to bar the way.

Slade glanced at his escorts, saw no evidence of any movement on their part, then dismounted and drew his shotgun from its saddle scabbard. Mounting to the porch, he stood off to the left side of the door, a stout log wall from gunfire if it came.

"This is a bad decision, Berringer," he called out through the door. "You're cornered and you don't have any reinforcements coming. Brody and the rest of them are dead in Stateline. You're the last name on my list, and one way or another you *are* going back to Enid."

No response.

Slade took a step back from the door and raised his shotgun, aiming at the upper hinge. Before he had a chance to fire, a deep voice at his back said, "Do you mean to kill him?"

Turning toward the sound, he recognized Joe Mockingbird from his last visit to the reservation. Mockingbird still carried his

.50-70 Sharps carbine tucked beneath one arm.

"I'd rather take him in alive," Slade answered. "But I'll leave that choice to him. If it goes wrong, I'll need signed statements from your officers as witnesses."

If they can write, Slade thought, now wondering if he would have to take them all to see Judge Dennison, a motley caravan crossing the plains.

"What charges does he face?" asked Mockingbird.

"Right now, accessory to moonshining and smuggling liquor. That could be upgraded at his hearing. Say accessory to murder."

"He will hang?"

"Depends on what comes out at trial," Slade said. "More likely, he'll do time. I'd guess about ten years."

"It's better if he lives, then," Mockingbird replied. "To understand captivity."

"Suits me," Slade said and turned back to the door, angling his twelve-gauge toward the upper hinge. The close-range blast of buckshot tore it free, a second doing likewise for the lower hinge. Slade guessed approximately where the inner bolts should be and fired once more, blowing a ragged porthole through the door and splintering its jamb. The door sagged slowly forward, then gave in to gravity and toppled to the porch, raising a minor cloud of dust on impact.

Two rounds left in Slade's Winchester, and Joe Mockingbird's Sharps carbine was a single-shot. They both wore pistols, though, and Slade thought that their long guns ought to get them through the gaping doorway.

If they weren't killed first.

Another moment's hesitation, wondering if Berringer was crouched in hiding with a six-gun pointed at the doorway. Or a shotgun. Hell, maybe he'd moved a Gatling gun in there since Slade's last visit on his way to Stateline. Anything was possible, but standing on the doorstep like a drummer selling tin pans door to door would get him nowhere.

Slade considered calling out to Berringer again, then rushed the door instead, slipped through it, ducking off to one side with his shotgun raised to cover Mockingbird as he came in. The man they sought was nowhere to be seen, but Slade heard something from the general direction of the study where he'd met with Berringer on both prior visits to the rez.

With Mockingbird a cautious step behind

him, Slade moved toward the agent's study, planting each foot carefully, unable to remember whether any of the floorboards squeaked. They didn't, as it turned out, and he reached the study door, stopped there, pausing to listen. He could hear Berringer moving on the far side of the door. Dragging a chair or something? Maybe setting up a barricade for his last stand?

Slade called out through the door. "This doesn't have to end in blood. Come out, and we can —"

Something hit the floor inside the office, followed by a gagging, thrashing sound. Slade tried the door, surprised to find it was unlocked, and pushed on through. In front of him, Frank Berringer hung wriggling with a noose around his neck, suspended from a rafter beam.

Slade dropped his Winchester, rushed in, and grabbed the hanging man around his legs. Tried hoisting him to take the pressure off his windpipe, but it wasn't doing any good. A half turn toward the open door revealed Joe Mockingbird, watching the grim tableau with something very much like satisfaction on his face.

"Help me, will you?" Slade called to him. "You need to cut the rope!"

Mockingbird hesitated for another second,

then leaped forward, climbed atop the agent's desk, and started sawing on the tight rope with a knife drawn from his belt. It seemed to take forever, but the rope eventually parted, Berringer's full weight descending onto Slade. The lawman spun and dropped his burden on the desktop, trembling fingers scrabbling to free Berringer's bruised neck from its noose.

Berringer gasped, drew breath, then started coughing, mixed with sobbing as he huddled on the desktop. Mockingbird still loomed above him, knife in hand, but finally, reluctantly, stepped down and back away from Berringer, leaving the breathless man for Slade to handle.

When he got his voice back, Berringer wheezed, "Kill me, will you? God, just get it over with!"

"That's not my job," Slade said. "Judge Dennison may want to see you swing, but not before you're tried and everything comes out. Who knows, you may get lucky. Say you get ten years. When you get out, you'd only be — what? Fifty? Fifty-five? Maybe somebody needs a dishwasher or janitor."

"Please!" Tears were streaming down the agent's face, his voice a battered whisper. "You can say I ran, or pulled a gun."

"Wouldn't be right," Slade said, steering his captive toward the exit, pausing on the way to grab his shotgun. "Every man deserves his day in court."

Slade found a crowd awaiting them outside Berringer's house. He counted half a dozen badges in the front row, tribal officers, with better than a hundred Cherokees arrayed behind them. No one spoke, and no one moved, eyes locked on Slade and Berringer as they emerged. It almost had the feeling of a lynch mob, minus any of the ruckus Slade had seen at other vigilante necktie parties in the past.

He turned to Mockingbird and asked, "What's this about?"

"They need to see him leaving in disgrace," said Mockingbird. "Unless you choose to leave him here, with us."

"He's not too popular, I take it?"

"He's a white man who has cheated us in every way he could. Now, we discover he has helped to make our people drunk and foolish, so that he can steal the only land remaining to us."

"Sounds like bad news travels fast," Slade said.

"You can't leave me here," said Berringer, a tinge of panic in his wasted voice.

"Thought you were anxious to be done

with living," Slade replied.

"But not like *this.*"

"Discriminating taste, I guess." Slade faced the silent crowd and raised his voice. "I'm taking this man to the court in Enid for his trial. He won't be coming back here, I can guarantee you that."

"They will send someone else," said Mockingbird, over his shoulder.

"Bound to," Slade replied. "But with this character's example fresh in mind, it may be someone better."

"You believe that?" Mockingbird inquired.

I wouldn't want to bet my life on it, Slade thought. But said, "Much as I'd like to make him walk, we'll need another horse."

And one was there, almost before he knew it. Slade helped Berringer mount up, then climbed aboard his roan. The crowd parted to let them pass, this time without an escort to the reservation's border.

Halfway back to Enid, Berringer said, "I suppose you'll shoot me now."

"Stop asking," Slade replied, "before you talk me into it."

"No, I just meant . . . Rafferty told you about Little Wolf, I guess?"

Slade pinned him with a glare. "What do you mean?"

361

"He *didn't* tell you? Christ."

Berringer wheezed, or maybe he was laughing at himself. Slade couldn't tell. The agent's comment brought to mind his recent conversation with the tribal officer. "Why don't you tell me," Slade suggested.

"He was always butting into things, you know? That Little Wolf. I'm not sure how he tracked the whiskey, timing the delivery, but he was waiting for the last shipment that came across."

"And?"

"And he tried to stop it. Thought he could arrest the driver and his escort, maybe. I don't know. They got the drop on him, and that was all."

"He's dead, then?"

"Dead and buried," Berringer confirmed. "Rafferty's men took care of it."

"How long ago was that?"

"Say four weeks now. About that, anyway."

"I guess you could try running, after all," Slade told him.

"What?"

"Your way out. Shot while trying to escape. No trial, no more embarrassment. I'm game if you are."

"Now, wait. I wasn't thinking clearly. Call it shock."

"Call it a public service," Slade replied.

"Go on. Your move."

Berringer blanched. "I won't. It's murder if you shoot me now."

"Guess I could live with that. And you're a little short of witnesses."

"You took an oath!"

"Did you?" Slade challenged him.

"For God's sake, Marshal —"

"God's no part of this or anything you've done, as far as I can see."

"Deliver me to Enid. I'll tell everything. You don't know all the men involved in this."

"It's not worth saving you for small fry," Slade replied.

"So, how about a senior agent of the BIA? And there's a U.S. senator."

"If I find out you're lying . . ."

"I can give you names right now," said Berringer.

"Don't bother. Don't say anything at all, in fact, from now until you see Judge Dennison."

Berringer seemed about to speak, maybe agreeing with the terms, until Slade aimed a warning finger at his face. That was enough to silence him and keep him quiet for the long ride back to Enid, where a cell was waiting for him and he'd have a chance to tell his story. Maybe even save himself by giving up the bigger men behind him. Certainly it wouldn't be the first time that a deal was made to grease the wheels of justice.

And the big men Berringer betrayed? No doubt they would have batteries of lawyers standing by to speak on their behalf, raising as much dust as they could to counter any claims the witness made in court. Would any of them finally be held responsible, except for Berringer?

At least *he* wouldn't wriggle off the hook. No matter what bargain he struck, Slade vowed that to himself. And to the memory of a departed friend. By one means or another, Berringer would settle up his debt.

20

"Five years? That's it?" Lee Johnson pushed his empty beer mug back and told the passing bartender, "I'll need another one of those."

"Five years," Slade said, confirming it. "A special deal for his cooperation."

"Jesus," Ben Oates muttered. "How much did he give 'em to get off that easy?"

Slade was drinking at the Wildwood, in downtown Enid, following the special hearing where Frank Berringer had filed his guilty plea on charges of malfeasance while in office, dodging other counts that could have seen him caged for twenty years if run consecutively.

"First he gave up an assistant deputy director of the BIA," Slade said. "Guy name of Morrison. He's been collecting five percent of everything Rafferty made from shipping liquor to the rez, and he was in for ten percent of any proceeds from the land deal when they had it all in place."

"Figures," said Johnson. "There's not many you can trust in Washington, these days."

"And he sold out the senator," Slade said.

"Which one?" Oates asked.

"From Arkansas."

"Broadbelly, is it?" Johnson asked.

"Broad*bent,*" said Slade, correcting him. "The judge is putting out a warrant for him, probably first thing tomorrow. Bribery, conspiracy, accessory to murder."

"Think that it'll stick?" asked Oates.

Slade shrugged and said, "Beats me. I'm done with it, once we get Berringer aboard that prison wagon."

"And they're takin' him *today*?" asked Johnson.

"Judge is in a hurry," Slade explained. "He thinks somebody may be scared enough to make a move on Berringer and shut him up for good. He's on his way to Fort Supply, first thing, then off to Leavenworth with army guards."

"All that over some 'shine," said Oates.

"And land," Slade said. "And nineteen people dead so far."

"Most of 'em had it comin', though," said Johnson. Then he raised his mug and made a toast. "To Bill and Luke."

And Little Wolf, Slade thought, sipping his beer.

"You're ridin' escort on this joker, to the fort?" Oates asked.

Slade nodded. "Me, Ingram, and Sykes. We'll be there overnight, head back tomorrow."

"Should be fun," said Johnson, "since you killed them soldier boys."

"I've thought about that," Slade admitted.

"Three of you against a couple hundred," Oates suggested, grinning with a fleck of foam on his top lip. "Could get a little heated."

"I suppose the colonel over there can keep a lid on his enlisted men," Slade said. "If not . . . I guess we'll see what happens."

"Well, it's been nice knowin' you," said Johnson, with a wicked smile.

"Thanks for the sympathy," Slade said.

"Hey, better you than me."

"Than either one of us," said Oates.

"You reckon there'll be any women at the fort?" asked Johnson.

"Couldn't tell you," Slade replied. "What difference does it make?"

"Well, Sykes, you know," said Oates. "Feed him a couple drinks, and he starts tryin' to impress the ladies. I remember one time —"

"Hate to break this up," Slade said, "but I should go and get some things packed for the road."

"Some linament for cuts and bruises, just in case," said Johnson.

"Toss some splints in, while you're at it," Oates suggested.

"Ask for beefsteak if they black your eyes," Johnson advised.

"Next round's on me," Slade said and left a dollar on the bar as he was leaving.

Out into the daylight, Main Street looked normal as he turned toward his hotel. It wouldn't take long, packing. He'd be ready within twenty minutes, then required to sit around and wait for Berringer, but it was better than another hour in the saloon with Oates and Johnson. Put those two together with some beer, you couldn't shut them up.

My pals, he thought and had to smile, despite himself.

Just one more trip related to the case, and he could let it go. Move on to something different.

Or just move on?

Leaving was still an option, but he couldn't think of anyplace to go, offhand. Something to think about while he was shadowing Frank Berringer to Fort Supply, and maybe ducking soldiers who were spoiling for a fight.

The gunman liked his chances of surviving, but that didn't matter to the men who paid his salary. He had a job to do, and they expected him to follow through on it, regardless of the risk involved. They weren't the kind of people you could cheat and walk away from it, unless you planned to spend the rest of what life you had left watching your back.

He'd chosen a rooftop across from the federal courthouse, secure in the knowledge that few — if any — people check the high ground while they're strolling through a town, eyeing shop windows, meeting friends along the way, or simply tending to their normal business. No one thinks about the sky above unless it's thundering or raining on their heads.

His weapon was a Winchester Model 1886 rifle, chambered for powerful .45-70 Government rounds whose 300-grain bullets traveled at 1,600 feet per second, striking with 1,700 foot-pounds of destructive energy. The gunman had those figures memorized, since killing was his business and he always used the most efficient tool for any given job.

Today, he would be firing from a range of

fifty yards, with gravity to help him put his rounds on target. One should do it, but he'd have the time for two shots, anyway, before the pigeon's escorts worked out where the fire was coming from. There'd never been a man he couldn't kill with two shots. Most took only one — or on occasion, when he had to do it quietly, a blade between the ribs.

Getting away when he was done would be a challenge, but the gunman had taken precautions. He had a fast horse tied behind the building that would serve him as a sniper's roost, and his pockets were filled with spare rounds for his rifle. Aside from the long gun, he carried two pistols — a Colt M1892 Army and Navy revolver chambered for .38 Long Colt rounds, and a brand-new weapon made by Hugo Borchardt in Germany. The Borchardt C-93 was a peculiar-looking gun, described in its brochure as "self-loading," and carried eight rounds of 7.65-millimeter ammunition — equivalent to .32 caliber — in a detachable butt-loaded box magazine. A practiced hand could empty those eight rounds within two seconds flat, and nothing in their way was safe.

And if all else failed, he also carried six half sticks of dynamite with two-inch fuses.

It all came down to waiting now, watching the courthouse and the street below until the marshals made their move. He'd have one chance to nail his target from the roof, and failing that . . . what? Flee the town and hope that he could meet the prison wagon on its way to Fort Supply? Or later, on the road to Leavenworth with half a dozen soldiers riding escort?

No.

He had one chance to do it right and get away. Maybe. Between the money he'd been offered for the killing and the fear or what would surely happen to him if he failed, the gunman had no choice. Do this, and he would be a hero to the men who mattered, all the way from Little Rock to Washington, DC. Fail and he would barely be a memory.

The gunman checked his pocket watch and saw that it was nearly one o'clock. As if on cue, the prison wagon made its creaking way along Main Street, two horses pulling it, a deputy of middle age atop the driver's seat, the metal cage behind him empty for the moment.

Not for long.

It stopped before the courthouse, driver waiting, and another pair of marshals came outside to have a look around. Armed as they were, they must expect a problem —

or at least suspect that someone might attempt to shut their captive's mouth for good.

And they were right.

The gunman raised his Winchester, its wood and metal warm from basking in the sun, and eased its hammer back.

Slade led Frank Berringer out of his basement cell with shackles and manacles clanking, walking slowly to accommodate the prisoner's shuffling gait. Although he'd been rushed through the process of arraignment, plea, and sentencing, Berringer had the look of someone who had been in custody for weeks. Forlorn, with shoulders slumped, feet dragging even more than ankle chains required, he struggled up the concrete steps with Slade beside him and emerged into bright daylight like a blind cave dweller.

"I suppose you're happy now," he said to Slade, as they began to cross the courtyard, on their way to Main Street and the wagon that would transport Berringer to Leavenworth, two hundred fifty miles away.

"Happy? How do you figure that?" asked Slade.

"To see me like this. Humbled and disgraced."

"You still don't get it, do you?" Slade

responded. "You disgraced yourself. It wasn't something done to you."

"And so justice is served!" Berringer sneered at the idea.

"Think so?" Slade asked. "I would've said that called for hanging."

He could see the wagon now, Dutch Ingram on the driver's seat, Fred Sykes holding the door open in back. Berringer started to reply, mouth opening, but then it kept on going, yawning into something from a nightmare as his skull exploded, spraying blood and tissue in a warm, wet cloud. Some of it spattered Slade, smearing the right side of his face, before his ears picked up the crack of gunfire from somewhere across the street.

You never hear the shot . . .

For Berringer, at least, the old saying was true. Slade let the nearly headless body drop, focused on spotting where the rifleman had fired from. He could see a puff of smoke just dissipating at the cornice of a rooftop catty-corner from the courthouse. The Hotel Deluxe, four stories tall, with a commanding view of Main Street, a figure barely glimpsed up there, just ducking out of sight.

Slade called a warning out to Sykes and Ingram, as he ran toward the hotel. "Sniper!

Top of the Deluxe! Get help and cut him off! We need him breathing!"

It became a blur from there, Slade running with his pistol drawn and people watching from the sidewalks, some faces that he recognized, distorted now by shock at what they'd witnessed seconds earlier. He didn't bother shouting at them to find cover. It was clear the rifleman had come to do a job and wasn't on a mindless shooting spree.

Halfway across Main Street, still watching the hotel's rooftop, Slade saw a small object detach itself and tumble toward him, trailing smoke. It barely registered until the cut-down stick of dynamite touched down and detonated, smoke and dust enveloping the street scene as a thunderclap hammered Slade's eardrums, slamming him to earth.

He struggled to his feet again, Colt still in hand, and almost got his balance back before a second charge exploded within twenty feet of him. There was no shrapnel from the blast, just dirt and grit that peppered Slade and briefly blinded him, some of it sticking to the fresh blood on his face and giving him the aspect of a scarecrow dipped in mud.

Ears ringing, sleeving filth out of his eyes, Slade stumble-jogged to the hotel and paused a moment at the entrance to an alleyway beside it. If the rifleman was still above him, tossing dynamite into the street, it meant he hadn't climbed down yet. Slade had a chance to catch him if he didn't stall too long or let his sudden dizziness betray him.

Mouthing a curse he couldn't hear, Slade started down the alley, wishing that he had his shotgun. It would be a neat trick, taking Berringer's assassin without killing him — but that was not to say Slade couldn't *wound* him if he had to, trusting Dr. Abernathy to repair whatever damage might be suffered in the process. All he needed was a captive fit to talk, say who had sent him, fix his boss up with a necktie party.

As for Berringer . . . well, it was justice of a sort. Slade wouldn't lose a wink of sleep over his passing.

Not unless he let the killer slip away.

The rifleman was in a hurry, but he didn't panic. He'd already caused enough confusion on the street below to buy himself some time. The quickest member of the team escorting Berringer was likely down and out, a double blast of dynamite enough to stun him if it hadn't shaken loose his brains.

And it was time to go, before the other

lawmen managed to get organized, call reinforcements, block his exit from the prairie town. Anxiety was foreign to his makeup, but he felt the sense of urgency that made him run across the hotel's flat rooftop, hanging his rifle on its sling across his shoulder as he started down a wooden ladder mounted to the wall.

His horse whickered below him, as if urging him to hurry. Rung by rung, he clambered down the ladder, hoping no civilian with a gun and misplaced strain of heroism would attempt to stop him when he reached the ground. The money he'd been paid covered one death, and while the shooter had no qualms about raising the toll, he didn't kill for free if it could be avoided.

Anyway, another shot would draw pursuers to him like a swarm of flies to dung.

His left foot came to rest on solid ground, immediately followed by his right. He started for his stallion and had nearly reached it when a hoarse and winded voice behind him ordered, "Stop right there!"

He couldn't clear the rifle fast enough to aim and fire it, so he pulled the Colt instead, spinning around and triggering a shot when it had barely cleared its holster. The revolver's double-action trigger saved a crucial second for him, and he didn't bother aiming. Barely even saw his target, truth be told, before the first slug cleared his pistol's muzzle.

He was fast — but not quite fast enough. His adversary had arrived with gun in hand, no time at all wasted on drawing, and his bullet ripped into the sniper's shoulder, spinning him around to crumple on all fours.

Make that all *threes,* since his right arm was numb and useless, pain just starting to send signals from the epicenter of his mangled shoulder. He could see the Colt revolver where he'd dropped it, but his right hand wouldn't answer orders from his brain. Behind him, cautiously approaching, his opponent warned, "Stay down!"

"Yes, sir!" the gunman answered, grinning fiercely through the pain. And as he spoke, his left hand slid inside his jacket, fingers seeking out the Borchardt C-93 in its snug shoulder holster. It was an awkward kind of draw, backward and upside down, but he'd rehearsed it, knowing you could never tell what might occur when there was gun work to be done.

The pistol had a safety lever on the left side of its frame, a hedge against an ac-cidental discharge, and it took some fum-bling to release it with his left hand, but the shooter got it done. He covered the procedure with a groan he didn't have to fake, slumped forward to disguise the twisting movement of his one good arm, and eased the Borchardt free of clinging leather.

Footsteps told him that his enemy was drawing closer. Perfect. It would spare him aiming. He could drop the lawman, climb aboard his horse, and get the hell away from there before he bled out in the dust.

And then what?

One thing at a time.

Rising, turning with a snarl of pain and rage, the gunman sprayed his target with a burst of rapid fire — or would have, if the lawman had been standing where he'd been a moment earlier. He'd moved, though, ducking to the left and crouching low, six-gun extended in a steady grip. Before the shooter could correct his aim and swing the Borchardt pistol left-ward, the marshal fired again — to kill, this time.

His bullet drilled the gunman's chest, lifted him off his knees, and tossed him over on his back. It should have hurt, but didn't, numbness gripping him, the semiautomatic weapon slipping from his hand. Impossibly, the sky revolved above him, clouds spinning for him alone like soapy water swirling down a drainpipe.

This is how it ends? he asked himself. And died.

"We don't know who he was," Slade told Judge Dennison. "No papers on him. Nothing in his saddle bags but ammunition and provisions for the trail."

"And money?" asked the judge.

"A hundred dollars, more or less. Not much, to sacrifice himself that way."

"I'm guessing he was promised more," said Dennison. "I wouldn't be surprised if there's a bank account somewhere, considerably fatter than it was before he took the job."

"I don't see how we'll ever find that, either, when we've got no name to start with," Slade replied.

"Sounds damn near hopeless," Dennison acknowledged.

"And the people Berringer gave up? What happens now, to them?" Slade asked.

"They'll have attorneys standing by to challenge the indictments. I suspect they'll win, under the confrontation clause."

"How's that?" asked Slade.

"The Sixth Amendment to the Constitution," Dennison explained. "Anyone accused of a crime has the absolute right to confront and cross-examine his accusers.

It's fundamental."

"Even when they have him murdered?"

"That's the rub," said Dennison. "We don't know who the *killer* is — or was — much less who hired him. Lacking evidence, it's just a heap of speculation."

"I'd have called it common sense," Slade said.

"Which isn't evidence. We can't go into court with an opinion, unsupported by a single solid fact."

"So it was all for nothing?"

"On the contrary. You cracked the moonshine ring and found Bill Tanner's killers. You cleaned out a nest of filth at Fort Supply, for which the army may or may not thank you, and you've helped the Cherokees."

Too late for Little Wolf, Slade thought. "It doesn't feel like much," he said.

"Look on the bright side," Dennison suggested. "If they'd killed you on their first try, Rafferty would still be riding high. His friends would still be looking forward to their payday."

"As it is, they just go on about their business, looking for another way to steal," Slade said.

"Don't be so sure. The BIA will likely fire Berringer's boss, for the appearance that it's cleaning house, if nothing else."

"There's still the senator," said Slade.

"Who's up for reelection in another year. Maybe the people will remember and decide to clean their own house."

"Will they even know about the charges?" Slade inquired.

Dennison smiled. "As luck would have it, I have friends in Little Rock. One of them manages the *Arkansas Gazette.* I wouldn't be surprised if he could get a feature out of this. Maybe a series."

"That's something, anyway."

"You need some rest, Jack. Take a couple days and let yourself unwind. If anything comes up —"

"You know where to find me," Slade said, already on his feet and moving toward the door.

"I do, indeed."

The desk clerk back at Slade's hotel looked like a man with something on his mind, but if there was, he kept it to himself. Slade put it down to gun-smoke syndrome, the attraction some folks felt toward killing even though the act itself repulsed them. You could see it on the faces of spectators at a shooting, morbid curiosity that verged on sick excitement. Or, he may have just had gas from eating too much barbecue at

Colter's Café, down the street.

Slade climbed the stairs, fatigue weighting his feet, wondering whether Lo Ming's laundry could could cleanse his shirt and vest of Berringer's bloodstains. Something to think about, but not this afternoon. He reached the second-story landing, turned down toward his room, and stopped dead in his tracks at sight of Faith Connover, standing in the hallway by his numbered door.

Slade felt his mouth go dry, his mind go blank. His legs felt wooden as he moved along the corridor, trying to think if he remembered how to smile.

"Clerk didn't tell me I had company," he said.

"I asked him not to warn you," Faith replied.

"Afraid I'd come up shooting?" Slade's pulse hammered as the stupid joke fell flat.

"More like afraid you'd turn around and run," she said.

"Not likely."

"Jack, we need to talk."

"Okay. You know —"

"Me first," she interrupted him. "I'm pregnant."

The employees of Thorndike Press hope you have enjoyed this Large Print book. All our Thorndike, Wheeler, and Kennebec Large Print titles are designed for easy reading, and all our books are made to last. Other Thorndike Press Large Print books are available at your library, through selected bookstores, or directly from us.

For information about titles, please call:
    (800) 223-1244

or visit our Web site at:
    http://gale.cengage.com/thorndike

To share your comments, please write:
    Publisher
    Thorndike Press
    10 Water St., Suite 310
    Waterville, ME 04901